A Devil in the Dark

THE PLANES
BOOK TWO

ELISE NOBLE

Published by Undercover Publishing Limited

Copyright © 2024 Elise Noble

v2

ISBN: 978-1-912888-93-1

Edited by Nikki Mentges, NAM Editorial

Cover design by Elise Noble

www.undercover-publishing.com

www.elise-noble.com

Love is the fire of life.
It either consumes or it purifies.

CHAPTER 1
Blane

"Go to hell," the blonde banshee screeched.

"At times like this, it's tempting."

"Don't you know who I am?"

"Unfortunately."

The woman with the slightly unfocused eyes and inch-long nails was Taylee M, hawker of diet pills, false eyelashes, and butt-enhancing "wunderwear," so my assistant reliably informed me. I glanced down out of curiosity as the doorman hustled her out of the VIP area. Well, she wasn't wearing the wunderwear tonight. One of her stilettos fell off, and the resulting shriek was audible over the thumping bass from the live band downstairs.

"You'll pay for this! Your stupid club is boring anyway. The service sucks, and the music's trashy, and…"

I turned away and surveyed the damage. A waitress was cleaning up the glass Taylee had broken, and the man she'd arrived with was studiously pretending he didn't know her. A few people were filming the scene, which she'd probably love. No publicity was bad publicity, after all.

"Life's too short to put up with a hellion like that," I muttered to a smirking Joseph.

"You're immortal."

"It's a figure of speech."

Plus there were plenty of regular humans in the club, and they shouldn't have to deal with Taylee M either. She'd been obnoxious enough before she began taking drugs, but snorting a line of coke had been the final straw. Or, in her case, the final rolled-up ten-dollar bill. Club Dead had a strict "no drugs" policy, and she'd broken the rules.

My rules.

I'd never had this problem in my former home. In Plane Three, my word was law. Plane Five—aka Earth—was full of rebellious souls. Yes, that was one of the reasons I liked it, but as my mother always said, every positive was balanced by a negative. Good and evil, light and dark, yin and yang, orange juice and vodka. Cecily Shepherd and Taylee M.

Cecily was in the VIP area now, sitting with her husband and a young singer she was trying to woo into performing at the charity benefit she was organising. For either starving puppies or sick children—I forgot which. Shep, her husband, kept one eye on the crowd as his wife spoke. Even though he'd left his gun at home, he never stopped being a cop. Six months ago, the sight of him on the mezzanine would have left me twitchy, especially when Taylee M had snorted a line of Colombian finest off the mirrored table. But one of Detective Shepherd's colleagues had become a friend, and both men understood that I had no tolerance for narcotics.

"Why didn't Shep arrest her?" Joseph asked. "Don't cops have quotas to meet?"

"Cece doesn't like it when he mixes business with pleasure, and besides, Taylee inhaled the evidence. I'm going back upstairs."

The main room of the cavernous nightclub had a ceiling that reached for the heavens, and my apartment sprawled above the masses, accessible via my private office suite on the second floor. Outside the office, a balcony spanned the width of the club, giving me a bird's-eye view of the bar, the tables, and the dance floor. The VIP mezzanine stretched off to my right, bringing our special guests closer to my personal fiefdom, but not close enough to touch. If the VIPs thought they were lording over the peons, they only had to glance up to see that they weren't quite as high in the pecking order as they might wish.

And thanks to my twenty-twenty vision—being the son of Earth's overlord did afford me certain advantages—I'd been able to witness Taylee's indiscretions from the shadows and deal with the problem before she cost the club its licence.

Club Dead had been my first purchase here in Plane Five. Okay, my second—it turned out that Vegas really was hotter than Hell, tar-burning pits and lava craters excepted, and if one was going to spend much time outside in Nevada, shorts were an unfortunate necessity. Joseph had nearly expired in his leather pants. On the whole, being a nightclub owner was satisfactory, but there were rare occasions when I missed my old home. Tonight was one of them.

So, why was I in Plane Five, you ask? An excellent question, and I had my father to thank for that. Several years ago, he'd banished me here to learn my lesson.

"Plane Three isn't meant to be fun, son," he'd told me. "Souls are sent there as a punishment."

"Yesterday's losing acidball team was far from happy."

Joseph had come up with that little game. I'd always wanted to try paintball, but for an added challenge, we'd switched out the paint for sulphuric acid from the volcano

3

crater. The winners were the folks with the most skin left when the buzzer sounded.

"Acidball, fire-walking, bungee jumping... This wasn't what the Celestial Council had in mind when they appointed our family to rule the eighty-sixth realm."

"*Russian roulette* bungee jumping," I corrected. The activity was so much more fun when you didn't know how long the rope was. Pick the wrong one, and...*splat*.

"And the Celestial Council definitely wouldn't have approved of Genghis Khan and Oliver Cromwell placing bets on the outcome."

"Don't forget Cathy." More formally known as Catherine the Great, but that was such a mouthful. "We're all for diversity and inclusion here in Plane Three."

"Diversity and inclusion? Then why was Robespierre sitting on the sidelines?"

"He twisted an ankle."

"*Everyone's* supposed to suffer." Father sighed. "Son, this isn't working. I gave you one more chance after the swimming pool incident, but you clearly didn't take my concerns on board."

I had; I just disagreed with his approach. Simply punishing everyone led to grumbling and rebellion, while the carrot-and-stick method had better results. The guests who learned to behave in a civilised manner earned privileges, and those determined to remain assholes spent their days breaking big rocks into little rocks in the shadow of Mount Malum.

"Okay, okay. I'll close down the sportsbook."

"No, you're going to take a trip."

"A trip where? Don't make me visit Plane Two again— you know I hate playing golf."

Although that did give me an idea. If we switched out some of the golf balls for, say, bomblets... Par four or bust.

"You're going to Plane Five. Sin City, to be precise."

"What the hell...?"

"If you see mortal transgressions for yourself, perhaps you'll take your job a little more seriously."

"But...but...who will run Plane Three in my absence?"

"Decima."

"*Decima*?" Oh, of course. My older sister had been desperate for a managerial position ever since she returned from backpacking around Alpha Centauri. And Decima had one big advantage over me when it came to running Hell—she was a bitch. Cathy would hate her. "How long are we talking here?"

"Until you learn the error of your ways. You can take Beauregard with you."

Joseph had been sniggering in the corner, but at my father's words, his mouth dropped open.

"What? Why me?"

"Because someone needs to keep an eye on my son."

Well, it had been eight years and counting. Every six months, my performance was reevaluated by my father's PA, which was invariably followed by an awkward meeting, a promise to do better, and a muttered, "Why can't you be more like your older sister?"

But the truth was, I was in no hurry to return to Plane Three. Initially, I'd treated Club Dead as a lab experiment, a microcosm of the human condition to be analysed and studied. A necessary but tedious learning experience. But now it had become home.

I headed for the door marked "Staff Only" and took the stairs that led to my private domain with Joseph at my heels. When we first arrived, he'd hated life in Plane Five, but after he'd stolen a lawyer's body and gotten his very own bar certificate, he'd stopped whining about our new place of residence.

In my office, I settled behind the desk and reached for the bottle of red I'd opened earlier. Alcohol was officially banned in Plane Three but enjoyed with great relish by my father, at least when my mother wasn't looking. Go figure. Anyhow, I was fond of a tipple. My second big investment on Earth had been a vineyard. Once a year, I took a vacation in Italy to sample the latest vintage. Spring was a lovely time to visit, but the next few months promised to be busy, so I'd probably go in September or October this time around.

"Drink?"

Joseph took a seat on the leather couch. "Why not?"

But I'd barely poured half a glass when my phone rang. I checked the screen. Barry McKee was calling. McKee managed Tilt, the private casino I'd bought three years ago after Father said I needed to expand my horizons. Actually, it was more of a poker club, although we also offered blackjack and baccarat. But poker was the main thing. The previous owner had been a Mafia boss who'd fallen on hard times, and although the clientele still included a few dubious characters, I'd say the members were ninety percent legit now.

Tilt catered to serious gamblers, wealthy ones, but not in the same class as the divas who wanted a butler to fawn over them twenty-four-seven. Yes, we'd collect our members from the airport and provide them with a luxury suite, a concierge, and a personal shopper, but if they wanted to swing naked in a chinchilla-fur hammock or have a cheetah dressed in a tuxedo greet them at check-in, let them go to the Strip.

What they did get was privacy. No bachelor parties, no nosy reporters, and absolute discretion from the staff. Drugs were still verboten, but if a guest wanted female company, we'd arrange it, even though Clark County frowned upon that particular activity. Discretion was the name of the game. Take Sheikh Mahbrouk, who'd flown in today, for example. Since gambling and alcohol were both *haram*, the Strip was off limits to him. He and several of his friends had been members of Tilt for years.

"Barry? Is there a problem? Did the sheikh bring his falcon again?"

The arrival of the bird had been a surprise to everyone last year, and the sheikh had insisted upon live food. When the assistant concierge had balked at going to Petco to pick up a dozen hamsters, I'd been forced to dispatch Joseph to hunt for rats in the warren of tunnels that ran beneath the city. He hadn't spoken to me for a week afterward. Hmm... Perhaps the falcon hadn't been so bad after all?

"The sheikh's falcon tried to eat his fourth wife's Maltese terrier, so he left the bird behind. But the sheikh lost a sock. It's possible the dog ate it, and he's refusing to play until the sock is found."

Great planes, the four-legged fiend hadn't been satisfied with the gourmet dog food they stocked in the kitchen?

"We can't get him new socks?"

"Apparently, this is his lucky pair. Kressie and the wife" —Kressie was the head concierge—"have taken the mutt to the veterinarian, and every spare person is searching the suite in case it hid the sock somewhere."

Slowly, I put down my glass of wine. These hiccups were just one more facet of life in Plane Five, and I'd admit to being intrigued as to what the sheikh would do if the sock was indeed in the dog.

"I'll come over."

~

Tilt was located off the Strip, far enough from the gaudiness to ensure one wasn't tripping over a tourist every five minutes, but close enough to get the full Vegas experience.

The twelve-storey art deco-style building was tiny compared to the gargantuan casinos the city was known for, but it served its purpose. The first floor housed the restaurant and spa, the second floor was home to the casino itself, and accommodation took up the rest of the space, sixteen suites per floor. Membership fees paid for most of the overheads, plus the house took a rake from every pot. The place turned a comfortable profit, with the added benefit that it allowed me to study earthly sins up close.

The problem?

I quite enjoyed them.

Returning to my former home held little appeal, especially when I considered the inevitable power struggle with Decima.

"Good evening, Melina."

The hostess in the lobby beamed at me. "Good evening, Mr. Blane. Can I help you with anything?"

"Has the sock been found?"

Her smile slipped away. "Not yet. Most everyone's up in suite 1204 looking for it."

I glanced into the restaurant on my way past, relieved to see everything running smoothly. Ditto for the casino. The quiet buzz of activity as I made money and other people lost it never failed to make me smile.

"Why is Rex dealing tonight?" Joseph nodded toward the three blackjack tables at the far end of the room. Only one was set up tonight since most of the guests were playing poker. "I thought Wren Gillebrand worked Tuesdays?"

Wren was missing? It didn't surprise me that Joseph had noticed, but it did surprise me that he'd noticed before I did. My gaze usually gravitated toward Wren the moment we set foot on the second floor. Although Joseph did have a teeny crush on Wren's brother, which was a little tricky because firstly, we hadn't been able to ascertain whether Kayden was gay or straight or ace or somewhere in between, and secondly, Joseph was a demon.

But his issues were trivial compared to mine. I very much suspected that the love of my earthly life, my dearly departed Nevaeh, had been reincarnated as a four-year-old child. Awkward didn't even begin to cover it.

And that was also why my gaze was the only thing I'd lay on Wren Gillebrand. Falling for a mortal only led to unbearable heartache. Been there, done that, experienced the agony.

Upstairs in suite 1204, a dozen staff were on their hands and knees, checking underneath furniture and behind the drapes. I spotted Vee Pelletier crawling out from behind the king-sized bed. Until recently, she'd been the best waitress on the VIP floor at Club Dead, but after we spotted her murderous ex climbing out of a limo in front of Circus Circus last month, I'd suggested she might want to work somewhere slightly quieter until we could ascertain why Voltaire was in town.

Over the past few months, Vee had also become a friend, and I headed in her direction. Joseph had stayed behind in the bar.

"How's the search going?"

Her roll of the eyes told me exactly what she thought of the sheikh and his lucky sock.

"Fifty bucks says it isn't here. I asked the sheikh to call his staff back home, but they can't find it either."

"Where *is* the sheikh?"

"In suite 1203 with a bottle of forty-year-old single malt and a headache. Barry's keeping him company."

"Did you check under the pillows?"

A nod. "Wait!" Vee turned to the room. "Did anyone check *inside* the pillowcases?"

When no one answered in the affirmative, she moved back to the bed and shook the first of the eight cream satin pillows out of its case. No sock. I grabbed the next pillow and checked it—not there either.

"What colour is the sock?"

"Lavender with a diamond pattern in yellow. The sheikh put the other one in the safe, but I have a picture." Vee held up her phone to show me the ugliest sock ever knitted. "Mariah's scouring the internet in case we can purchase a duplicate pair, but the closest she's found so far are more argyle pattern than harlequin."

"Keep trying."

"We will, but wouldn't it be weird if we bought a new pair and then he found the old one?"

"Yes, but is that better or worse than having to launder a partially digested sock?"

Barry poked his head around the door. "The sheikh wants to know if there's any news?"

Vee shook her head, and his shoulders slumped. He stepped back, but before he could leave, I held up a hand.

"Where's Wren Gillebrand?"

"She didn't show up today."

"Did she call in sick?"

"Nope. Kressie tried getting in touch with her, but she didn't pick up."

Of all the people with the potential to go AWOL, Wren would have been at the bottom of my list. She'd worked at Tilt for over a year, and she'd never been even a minute late. Do you know how hard it is to hire a good blackjack dealer who shows up on time? Wren's predecessor had once been an hour late because her pet goat ate her car key. Oh, and it got worse. Since the key only had to be in close proximity to the car for the engine to start, she'd stuffed the goat into the back seat and brought it to work with her. Halfway through her shift, alarms began going off in the parking garage, and the escaped goat damaged six luxury vehicles and shit all over the floor before Joseph managed to catch it.

We needed to get Wren back.

Fast.

"How about yesterday? Was she here?"

"No, but it was her scheduled day off. Vee here offered to swing by Wren's apartment after her shift, but I'm not sure that's a good idea. I mean, if she goes alone and there's a problem..."

If there was a problem, then Vee was probably the best person to handle it. Because Vee had a secret. She was a vampire, and as long as she obtained an appropriate amount of sustenance, her strength was far superior to any man's. Plus if she got shot at, she just regenerated, which was fascinating to watch. But of course, Barry didn't know that.

What time was it? Almost two a.m. I could head over to Wren's apartment with Joseph and check out the situation myself. That might earn Joseph brownie points when it came to Kayden, but if Wren had split up with a boyfriend or gotten hormonal or suffered another disaster that involved tears, then Joseph was the wrong person to deal with the issue. And so was I, quite frankly. If I waited another two hours, I could accompany Vee, and Vee could bring tissues.

And in the meantime, we'd all wait with bated breath to see if the fourth Mrs. Mahbrouk's pet pooch vomited a sock.

I felt in my pocket for the Kansas State Quarter—the one with the error that said "In God we Rust"—that Nevaeh had gifted me for my thirtieth birthday. Or rather, what she thought was my thirtieth birthday. I was actually

ELISE NOBLE

several thousand years old, but the right moment to explain that had somehow never arisen. Anyhow, she swore the coin was lucky.

Heads, and I'd go to Wren's place with Joseph; tails, I'd wait for Vee.

The quarter flashed and glinted under the chandelier as I flipped it. What was it to be?

CHAPTER 2

Blane

"Is this the place?"

Vee checked the piece of paper with Wren's address. "437A, yes."

Sheikh Mahbrouk had found his missing sock stuck to the inside of his pants, the dog had been chauffeured back from the veterinarian, and now we had another mystery to solve. A more important one. Wren Gillebrand lived in the left side of a narrow duplex, a home built half a century ago and barely maintained since. Pale paint that might once have been blue or green or white or cream peeled from the siding in the glow of a yellowed streetlight, and skeletal weeds had taken over the front yard. Some were higher than my waist, while others were flattened. Had a second vehicle been parked there recently? One car remained in the driveway, a Prius with a dent in the trunk. Wren's?

I exited my Bentley—a new addition and one that Joseph had chosen—and moved to get the passenger door for Vee, but she climbed out before I could open it. At least I'd tried to be a gentleman. It was surprisingly easy. Soon after I left Plane Three, I'd watched a bunch of old black-

and-white movies for tips—my little sister, Aurelia, assured me that those men lived up to earthly ideals. Open doors, hold the umbrella if it rained, challenge a stranger to a duel if he insulted your masculinity. Although it seemed the duelling was considered a little old-fashioned now. The one time I'd issued an invitation, the fellow had asked me if I was on crack and then fired a gun at me without taking ten paces first. Of course, being immortal, I did have an advantage, and the look of shock as I'd sucked his soul out of his scrawny body had been mildly amusing.

Upon closer inspection, each half of the duplex had been subdivided into two, which meant Wren's apartment was tiny.

"Upstairs or downstairs?"

Vee checked the metal plates by the doors. "437A is downstairs."

The apartment was dark, which was relatively normal for this time in the morning, but when I knocked on the door, there was no movement inside. I tried again, harder, possibly too hard, because the upstairs window opened and a sour-faced chap leaned out.

"Shaddup, would ya? People are tryin' to sleep."

"We're looking for Wren Gillebrand."

"Who?"

"Your downstairs neighbour."

"Oh, her. She took off hours ago. Slammed the damn door on her way out."

"Was she alone?" Vee asked.

"Didn't see nobody else."

"Do you know where she went?" I considered it unlikely since he hadn't even been aware of her name, but I figured I'd voice the question.

"Do I look like a psychic to you?"

I had to concede that he didn't. The only true psychics

were the five conquisitors, all female, and their powers only worked in limited circumstances. They'd escaped their celestial bonds in the late seventeenth century, and although physical gender reassignment had become a thing now, I couldn't imagine any of them slumming it in a place like this. Delilah, in particular, was notoriously vain.

Anyhow, the man upstairs didn't seem to expect an answer because he closed the window with a *bang*. Vee listened for a moment, head tilted to one side, a waterfall of turquoise hair cascading over her shoulder. She changed the colour every couple of months, usually to something outlandish. Pink, purple, yellow, green... Although the yellow hadn't lasted long, probably because with her pale skin, she'd looked like a fried egg.

"He's gone back to bed."

Ah, yes, there was Vee's enhanced hearing at work. When my Great-Uncle Tiberius had created vampires, he'd upgraded their senses to assist with their designated job as part of Plane Five enforcement. At least, that had been the plan. The system had fallen apart years ago, and now Vee spent her days relaxing in a Las Vegas penthouse and her nights roaming the city. At least she didn't need to hunt for meals anymore. Her cop boyfriend provided drinkies on demand, a recent development that still baffled me.

"At least we know Wren left of her own volition," I said.

Although I confess, I did feel slightly let down. At Club Dead and Tilt, I strived to maintain good employee relations. Joseph told me I wasn't the most approachable person in Plane Five, but would it really have been so difficult for Wren to send an email?

"Did she?" Vee asked.

"The neighbour insinuated that she left alone."

"There's more than one way to coerce somebody into acting against their will. I only met Wren a handful of times, but she didn't strike me as the kind of person who'd quit her job without notice."

"You think she was forced into departing?"

"I think we should try to find out. Does she have family? A boyfriend? Girlfriend?"

"She has a brother. Kayden. He picks her up from Tilt on occasion."

"Where does he live? Do you have a phone number? Maybe in her employee file?"

"I tried calling before we left, and he must have changed his number because it was out of service." But Wren would have his new contact details. Perhaps she'd noted them down somewhere? Otherwise, I'd have to pay him a visit in person—Joseph would dig up the address. He was good at that sort of thing. I scanned the apartment windows, but they were all closed. "Do you know how to pick a lock?"

"No, do you?"

"How hard can it be?" I reached forward and slid two bobby pins out of Vee's hair, then bent the ends a bit. Would that work? This was where bringing Joseph along would have given me an advantage—he'd know how to break into an apartment. He spent his spare time studying the habits of Plane Five's least desirable citizens. "They do this all the time in the movies."

"Movies aren't real."

"Shhh."

I poked the first wire into the lock and wiggled it. Was there supposed to be a *click* or something? At least the neighbour had returned to bed. The second wire didn't make much difference, and I began to wonder if Vee was right, a thought that pained me. I didn't enjoy failure. It reminded me of my childhood. Perhaps a YouTube video might provide a few practical hints? A man could find anything on the internet, or so Joseph said.

Ten minutes later, I realised that lock picking was more complicated than I thought. Turned out some oddballs actually did this for a hobby, which was an interesting revelation. Cylinders, plugs, shear lines, driver pins... I was on the third video, learning about tension wrenches and rakes, when I heard the first *whoop* of a siren nearby. *Very* nearby. Right outside Wren's apartment, in fact.

Well now, this was awkward.

"Sir, is there a problem here?"

What were my options? I could slide through a portal to another plane, but that might cause more problems than it solved, not least for Vee, who'd be left behind. Hold on, where *was* Vee? I hadn't seen her since the end of the first instructional video.

"Sir, is this your home?"

Or I could namedrop Detective Callahan—he'd know I had a good reason for attempting to break into Wren's apartment.

"Sir?"

Or I could bullshit.

"Yesh, this ish my home." Did I sound drunk? Alcohol didn't have much of an impact on my immortal soul, so I channelled one of the idiots who'd been lurching around the dance floor in Club Dead earlier. "I losht my key."

"Sir, I'm gonna need to see some ID."

I patted my pockets, stalling. My ID was an excellent fake, but a fake nonetheless. The US government didn't hand out social security numbers to beings from other planes. They had annoying rules about birth certificates or equivalent documentation. And even if I possessed the required documents, I was so old that they would have been chiselled into stone or inked onto papyrus.

"I think I left my—"

"I found it, honey!" Vee appeared from the darkness. "I found the spare key."

She brushed past me and slotted it into the lock, deftly removing the bent bobby pins with her other hand as she did so. A jiggle, a *click*, and the door swung open. She turned to beam at the cop.

"Are you here to look for the loose dog, officer? I haven't seen it today, but it was running around yesterday morning."

"Uh, no. I don't know anything about a dog."

Vee wrapped her arm around my waist and stared at him, expectant. "Then why are you here?"

"We received a report of... Never mind. I see there's been a mix-up. You have a good evening, ma'am. Sir."

Vee pulled me inside Wren's apartment and closed the door, and we waited in silence as she listened. After thirty seconds, she nodded.

"He's gone."

"That's a relief. Things could have gotten awkward if I'd sucked out his soul."

"What? You wouldn't...?"

"Relax, I'm kidding. Where did you get the key?"

"It was under a broken flowerpot in the backyard. I figured that seeing as Wren lived alone, she might have hidden a spare for emergencies. Or it could have belonged to the grouchy guy upstairs. We had a fifty-fifty chance."

Reasonable odds, and what was life without a little risk?

"Good thinking."

"Picking locks was harder than you figured, huh? What happens if you lose a key in Plane Three?"

"We don't have traditional locks. If a resident acts out, we bind them using cosmic string."

"How does that work?"

"In all honesty, I'm not certain of the mechanism." I

waved a hand. "I just picture the energy wrapping around them, and it happens. We should look for Kayden's phone number. Do you think the upstairs neighbour reported us?"

"No, he's snoring right now. But I saw drapes twitch in the apartment block next door, so I'm guessing there's a bored insomniac who likes to watch over the neighbourhood."

I switched on a light. If someone had watched us enter the building, it would be strange if the place stayed in darkness. Wren's home was small and neat, a reflection of her personality, decorated with functionality in mind rather than style. There were only four rooms—a bedroom, a bathroom, a small kitchen, and a living-slash-dining room. I spotted a calendar pinned to a corkboard beside the refrigerator.

"Wren didn't expect to leave tonight. She had this evening blocked out for work, and a dental appointment at nine thirty tomorrow. Then lunch with Caria. Any idea who that is?"

Vee shook her head. "She never mentioned the name to me. There's milk in the refrigerator, leftovers as well. Either she's intending to come back soon, or she ran with little thought at all."

The bedroom told another chapter of the story. The closet was open, drawers too. Items of clothing were scattered on the bed as if she'd discarded them in her hurry to pack. Toiletries were missing from the shower, and there was no phone charger in sight, no laptop, no purse. She'd taken the essentials and left the rest.

A heart-shaped Post-it was stuck to the mirror.

Yoga with Caria, 2 p.m. Friday.

"Caria must be in Wren's yoga class, but there's no indication of where it takes place."

"She goes to the Fitness Factory at the community centre on Madison. Cheap à la creep, she said."

"What does that mean?"

"The classes are good value, but a bunch of weirdos take advantage of the low joining fee. The week before last, a sleaze kept making lewd comments about her downward-facing dog."

"Could he be involved in this?" I gestured at the empty apartment. "Maybe he followed her home?"

"I doubt it. The instructor threw him out, and he was so busy yelling obscenities that he didn't look where he was going, fell down the steps, and got hit by a truck in the parking lot. The EMTs seemed to think he'd be in the hospital for a while. Wren actually considered sending a 'Get Well Soon' card—out of guilt, I assume—but I guess I must have looked aghast because she quickly changed her mind."

"Maybe I should start offering gym memberships as an employee benefit?" At a facility that vetted its members to avoid creeps. If Wren wanted to contort herself into awkward positions, she should be able to do that in peace.

"Have you ever considered opening a gym?"

"Exercise isn't really my thing."

"The six-pack just...happens?"

"I have good genes."

"Well, I—" Vee paused for a moment, a finger to her lips. "Did you hear that?"

"Hear what?"

"Footsteps. There's somebody outside." Another pause. "No, two people."

Now I heard it too. The metallic scrape of someone fiddling with the lock, and they had either a key or considerably more practice with a set of picks than I did because a moment later, the front door opened with a *creak*.

"Wren?" I whispered.

"No, they're men. Stay or go?"

Vee tiptoed over to the bedroom window, and we both let out a breath of relief when it slid smoothly open. Now we had a decision to make. The window was around the corner from the front door, which meant we could sneak out into the backyard unseen, wait for Wren's visitors to leave, and then follow them. Alternatively, if we hid in the bathroom, we could jump them and ask a few questions. Vee and I could easily overpower two men, even those who thought they were tough guys. We'd both been blessed with strength and speed no human was able to match.

But would they talk? Joseph informed me that some mortals had a stubborn streak, no matter how much pain was inflicted. And with curious neighbours above and to the side, we'd have to keep the interrogation quiet.

If we hung back and followed, who knew where they'd lead us? Were they common or garden burglars? Or up to something more nefarious? With Wren missing, the latter seemed quite possible. But daylight would soon be upon us, and whenever the sun's rays touched Vee's skin, her epidermis began smoking. She wouldn't be able to join me on an escapade across the city.

"Are we leaving?" Vee asked, tapping her watch. She swung a leg over the windowsill as footsteps came closer, leather-soled shoes on laminate. "Would you mind making a decision? Any time today is good."

CHAPTER 3
Blane

"Let's see what they have to say," I suggested to Vee. "We can surprise them from the bathroom."

If the men left, who knew where they'd go? On a normal day, I could have climbed into my car and followed, but on the way over, I'd noticed that the gas tank was almost empty. One more reason to chat in situ.

But Vee shook her head. "I have a better plan. Let's meet them at the front door."

Hmm, an interesting idea, and one that had the added advantage of cutting off their escape route should they try to run. And they'd left the door open, the fools. It only took a moment for us to slip out the window and get ourselves into position.

"Knock knock," I called, loud enough to be heard but not loud enough to disturb the neighbours again.

Why not try the civil approach first? If they tried to scarper, *then* we'd overpower them. Bundling them back inside wouldn't take more than a second.

Movement in the apartment stopped.

"Wren?" I called. "Are you there?"

Frantic whispers came from inside, and Vee giggled softly.

"They're trying to decide whether to climb out the window, barge past us, or pretend they're meant to be here," she said softly. "Okay, the guy with the deeper voice is complaining that he won't fit through the window."

How unfortunate.

"Wren, it's Chad. Are you okay? Your door was open."

"Chad?" Vee mouthed.

"Might as well use the name of somebody I don't like."

"The smaller man is going out the window."

"Let him. We only need one."

"Are you sure?"

"It might even be better—no witnesses."

We stepped over the threshold and closed the door behind us just as the second man came barrelling out of the bedroom. He'd planned to flatten me, that much was clear, but he stopped short when he saw Vee. An enforcer and a gentleman? Or just easily distracted?

Whatever, we used his hesitation to our benefit. I grabbed one arm, Vee grabbed the other, and we pinned him against the wall. He struggled. Boy, did he struggle. His eyes said "fuck you," and his body said "steroid abuse." Muscles in his arms bulged, but anger turned to fear when he realised we were both considerably stronger than we appeared.

"Wren, you look different," I said. "Have you changed your hair?"

He spat in my face. Well, if that was how we were going to play things... I kneed him in the genitals, then dodged to the side as he vomited. Mortals were strangely sensitive about that particular part of their anatomy. Admittedly, I wasn't fond of physical altercations, but thanks to the abundance of heat and fire in Plane Three, I'd built up a reasonably high pain threshold. Earth had a much more refreshing climate, Las Vegas excepted, which was yet another reason I hadn't been too sorry when my father relieved me of my previous job.

But the vomit smelled, and someone would have to clean that up before Wren came home. Thank goodness Joseph was duty-bound to serve me.

"That's not very friendly," I told the stranger. "Care to tell us what you're doing in Wren's apartment?"

"Go to hell."

"I've been there many, many times, and it's not as bad as you might think."

"You tryna be clever?"

"*I'm* asking the questions. Why are you here?"

Silence.

Vee tried a different approach. "We're just worried about our friend. Either you're also a friend, and you're worried about her too, or you're here for a different reason. Can you see our dilemma?"

"Fine, sure, I'm a friend of hers. I came to check up on her when she didn't answer the phone."

"Did her sister call you? I know she's anxious too."

"Yeah, yeah, her sister called me."

"Funny—she doesn't have a sister. Now, why are you really here?"

"You bitch."

The man lunged forward, and I learned an important lesson: the next time I took a prisoner, I needed to check his pockets before any discussion took place. A knife had found its way into the man's hand, a nasty-looking switchblade. Vee slammed him back against the wall, but not before he slashed her cheek.

Now the drywall was cracked—another job for Joseph —and curses spewed from the man's lips. Curses that slowed considerably as Vee's cheek healed before his eyes.

The words trickled to a blessed stop entirely when she grinned, revealing elongated canine teeth. Clearly, she was peckish. When she'd recently indulged in a good meal, her smile was picture perfect.

"Do you want to try that again?" Her fingers dug into his shoulder, her nails as sharp as talons. Today, she'd painted them turquoise to match her hair.

"W-w-who are you people?"

Better. Yes, this attitude was *much* better.

"Where's Wren?"

"I-I-I don't know."

"Why are you here?"

"Some guy hired me to pick her up, that's all."

"What guy?"

When he hesitated, I got into the spirit of the game and let my hand heat. I could brand a man with my touch, or spark the little fires necessary to keep Plane Three at a summery hundred degrees.

"Hey, what are you—"

"She asked you for a name."

"I don't know the damn name! A guy in a bar, he gave me a hundred bucks and promised another five when I did the job."

Okay, now we were getting somewhere.

"Do you make a habit of doing illegal work for men you don't know?"

"Rent keeps going up, man. I gotta make the cash somehow."

"You haven't considered getting a legitimate job?"

"That don't pay shit, and you have to work eight hours a day if you wanna eat more than rabbit food."

Oh, my heart bled. Metaphorically, of course—my internal organs recovered as quickly as Vee's skin did on the rare occasions they got damaged.

"So presumably there was meant to be a handover? Where and when?"

"Power Zone on South Thirteenth."

"What's that? An appliance store?"

And where was South Thirteenth Street? In Fremont East, if I wasn't mistaken.

"A gym."

"And the time?"

"They didn't say, man. Just told me to press the buzzer and ask for Zion."

"You were meant to do that tonight?"

"Tonight, tomorrow night... They gave me the address and told me to drive her there."

He made himself sound like a fucking chauffeur, but no doubt Wren would have been unconscious or possibly tied up. If I'd been able to nominate residents for Plane Three, this entitled prick would have made an excellent candidate, but sadly, my responsibilities had never extended that far.

"Which gym do you go to?" Vee asked.

"None of your fuckin' business."

And we'd been getting along so well...

"Answer the question." I raised the temperature again, and his skin began to sizzle. A yelp, and he immediately became more cooperative.

"Body Rock! I go to Body Rock."

"Have you ever been to Power Zone?"

"Nah, man. I've driven past it, but I've never been inside. That place is full of mean motherfuckers."

"Interesting that you don't include yourself in that collective." I ran a fingertip down the man's cheek. "Underneath this tough exterior, you're just a pussycat."

"Fuck you." Then he looked between us. "Uh, sorry. I didn't mean that."

I laughed. Toying with humans could be so

entertaining. But the fact that this man had seen more of Vee and me than we would usually show to mere mortals did present us with a problem. Sure, we could let him go, allow him to walk out of Wren's apartment under threat of retribution if he breathed a word about our presence, and I was almost certain he would obey. He was hired help, not a loyal foot soldier. Or if we knocked him out before we left, he'd probably assume he'd dreamed the whole nightmare, apart from the handprint burned into his face, anyway.

The other option? Well, removing a human soul from its host body was child's play when you were the former Lord of the Underworld. Did I mean death? Death was such a final word. So many negative connotations. His essence would be freed from this abomination of a body that he'd spent so long abusing, his soul granted the freedom to make a fresh start. Vee still got a little touchy about these things, but that was only because she hadn't visited the other planes. Hadn't seen the celestial world for herself. Her experience of the human race was limited to Earth's Plane Five, which was such a tiny part of the universe. Reincarnation was nearly as old as time.

Decisions, decisions... When Vee glanced my way and raised an enquiring eyebrow, I knew she was having similar thoughts.

"So..." I said. "How hungry are you?"

CHAPTER 4

Blane

"I promised Jack that I wouldn't mess around with strangers anymore."

Ah, a vampire with a conscience. A true novelty. And in all likelihood, Vee was also the only vampire in Plane Five who was dating a cop. Jack Callahan was a detective with the Las Vegas Metropolitan Police Department, and he was far better at keeping secrets than I'd ever imagined. When a friend of mine was murdered in Club Dead earlier in the year, he'd headed up the investigation, and the killer wasn't the only person whose dark side had been revealed. Perhaps it was Callahan's near-death experience that made him bite his tongue? Or maybe a touch of fear?

Whatever, Callahan was dating Vee now, so she no longer had to suck blood from drunkards and drug addicts, and he didn't have to investigate any reports of unexplained puncture wounds. Although Vee had always been careful while dining out, I had to concede. Her saliva contained a healing enzyme, and provided she didn't drink past the point of death, the holes disappeared fast.

"A sip won't hurt."

The prisoner's gaze pinged between us. "What you talkin' about?"

"Your fate," I told him. "We wouldn't want to let you go, only for you to spill the beans about our meeting to Zion."

For the first time, the man seemed to realise he might be in serious trouble.

"Hey, I'm not gonna do that, I swear. You can trust me."

"Can I? They say there's no honour among thieves, and I'm sure the same holds true for kidnappers."

"I wasn't exactly gonna kidnap the girl. It was more of a relocation."

"You still planned to take her against her will."

"How many other young women have you 'relocated'?" Vee asked.

"She was the first. I'm a good guy, honest. I just needed to make a few bucks."

Really? A good guy? Well, we'd see about that. Did you know that you can tell a person's character by the shade of their soul? In the planes, we referred to it as karmic tint. The darker the soul, the more negative karma had accumulated over its lifetime. Theoretically, two separate Earth-based teams—the Electi and Opus Vi— were meant to weed out those folks and send them to Plane Three so they didn't find their way back to the mortal world. The Electi had the power to condemn the dark souls right away—do not pass go, do not collect two hundred dollars—while Opus Vi sent them to face Ad Tabulam, a council that sat in final judgment. Ditto for the light souls, the best of which took on the appearance of a rainbow with the accumulation of significant positive karma. The pure-white souls were...disappointing. Not bad, but not good either. They'd gone through life turning the other cheek, only helping their fellow citizens when there was something in it for them too. In centuries gone by, they were known as nobility, but now they'd evolved into socialites, wellness gurus, and social media stars.

Anyhow, Factora Angelus should have been nominating the rainbow souls to spend eternity in Plane Two as reward for their good works. The problem? Both Opus Vi and Factora Angelus had gone AWOL, and the Electi had only recently gotten their act together after several centuries of absence. As a result, Planes Two and Three were underpopulated, while Plane Five was full of assholes.

And Ad Tabulam spent much of their time playing cards.

So, was this man a good guy, as he claimed? Was his attempted "relocation" of Wren a one-off? Fortunately, I had a way to tell.

When my siblings and I were created, the Celestial Council had bestowed a gift upon each of us. My ability to move souls around had been useful in the unruly environment of Plane Three, but in Plane Five? Not so much. Tonight might be a rare exception. With a flick of my wrist and a touch of concentration, I separated Wren's visitor into his constituent parts—the meat-covered skeleton that was stuck here on Earth, and the soul.

Vee gasped as the body crumpled to the floor.

"What did you do?"

"I'm just checking something."

Hmm, that soul looked pretty dark to me. A little extra focus, and it stretched apart into its two components: the secondary soul that contained a person's memories, likes and dislikes, that sort of thing, and the primary soul that held the human essence: the subconscious and the conscience. Yes, I'd been right.

"See? He has the midnight of primary souls. Prussian blue and heading toward indigo."

The darkest souls were almost black. This man wasn't quite there yet, but he was well on the way. His essence shimmered under the lights of Wren's hallway, a malevolent shadow. His secondary soul—the image of him in life—looked on, and it wasn't happy. More incredulous than angry, but give it time.

"Put that back!" Vee screeched.

"Why? So he can do even more damage here in Plane Five?"

"Because...because you can't kill a man in Wren's freaking apartment."

"It might actually be advantageous. The cops would come, and then they'd search for her."

"They'd also search for us. The neighbour upstairs saw our faces, and so did a police officer, remember?"

She did make a good point. I didn't want to draw any unwanted attention to my presence here. Detective Callahan had been remarkably understanding about the whole situation, but his colleagues might not share the same attitude.

"Okay, then we can take him somewhere else. If we carry him between us, it'll look as if he's walking."

"Forget the location; we shouldn't kill anyone, period."

"Then what do you propose we do?" I ticked off the points on my fingers. "This man is a criminal, he's a liar, and he's an all-around nasty piece of work. He's only going to hinder our search for Wren, and I won't risk him speaking to Zion."

"I'm dating a freaking cop."

"Unfortunate, given your purpose."

Rumour said that vampires had been an early prototype of the Electi, a theory borne out by the fact that for years, the only newcomers to Plane Three had been a trickle of European ingénues, glowing souls with bewildered expressions who reported spending time with a charming Frenchman before they woke up dead. I had a suspicion that the Frenchman was Vee's estranged husband, Voltaire. But that was an issue for another day.

"Enough with the 'killing is your destiny' crap. I'm an artist, and when I'm not painting, I'm a cocktail waitress." But Vee took a step closer. "Is that really his soul? Why is it in two parts?"

"Conscious and subconscious. When the soul is assigned a new body, the conscious part gets wiped, and they're given a fresh one. But the subconscious is the important part. That dictates a person's nature, and his is disappointing. Definitely a candidate for Plane Three."

Vee reached toward the pulsating shimmer, then paused, her finger outstretched. "What would happen if I touched it?"

"Nothing. You can't interact with it outside its host body, and you can only see it because I'm holding it here. There are trapped souls everywhere in Plane Five, so I've heard, but those are only visible to the Electi."

"Your Uncle Tiberius was a real asshole, did you know that?"

Ah, Great-Uncle Tiberius. The flawed genius who'd dreamed up this convoluted system. Several thousand years ago, he'd decided to decentralise parts of the soul management process, and he'd succeeded to the point where each team had no damn clue what the other teams were doing. Then he'd vanished.

"You'll hear no arguments from me."

Vee waved a hand through the man's soul, curious. "The darkness is bad, isn't it?"

"Indeed."

A shudder. "I feel it."

"Good. You're supposed to. What's it to be, Vee? I can't hold him here forever."

Ten minutes or so, that was my limit. After that, I had to either put the soul back into a body or let it pass to another plane.

"Why don't we just tie him up and give the information to Jack? Let him look for Wren?"

"Because your dearly beloved has procedures to follow. All those pesky rules. Firstly, we'd have to submit statements explaining that we'd broken into Wren's apartment, and secondly, this fool would be out on bail before you could blink. If he vanishes quietly, he won't be able to warn Zion, and we'll have a better chance of finding Wren."

"I don't like this. What if Jack finds out?"

"I'm not going to tell him. Are you?"

"Killing is still wrong."

"I was the Lord of the Underworld, Vee. I checked my morals at the door."

"Does Plane Three even have a door?"

"Okay, so it's more of a portal." A one-way trip for the damned. I was one of the few who could leave at will. "Don't think of it as death. Think of it as recycling. He'll get a new body; it'll just be a smaller one, and he'll struggle to do so much damage for the next decade or two. We'll be doing him a favour. Aren't your school years meant to be the best time of your life?"

"I'm not the right person to ask; I went to school two hundred years ago."

"And the Celestial Academy was on a par with Plane Three."

"For the record, I hate this idea."

"Does that mean you're on board?"

"What if I say no?"

"Then you'll want to close your eyes for the next part."

"You're such an asshole, Blane."

"Now you sound just like my older sister."

"How are we going to get him into the car?"

I knew she'd come around. "Relax, I have a plan for that."

"Do you have a plan for finding Wren? Because I can't see any clues around here."

"If she's on the run, she probably went to stay with her brother."

"Does he live in Vegas?"

"I'm not sure."

"The sun will rise soon. I don't have time to hunt for him."

"I can take Joseph."

He'd love to go, but he'd undoubtedly insist on swinging by the barber on the way. Another delay. When he stole the lawyer's body, he'd somehow managed to inherit the man's vanity as well. Although perhaps we should speak with Zion first? Find out more about the man? If Wren was still in danger of being abducted, she wouldn't want to come back to Vegas.

With a sigh, I pushed the souls back into the man's flesh and chuckled at his bemused expression when he opened his eyes and found himself on the floor. Several seconds passed before he got his bearings and scrambled to his feet.

"What happened? What did you do to me?"

"Absolutely nothing. I guess you must have been overwhelmed, because you fainted."

"Fainted? No fucking way."

"We're a little concerned you might have a medical issue, and neither of us wants to be blamed for your untimely demise. If you give us your assurance that you'll play no further part in Wren's life, we'll drive you home and forget about the whole thing."

As I'd hoped, he seized the lifeline I offered. Too bad I'd had an eternity's practice at lying.

"Yeah, sure, sure, I promise. Like, Wren who?"

Did anabolic steroids rot a man's brain, or was it the other way around? Did he have to be a fool to take them in the first place? In truth, it didn't matter either way, and I held Wren's front door open for the man, ready to grab his collar if he tried to run. But good little soldier that he was, he just followed me to the car.

"Nice wheels."

"You think? I was worried the Bentley might be too flashy."

"We're in Vegas, man."

"An excellent point." I opened the rear door, pleased that Joseph had shown the foresight to select the tinted rear windows. "You'll have to give me directions to your place. Don't forget to wear your seat belt."

Vee climbed into the front beside me, and as soon as we pulled away, I flicked our passenger's soul out of his body again. This time, I let it go.

"Enjoy Plane Four, you dumb chump."

After a quick look behind her, Vee clasped her hands in her lap.

"Which one is Plane Four? I forget."

"Humans call it Limbo. Do you want a drink? His heart will beat for a few more seconds while it catches up with the program."

"Nothing tastes as good as Jack."

"So you're not going to indulge?"

Another glance.

"You could give Callahan a night off."

"I thought we didn't want him asking questions?"

"True."

"Maybe I'll just have a mouthful. I need to give the punctures a moment to heal before he breathes his last."

A moment later, she scrambled into the back seat, gone in the blink of an eye. I watched in the rear-view mirror as she bit into the man's carotid artery and drank, making a face when his blood didn't taste as good as she hoped. Vee so badly wanted to believe that she was still human, that her own karma was firmly positive, but at heart, she was undeniably a vampire. She couldn't change her raison d'être any more than I could.

"Don't break the speed limit," she instructed between mouthfuls.

"Yes, Mom."

But I lifted off the gas. Neither of us wanted to answer awkward questions about why we had a dead body strapped into the back seat of the car, even if a precise cause of death could never be established. I drove to the outskirts of the city, keeping an eye on the horizon. There was a faint yellow glow, but the sun wasn't ready to make an appearance quite yet.

"Did the hole heal okay?" I asked Vee.

"I do know what I'm doing, thank you very much. Unlike some people with their handprints."

When I spotted a tangle of scrubby bushes by the side of the road, I pulled to a stop and tucked the car in alongside. It was still too early for much traffic, and it only took the two of us a moment to dump the body into the undergrowth. The wildlife would be feasting before dawn.

And I had a choice to make—where should I go next? Should Joseph and I have a chat with Zion? Or was it better to head directly for Wren's brother's place? I knew what Joseph's answer would be, which was why I didn't ask him. No, this decision would be all mine.

CHAPTER 5

Blane

I f I ever returned to Plane Three, I had a great idea for a new game. Who on earth invented parallel parking, anyway? The idea of trying to wedge my Bentley into a space barely a foot longer than the car itself... How did people do this?

"Do I have room on that side?" I asked Joseph.

"Uh..." The *crunch* of alloy on concrete made me cringe. "No."

Great. Another scratch to go with the dozen I already had.

Plane Three's earthly equivalent would be a home without sufficient off-street parking. Fortunately, I didn't live in one—Club Dead had a generously sized parking lot to the rear—but Kayden Gillebrand did. According to the information Joseph had tracked down, Kayden inhabited a narrow duplex in the south of Mesquite, not too far from the golf club he worked at.

"Why don't you try parking farther along the street?" Joseph suggested.

Firstly, because there were cars as far as the eye could see, and secondly because that would mean admitting defeat.

"It'll fit in here."

At least the camera in the rear bumper would tell me if I was about to hit the ugly SUV parked behind me. Why did vehicles have to be so big? My next car would be a sporty two-seater, something small and fast. Or a motorbike. Although, hmm... If I had to dump another body, where would I put it? How big was the trunk on a Ferrari?

"I thought you were going to practise reversing?" Joseph said.

"I didn't get time, okay?"

"If you added up all the time you spend trying to park, I bet you've wasted a month of your life."

"I'm immortal. Time is irrelevant."

"Fine, a month of your pretend human life."

"I hate this damn car, and it's not my fault Plane Three doesn't have on-street parking, so—"

"Hey, the front door just opened."

I stomped on the brakes, and sure enough, Kayden Gillebrand was standing in the entryway, his arm around a slender brunette. A slender *female* brunette. Joseph's sigh of disappointment as Kayden kissed her settled heavily over the custom-tailored suit he'd insisted on changing into for our visit.

Oh dear.

"I'm sorry you had to see that. But at least now you know, huh? When we get back to Vegas, why don't you try one of those dating apps?"

"I did. The last guy said he was a successful businessman who enjoyed dirty weekends, and it turned out he owned a sewage cleanup company. Right after dinner, he got an emergency call and had to go remove contaminated water from someone's bathroom."

"Ouch."

The brunette was jogging in our direction now, and as she came closer, she waved. Her lips moved. I rolled down the window to hear what she was saying.

"Don't worry; I'm just leaving."

What did she want me to do? Offer congratulations for her escape?

"I wasn't worrying."

She gave a nervous laugh and held up a key. "That's my SUV right behind you. Give me a second, and I'll get out of your way." A pause. "You didn't scratch it, did you?"

I expected a snarky comment from Joseph, but he was still sulking.

"No, just the kerb."

Perhaps I should have taken driving lessons before I obtained my first car, but it had been so much easier to simply buy the licence from a slightly shady guy I met in a bar and take to the road. I'd spent plenty of time trundling around in my father's golf cart in Plane Two, so it wasn't as if I'd had no experience of driving whatsoever, but parking had turned out to be more challenging than I expected. Were parking lessons a thing? When Joseph got over his snit, I'd ask him to look into that.

After the brunette left, I abandoned the Bentley in the vicinity of the kerb and climbed out, stretching my arms over my head. It had been a long couple of days. Luckily, I didn't need much sleep—immortality did have its plus points—but I'd tweaked a muscle entertaining a pair of pretty blonde dancers last week, and sitting around for long periods left me uncomfortable. Decima could fix the problem in an instant—healing was her superpower—but that would mean swallowing my pride and asking her for help. No, I'd try a masseuse first.

"Do you want to wait in the car?" I asked Joseph.

"No, I'll come with you."

Kayden Gillebrand opened the door a second after I knocked, almost as if he'd been waiting. Or maybe he'd just been watching TV? The door opened directly into a minuscule living room, and a soccer game was playing on a giant flatscreen opposite. Did people partake in soccer at this time in the morning? Or was it pre-recorded? Several years ago, I'd started a soccer league in Plane Three, but I heard Decima had discontinued it. Even though the games were played with flaming skulls rather than regular balls, she'd still considered that the guests were having too much fun.

"Babe, what did you forg—" Kayden stopped abruptly. "Do I know you?"

"Not exactly, but Wren works in my casino. We've met once or twice."

Kayden gave me a harder look. "Right, yeah. Dane?"

"Blane, and do you remember Joseph?"

"Uh, maybe? Why are you here?"

"Call it a welfare check. Wren didn't show up for work last night, which wasn't like her."

Kayden fidgeted, but instead of the worry I'd have expected from a man who'd just found out his sister was missing, I got a flash of alarm followed by an indifferent shrug.

"She probably ate something bad," he said.

"That's possible, but she's not in her apartment, so I thought she might have come here. Did she?"

"I haven't seen her since last week." His mouth twisted. "Is this normal? You know, checking up on people?"

"Being concerned for the wellbeing of my team members? Of course. But Wren's the first employee to disappear. Have you spoken with her?"

"No, man," he said, but he was lying. Kayden Gillebrand was nervous, but of us rather than the fact that his sister had gone AWOL. "Maybe she's staying with a friend?"

"Any idea who?"

Again, Kayden shifted from foot to foot. "We don't really talk about that stuff."

He knew more than he was letting on, but it was also clear he wasn't going to spill the beans to us. Which meant that either Wren's predicament was something to do with work, or it was serious enough to keep secret from everyone. Serious enough that she'd walk out of her job because of it.

Could there be a problem at Tilt? I didn't think so, but more importantly, Vee hadn't mentioned any issues, and she was closer to the employees than I was. They thought she was one of them. Which technically she was, but she also wasn't. Vee and I had grown close over the past few months, and if she had any concerns about the poker club, she would have mentioned them to me before we dispatched the bodybuilder last night.

The bodybuilder... Why had he been sent to kidnap Wren? Yes, his presence meant that the problem was elsewhere.

And Kayden was covering for his sister.

I couldn't force the truth out of him, not with Joseph present anyway, and Wren wouldn't be too pleased if I strong-armed her brother either. No, we'd have to back off temporarily. But I wouldn't give up. I'd already lost one colleague recently—okay, so Serenity had been a freelancer rather than an employee—and once again, I'd experienced a little of the pain mortals suffered. It wasn't a feeling I enjoyed.

"If you see Wren, could you ask her to call me?" I held out a business card. "I just want to know she's okay."

"Sure, I'll tell her." His eyes widened. "Uh, I mean, if I see her, I'll pass on the message."

Oh, he definitely knew where she was.

"Thanks, I appreciate it."

Would Kayden call his sister? Joseph had enhanced hearing, and if he hid in the yard, he'd be able to eavesdrop on the conversation. Or perhaps Kayden would pay Wren a visit? If we stuck around in Mesquite, we might be able to pick up a clue.

Or we could head back to Vegas and pay Zion a visit— we knew he was involved somehow.

Decisions, decisions... Running Plane Three had been so much more straightforward than navigating life here on Earth.

CHAPTER 6
Blane

"**D**id you see the bag in the hallway?" Joseph asked.

"What bag?"

I'd been focusing on Kayden Gillebrand's reactions, not his surroundings.

"The duffel bag next to the side table. Either Kayden's going to the gym, or he's going on a trip. And Wren said he doesn't go to the gym."

"You asked her that? What, did you think you'd join and accidentally-on-purpose coordinate your workouts with his?"

Joseph's reddening cheeks said that had been precisely his plan. The joys of inhabiting a human body—there was no hiding his true thoughts. In demon form, darkness and shadows, he was a lot harder to read.

"If you're going to belittle me, I'm going home."

"Home to Las Vegas, or home to Plane Three?"

"Vegas, of course. Who would want to spend longer than five minutes with Decima?"

"I thought you enjoyed torture and bondage and all that shizzle?"

"Not with her." He shuddered. "Never with her. Do you want my help or not?"

Joseph might have acted annoying at times, but his loyalty was unquestionable. Plus he *had* spotted the duffel bag.

"Yes, I want your help." I sighed because humility didn't come naturally to me. Other than the occasional moment of grovelling to my father, I'd never had to apologise for anything in Plane Three. "I'm sorry I belittled you. You really think Kayden's planning to take a trip?"

"Yes, and since he doesn't travel for work, I bet he's going to see Wren, wherever she is."

"He might be going on vacation."

"When his sister's in trouble?"

A fair point.

"You think we should follow him?" Because that might present a problem. "This car isn't exactly subtle."

Joseph nodded his agreement. "And it's possible he noticed when you spent ten minutes trying to park outside his residence, ergo he knows this is your car. One glance in the rear-view mirror, and he'll realise we're behind him."

"Please, spend even more time criticising my driving abilities. Why don't you try doing something constructive?"

"Like what?"

"Like finding us another vehicle?"

"In Mesquite?"

"Well, we don't have time to drive back to Las Vegas, do we?"

"Why can't *you* find another vehicle?"

"Because...because..." The simple answer would have been that I was the boss and he was required to serve me. In

Plane Three, that excuse would have worked, but I'd discovered the power balance wasn't so simple in Plane Five. Freedom was a big deal here. Wars had been fought and lost based on the concept. And much as I hated to admit it, I was grateful that Joseph had accompanied me on my journey. Before Vee came along, he'd been the only soul I was able to talk with freely, the only creature who knew my secret. With everyone else, I had to wear a mask. Over the past several years, Joseph had become a friend as well as a servant, and I needed to keep reminding myself of that fact. "Because you're better at procuring chattels than I am. *Please* would you find us another vehicle?"

That drew a smile out of him. "Fine. I'll arrange alternative transportation. You need to move the Bentley somewhere else and watch the house."

If I could find a reasonably empty field or a grocery store with a generously sized parking lot, I might be able to squeeze the car in with only two or three attempts, but I had a better idea.

"How about you take the Bentley, and I'll call you if Kayden leaves?"

"*When* he leaves."

I only hoped that Joseph was right in his assumption. In Plane Three, he'd been a bureaucrat, more concerned with arranging schedules and monitoring the usage of consumables than with performing psychoanalysis. It was only when we came to Earth that he'd developed an interest in the human mind. But his twin sister had been a member of my enforcement team, so maybe when their souls were cleaved during creation, some of Grimalda's investigative abilities had rubbed off on him?

"Okay, *when* he leaves."

"Joseph, tell me you have a vehicle?"

Fifteen minutes after I'd hunkered into position behind a neighbour's trash can—it smelled disgusting, by the way—Kayden Gillebrand scurried out of his home carrying the duffel bag and climbed into a small black car parked fifty yards down the street. His steps were fast, his frame tense. The man was definitely unhappy with the current situation.

"Just finishing the negotiations."

"Hurry, he's getting into a vehicle."

"Be there in one minute."

"Make it thirty seconds."

Kayden's car engine coughed into life as I heard a shout from behind me.

"Freeze, mothertrucker!"

It might have been early March, but this was Nevada. Freezing was highly unlikely. I turned to find a tiny grey-haired lady standing on the porch of the house behind me, and she was pointing a gun in my direction.

"Be careful with that thing. You might shoot me."

"That's the whole point, asshole. What you doin' over there by the garbage cans? Are you one of them dumpster divers?"

"How many dumpster divers do you know who wear six-thousand-dollar suits?"

She considered that for a moment. "Are you a burglar?"

Kayden's car backfired as he pulled out of the parking space, and the woman jumped three inches in the air, squeezing the trigger as she did so. It seemed her aim was better than her judgment because damn, that stung. And now the suit was worthless because the jacket had a hole in it. I pulled out my pocket square—at least it served some purpose—and used it to blot up the blood that had seeped out of my chest before my body healed. Joseph was going to laugh his head off when he found out about this.

"You shot me. You actually shot me."

The woman had turned pale now, and the gun slipped out of her hand, then landed with a *clunk* on the wooden porch. At least the damn thing didn't go off again.

"I shot you," she whispered, clutching at her own chest.

For the love of Dad, I didn't have time for this. "Yes, exactly. You need to take more care when handling a firearm."

A man ran out of the house next door, barefoot in pyjama pants, still with blobs of shaving foam on his face.

"What happened? I heard gunshots."

"It was a car backfiring, but the noise scared your neighbour. I think she's having a turn."

"Margaret, are you okay?"

"I...I..."

"Maybe you should sit with her for a while? Get her a glass of water?"

"Sure, I'll do that. Hey, is that blood on your shirt?"

"No, I spilled ketchup on it earlier." I gave a nonchalant shrug. "They never give you enough napkins at the drive-through. Nice meeting you, Margaret."

I strolled out of the yard just in time to catch sight of Kayden turning right at the end of the road. Was I worried that Margaret might spill the beans about my immortality? No, not really. Who would believe her? Either she'd keep her mouth shut, or she'd be written off as delusional. Or perhaps those chest pains would fast-track her to Plane Four and she'd forget all about me?

Now, where was Joseph? If we didn't set off after Kayden right now, we'd lose not only him but our best lead to finding Wren. I was about to call him again when I heard rattling, the sound of an engine in its death throes. A horn sounded behind me, more of a wheeze than a *toot*, and I turned to see a pickup that had once been white but was now more rust-coloured belching its way in my direction, leaving a trail of smoke in its wake.

And worse, Joseph was behind the wheel.

Tell me he's kidding.

He juddered to a halt beside me. "Hop in."

"*This* is your idea of staying inconspicuous?"

"There are a couple of ball caps on the seat. The guy threw them in for free."

Could this day get any worse?

"Tell me you didn't pay money for this rust bucket?"

Yes. Yes, it could.

"No, not actual cash. I traded the Bentley for it."

This had to be a joke. "You swapped my luxury sedan for a truck that's only one pothole away from a merciful end at the junkyard?"

"You said you hated the Bentley. Are we going after Kayden, or aren't we?"

I sucked in a breath. Some days, I was glad I'd come to Plane Five. Happy to be living among mortals and experiencing their sins for myself. But other days, this one included, I longed to be back in Plane Three, wrangling unruly souls and keeping the fires of Hell stoked. If I ever returned, I was going to somehow take this truck with me and make the next miscreant to rub me up the wrong way drive it for all eternity.

"Yes, we're going after Kayden."

I yanked on the door handle, and it came off in my hand.

"The guy said that handle can be temperamental—just clip it back on and lift as you pull."

Suddenly, dying from a gunshot wound seemed the lesser of two evils.

"Never again am I putting you in charge of transportation."

Joseph just grinned as we lurched away from the kerb. "Okay, next time we'll take the bus."

CHAPTER 7

Blane

By a miracle, we made it to Saint George, Utah, without the suspension falling out of the truck. Kayden didn't seem to be a fan of the rear-view mirror because he failed to notice us in the distance when he pulled into the parking lot of the Rest-E-Z Motel and slotted his car neatly into a space at the far end of the single-storey cinderblock building. The place was a dump—mustard-yellow paint peeling from the walls, a buzzing neon sign that blinked on and off at random intervals, and assorted trash blowing along the walkway that ran in front of the rooms.

Kayden climbed out of his car and glanced both ways, trying to get his bearings, it seemed. After a moment, he hefted the duffel bag, walked to room six, and knocked on the door. It opened a second later, as if the occupant had been waiting.

"There she is," Joseph murmured.

Why had Wren come to this awful place? Whatever happened to make her leave Vegas, it must have been truly terrible.

"We should talk with her."

"You don't think we should wait until Kayden leaves?"

"What if she goes with him? This truck isn't going to make it much farther. If they decide to drive to, say, Wyoming, we'll be left smoking at the side of the highway."

"Maybe I could source another vehicle?"

"What would you come back with this time? A bicycle?"

Joseph folded his arms and huffed. "Fine, we'll speak with them."

"I'll knock on the door, and you can go around the back in case they try to escape through the window."

"You really think they'd do that?"

Who knew? I mean, I'd seen it in a movie once, plus Wren's wannabe kidnappers had tried the same trick, so it seemed a reasonable possibility. And these shoes weren't designed for running. Not that I wanted to run anywhere—I'd get hot, and I couldn't take off my jacket because of the bloodstain on my shirt, which had spread out from the bullet hole in the shape of Montana. Dammit.

"Just go around the back."

"What if I stay here and listen in on the conversation?"

I'd already been shot once for loitering today, and I didn't particularly want it to happen a second time, even to Joseph. He'd never stop whining about it. And the truck parked next to us came complete with a rifle rack and a bumper sticker that said *Gun control is hitting your target*.

"We have the element of surprise right now. Let's not waste it."

I gave Joseph a few minutes to get in place, then climbed out of the truck. When I closed the door, the handle fell off again. Was our roadside assistance coverage up to date? Because we were going to need it on the drive back.

As I paused outside the door to room six, the murmur of voices came from inside, plus the sound of quiet sobbing.

Wren? Something wrenched in my chest, a lurching pain I hadn't felt since my days with Nevaeh. When I saw Wren two days ago, she'd been happy. What had Zion done to her?

I knocked on the door, and the voices stopped abruptly.

"Who's there?" Kayden called.

Should I try the old "room service" trick? Hmm... In this place, no one would believe me.

"It's Lucian Blane."

Silence, then muttering. After a long moment, footsteps approached, the door cracked open, and Kayden peered through the gap. His expression said *Ah, shit.*

"What are you doing here?" he demanded.

"As I said before, I'm performing outreach on behalf of the employee relations team."

"How the hell did you get to this place?"

"In a truck, unfortunately."

"Mr. Blane?" Wren appeared, her pale cheeks stained with tears. "I'm so sorry I didn't call."

"That doesn't matter. I just need to know you're okay. Can I come in?"

Kayden turned to his sister, and when she nodded, he opened the door wide enough for me to step through. The inside of the motel room was as bad as the outside. The carpet, bedspread, and drapes all bore dubious-looking stains, and someone had earned seven years of bad luck for cracking the mirror. Was I superstitious? Not really, but my father moved in mysterious ways.

"What happened, Wren?"

"I...I don't know where to start."

Nowhere, if Kayden had his way. "Do you trust this asshole? He must have followed me here."

"I don't trust anyone at the moment."

I offered what I hoped was a winning smile. Years ago, after Joseph told me I reminded him of Jack Nicholson's

Joker when I grinned, I'd taken to practising in front of the mirror, and I liked to think I'd turned into Bradley Cooper with a hint of a young Zac Efron. Wren didn't recoil in horror, so I had to be doing something right.

"If I wasn't on your side, I'd have returned to Vegas and told Zion where you were, not knocked on the door to offer help."

Now she shrank back. "Z-Z-Zion? What do you know about Zion?"

"When I went to your apartment to look for you last night, one of his acquaintances decided to drop by. You might want to invest in a better lock."

I left Vee's name out of it. Better for Wren to remain blissfully unaware of Vee's dietary preferences.

"You spoke with him? What did he say?"

"Not much, only that he'd come to take you to Zion. Don't worry about him returning; he's resigned from the job now."

"If Zion's looking for me, he'll just send somebody else."

"How do *you* know Zion?"

"I don't. I only know *of* him." Wren shuddered. "He's a psycho."

"If you don't know the man, then why did he send a buddy to kidnap you?"

Wren glanced at her brother, and Kayden shrugged. An unspoken conversation took place, some sibling thing—I communicated with Aurelia that way, but never Decima. With Decima, I mostly wondered how we were related at all.

Wren's answer shouldn't have been important, but as she underwent an internal struggle and bit down on that plump pink bottom lip of hers, I found myself growing tense. I wasn't exactly human, and yet I'd adopted some of their little foibles. Pride, for example. Her perception of me mattered.

Finally, she came to a decision.

"My friend Caria was dating a guy named Laurent. He's the one who knows Zion. Zion used to come over to his place sometimes, and Caria always tried to avoid him. She said he was a nasty little thug—and I heard bad things about him too—but when she told Laurent he gave her the creeps, Laurent just laughed and said she was overreacting."

I let out the breath I'd been holding. Wren *did* trust me, at least a little bit.

"That still doesn't explain why Zion came for you."

Wren sank onto the end of the bed. "As a favour for Laurent, I guess. Caria saw something she shouldn't have, and she told me about it. Now I'm a loose end. A problem that needs to be fixed."

"What did Caria see?"

Wren lost a shade of colour, and her voice dropped to a barely audible whisper.

"She saw a murder."

CHAPTER 8

Blane

A murder? Was that all? For a moment, I thought Wren was going to come up with something dramatic like, say, the unexpected transformation of a werewolf. Which weren't supposed to exist, of course. Damn my Great-Uncle Tiberius and his little experiments. The whole pack of werewolves had escaped centuries ago, and no one knew where they'd ended up. There were rumours, but several years ago when Joseph and I got curious after a slew of sightings and took a vacation to the Carpathian Mountains, the only thing we'd found was a very lost husky.

I had to be grateful to the dog, though. That grouchy mutt was the reason I'd met my dear Nevaeh.

"A murder? Well, that should be straightforward to rectify. All you need to do is tell the police everything you know, and they'll take it from there. If you need an introduction to a detective in the LVMPD, I'm sure—"

"No! No, no, no, no, no. Are you crazy? No cops."

Wren eyed up the door, but thankfully, I spotted Joseph

loitering outside. If he rugby-tackled her in the walkway, that would be awkward, but not as awkward as having to chase her in a truck with a faulty muffler.

"What's wrong with the police?"

I thought mortals were fond of law enforcement? Cops were by far the most popular type of stripper, and humans even had a hotline to call them. Actual cops, not stripper cops. Although that could be an interesting idea for a new business venture. Press one for a cop, two for a fireman, three for a cowboy...

"Because Laurent *owns* cops. Caria went to meet a detective from the LVMPD, and she never came back. Now Laurent has her."

"Maybe he spotted her on the trip over there?"

Wren was already shaking her head, and her curtain of glossy chestnut hair rippled. "You don't understand. He made her call me. She was supposed to lie, to say everything was fine and I should come over to her place for coffee, but at the last moment, she told me the cop called Laurent and he picked her up. She screamed at me to run, and then I think...I think he hit her. The line went dead."

"So you ran?"

"What else was I meant to do? I just packed a bag and took the first bus out of town. I'm so s-s-scared, and I'm terrified for Caria. What if he kills her too?"

Kayden put a comforting arm around his sister's shoulders. "Nah, he can't kill her, not when he might need her to contact you again. As long as you're in the wind, he has to keep her alive."

"Do you really think so?"

"If I was a sicko trying to avoid prison, that's what I'd do."

Kayden's theory did make a certain amount of sense. If

Caria was still breathing, then Laurent could use her as bait or a bargaining chip. If her soul went to Plane Four, Wren would have no incentive to stay in line. She could take out a full-page ad in the *Las Vegas Review-Journal* with all the juicy details of Laurent's crimes.

"So what's the long-term plan?" I asked. "You're going to live in a motel in Utah?"

Granted, I wasn't well acquainted with Wren's finances, but she'd never struck me as the type of woman who had spare cash lying around. Although I paid my staff above-average wages, rent wasn't cheap in Vegas, and Wren didn't have anyone to split living expenses with. Perhaps once she'd evaluated, she'd move in with her brother? Or head to another city in another state? I'd cover the costs for a few months to help out because that was what a responsible human would do, but she'd have to find a better place to hole up than the Rest-E-Z Motel. Was there a Four Seasons nearby?

"How can I stay here? Caria's still with that monster, and I have to find a way to get her out of there."

Quite understandably, Kayden didn't like the idea of Wren running into the arms of the Grim Reaper. Who was mostly a myth, by the way. I say "mostly" because rumour said that one of the Electi had made a particularly poor choice when it came to selecting an outfit on All Hallows' Eve several centuries ago and accidentally turned into a bit of a legend.

"You're going back to Vegas?" Kayden said, shaking his head. "No way."

"Caria's my best friend. I can't just abandon her."

Wren thrust her phone at me, a photo filling the screen. She and a pretty blonde were grinning for the camera, arms around each other's shoulders.

"If Laurent's as dangerous as you think he is, then you'll both wind up dead." Now Kayden was as pale as his sister. "You have to stay here, at least until I can find someone to take over my lease."

"You can't leave Mesquite. I mean, you love your job."

"I also love my sister."

His loyalty was touching. I'd stayed in a whole different plane to get some space from my family, but then again, they were immortal, so what did I know? Although I did miss my little sis. Aurelia was quiet and easygoing, and she spent most of her time in the library. My older sibling, on the other hand...

"You really should consider telling the police," I suggested. "Vee Pelletier is friendly with several trustworthy—"

"No. A thousand times, no. Cops stick together. You know who they protect and serve? Each other."

Not all cops, but Wren seemed to possess the same stubborn streak that Nevaeh used to have. I had as much hope of changing her mind as I did of convincing my father to let me hold a drag race in Plane Two. Tyre marks across one of his beloved golf courses? The *horror*. Which left only one solution. Joseph and I would have to find Laurent and deal with him ourselves.

"Where does Laurent live?" I asked. "Do you know?"

"Caria told me he has properties all over the country. A huge home on the outskirts of Las Vegas, an apartment in New York, a beach house in California, a villa in Florida, a yacht, even a ranch somewhere." Wren hiccuped a sob. "She said he was so charming at first, and then he gradually got more commanding. But not so much that she was scared, you know? She liked a man who knew what he wanted, but...but..."

"How are you going to check those places?" Kayden asked her.

"I don't freaking know!"

"I'll take a look," I offered. "I know people in Vegas."

It wasn't as if this would be my first rodeo—I'd accidentally gotten involved in a murder case earlier in the year —and detective work would give me a break from running my dens of sin. Plus death wouldn't be an issue, not for me anyway. If Joseph helped, he'd have to remember to take care of his body. When we first came to Plane Five, he'd purloined a meat suit from a handsome-in-a-pretty-way drug addict on the cusp of an overdose, then broken the legs jumping down a flight of stairs because he didn't realise humans were quite so fragile. As for me, my body and soul were fully integrated. I'd be just fine.

Wren looked at me with big blue eyes, and I regretted using my handkerchief to soak up blood earlier because I wanted to wipe her tears away.

"You will?" Wren asked, incredulous. "You'll really look for her?"

"Why would you?" Kayden asked, sounding more than a little suspicious.

A fair question—no sane person would put themselves in harm's way. But I wasn't entirely a person, and there was some debate over whether I was sane as well. Should I try to explain that? No, of course not.

"Do you realise how difficult it is to find a good blackjack dealer in Vegas? The mediocre ones are a dime a dozen, but Wren is top tier." That wasn't even a lie. "Plus I prioritise my staff's wellbeing, which includes taking care of them in their hour of need. Wren, do you have a place to stay? My apartment has three spare bedrooms."

"Aw, hell no," Kayden said. "You want to get into her panties? Wrong time, wrong place, asshole."

What? Why were humans so obsessed with sex? Granted, the act was a pleasurable way to spend a few hours, but it was so easy to find women willing to get naked with me that they held little allure. With Nevaeh, I'd been addicted to the spiritual connection as much as the physical one. And the fun. When we first met, I'd been covered in mud, carrying a skinny dog that wasn't too fond of me, and she'd nearly died from laughing.

"No, of course not. If I wanted to commit carnal sins, there are plenty of women in Club Dead every night who'd be only too happy to oblige. Would you rather stay here, Wren?"

"I...I don't know. I mean, I want to jump on an airplane and fly the hell out of the USA, but Caria's in Las Vegas."

"Well, seeing as I have security staff downstairs and door locks that work, you'd be safer in my apartment than in yours. Or we could find you a hotel room." I glanced around, and ugh, there was mould on the ceiling. "A *better* hotel room. If you'd rather stay with a woman, I'm sure Vee Pelletier would oblige, but she's dating a cop, so..."

Wren shuddered. "No cops." Then to her brother, "I'd feel safer with someone I know."

"Kayden, you need to watch your back too. If Laurent is serious about getting to Wren, he could use you as leverage in the same way he's using Caria."

Wren lost the little colour she had left. "Oh my gosh."

"I'll be okay," Kayden said, but he didn't sound convinced. Hardly surprising—he wasn't a tough guy; he was a greenkeeper.

"Maybe keep a set of golf clubs around?" I suggested.

"You should go on your vacation," Wren told him. "Kayden's meant to be flying to Hawaii with his girlfriend the day after tomorrow."

Another nail in Joseph's heart. "That would solve the

problem temporarily. Laurent's unlikely to look for him there."

"Go on vacation? Are you joking?" Kayden glared at me. "What about Wren?"

"I'll keep her safe. You have my word on that."

He rolled his eyes. "Right. Just like that, you'll keep her safe. What's in it for you?"

"As I already said, Wren's an excellent blackjack dealer."

"You expect me to believe that? I'm not letting my sister put her life in the hands of a stranger."

"A sensible approach. Thankfully, I'm not a stranger. I've known Wren for months."

"Oh yeah? What's her favourite flavour of potato chip?"

I nearly told him she preferred corn chips, based on the collection of snacks on her kitchen counter, but I bit my tongue. Wren might get curious about how I knew that, and I wasn't planning to confess that I'd broken into her apartment. Well, not *broken* into—there was a key involved —but...

"We've never discussed potato chips."

"Then you don't—"

"Can you two stop fighting?" Wren begged. "Please? Kayden, you saved for years to go on this trip, and didn't you buy a ring for Sarah?"

Ouch. Those nails were going in with a sledgehammer now.

"Yes, but I'd never forgive myself if something happened to you."

"It won't, not if I stay with Mr. Blane. He said there's security, and no one will be looking for me at his place."

"I don't know..."

"If you waste all the money you spent, I swear I'll go right back to my apartment and stay there."

That little flash of fire reminded me of my dear Nevaeh,

and nobody ever won an argument against her. Kayden stood no chance.

His shoulders sagged. "Fine. But if you change your mind, call me and I'll come right back." He cut me a sideways glance. "Day or night, I'll be there. You have to promise."

Wren managed a shaky smile. "I promise."

CHAPTER 9

Blane

Wren looked peaceful in sleep. On the ride back to Vegas yesterday, her features had grown more pinched the closer we got to the city limits, and when she stumbled out of her brother's car—she didn't have her own, apparently—and through the back door of Club Dead late in the evening, she'd worn the look of a condemned woman. Scared yet stoic, ready to accept her fate, whatever that fate may be.

Two days of running, and she was ready to give up.

Or maybe she'd been running her whole life? When Joseph asked Kayden about their parents, Wren had gone rigid beside me in the back seat, and Kayden had shaken his head and said they weren't in the picture. Hadn't been for a long time.

Well, *I* wasn't giving up on her.

Not when I needed her back at her blackjack table, charming Tilt's patrons into parting with their chips.

The lines on her forehead were smoother now, her lips parted slightly as she breathed softly. And before you assume I was a creep who'd snuck into her bedroom, I should mention that she'd passed out on the couch last night within three seconds of sitting down, and when I tried to wake her, she'd just mumbled something incomprehensible and keeled over sideways. Draping a blanket over her and leaving her there to rest had seemed like the best option.

I checked my watch, a platinum Hermès that Joseph had dredged up from his lawyer-host's closet along with the flashy Cartier he favoured. Nearly nine a.m. What was keeping him? He'd headed out to fetch breakfast an hour ago, something light from the French bakery along the street —far better than the packages of ramen in the duffel bag Kayden had schlepped to Utah—but instead he'd gone AWOL. And now Wren stirred, stretching languidly like a cat before she opened her eyes.

"Oh, crap," she muttered, then closed them again.

"Is my apartment really that bad?"

The interior designer I'd hired had described the decor as "modern with a twist." The twist, presumably, referred to the oversized armoire and the giant bookcase with the rolling ladder that my little sister had fallen in love with in an antique shop and insisted I purchase for her to enjoy on her occasional visits. I never had been able to say no to Aurelia.

Wren's entire body shuddered as she sighed. "I was hoping the last forty-eight hours were just a bad dream."

"Sorry to disappoint."

Another sigh, and her eyes flickered open again. They were the most vibrant azure blue, but the fire that used to lurk within them as she dealt cards in Tilt had been all but extinguished. Those sparkling flecks of silver had faded away.

"I guess I should start by saying thank you," she said.

"For what?"

I hadn't done anything, not yet. When Joseph deigned

to return, we'd have a chat with Zion and see what he had to say, but at this rate, we'd be paying a home visit and rousing him from his bed in pyjamas. I could have walked to the bakery and back ten times by now. Or made croissants from scratch, probably.

"For caring. For not being angry when I didn't show up for work."

I was a tiny bit annoyed, mainly because I'd had to suffer the indignity of riding in that abomination of a truck, plus a perfectly good suit had been ruined when I got shot. But I kept that to myself.

"Next time, just talk to me before you flee the state, okay?"

Her bottom lip quivered, and dammit, I knew what that meant. Where had Joseph left the tissues? I didn't carry a handkerchief in my pocket when I was in my apartment, but perhaps I should start?

"Don't be upset. There's nothing we can't fix, I promise." Even as the words left my mouth, I regretted them. I used to make that same promise to Nevaeh, but it turned out to be a lie because I couldn't fix her. *Don't think of the past.* Even Great-Uncle Tiberius hadn't managed to invent a time machine, although if he had, we'd have faced unmitigated disaster. One wrong calculation, and some poor fool would have been stranded with the dinosaurs. Although if he'd convinced Decima to volunteer... I swallowed a sigh of my own, then gave Wren an awkward pat on the shoulder. "I'll start asking questions about your friend, but first, I need you to tell me everything you know."

"But I hardly know anything."

"You probably have more information than you think locked away in that pretty head of yours. I'd suggest discussing it over breakfast, but Joseph disappeared before he could pick up the pastries."

Wren sat up straighter. "Disappeared? What if something happened to him? What if—"

"Relax. He's fine. He probably got distracted by some shiny trinket or another." Joseph was a magpie. In Plane Three, demons weren't allowed material possessions, so from the moment we arrived in Plane Five, he'd made up for lost time and begun buying mountains of unnecessary tat. His apartment was a treasure trove of tchotchkes. A bronze statue of a giraffe? Check. An extraordinary number of shoes? Check. A trapeze? Check. I didn't begrudge him. We were here to learn about sin, after all, and greed certainly counted.

"Are you sure?"

"Positive." If the worst happened and Laurent or Zion or one of their minions caught up with Joseph, he'd just shed his borrowed body, deal with the problem, and find himself a new carcass. "Can I offer you a coffee?"

"Do you have decaf?"

"No, what's the point of that?"

"It's healthier?"

"Living forever is overrated."

"I suppose that right now, I'm just worried about living until next week. Do you have juice?"

"Orange juice or pineapple juice?"

"Either one is good."

There was an open carton of OJ in the refrigerator, and I snorted as I poured two glasses. Decaf. Pah. Regular coffee was a vile-tasting liquid blessed with magical properties. Without the artificial stimulants, it was worthy only of being poured down the drain.

Back in the living room, I took a seat on the coffee table in front of Wren. "So, tell me more about this murder. Who died? Actually..." I held up a hand. "Wait a moment."

If there were tears, I didn't want them to drip on the

leather couch, and it only took a moment for me to fetch a handkerchief from my dressing room. I offered it to Wren.

"Here. Now you can start."

Good call on my part. She sniffled before she even began speaking.

"The woman who died, Caria didn't know her name, but she was a dancer. A dancer at the Pink Squirrel. Do you know it?"

"Only by reputation."

The Pink Squirrel, also known as the Randy Rodent, was a strip club near the aptly named Naked City, a charming part of Las Vegas where muggings were rife and cab drivers refused to venture at night. I'd once made the mistake of taking a shortcut through the area after sundown, and a gang of youths had tagged my Mercedes at a stoplight.

"Caria thought that maybe Laurent owned it, or part-owned it, or had some kind of interest in the place." Wren crinkled her dainty ski-jump nose in disgust. "He said he had business there that night. Just sit at the bar and have a drink, he told her. Watch the show. So she did, but after the third sleaze assumed she worked there and groped her, she'd had enough, and she went to tell Laurent that."

"And she walked in on something she shouldn't have?"

Wren nodded. "They were in an office out back, and she said the girl was just...lying there. On the floor. And then Laurent said, 'Get rid of the trash,' and stood up to leave, so she freaked out and ran."

"To your place?"

"No, back to the bar. She figured that if Laurent knew what she'd seen, he might do the same to her, so when he reappeared, she said she had a migraine and asked him to take her home." Smart lady. Well, smart apart from dating a murderous psychopath, anyway. "*Then* she came to my place, and when she got there, she was so pale I nearly called an ambulance, and she puked twice before she managed to talk. Just pushed past me in the hallway, ran straight to the bathroom, and bleurgh. She was crying too, and I thought that maybe she'd broken up with Laurent because last week, she was all gooey over him, but the reality was so, so much worse. I mean, it's crazy, don't you think? That a businessman can kill a person like that? She said he was so calm, and that scared her more than anything."

"Yes, it's absolutely insane."

Mental note: do *not* rearrange any souls in front of Wren.

"What am I gonna do, Mr. Blane? Caria's missing, I'm freaking terrified, and I can't hide here forever."

"Leave it with me. And it's Blane, not Mr. Blane."

It had been Blane since my school days, when there had been two Lucians in my class at the Celestial Academy. To save confusion, we'd begun using our house names rather than our given names, and I'd been Blane ever since. Only my family and Nevaeh called me Lucian.

Wren grabbed my hand, then realised what she'd done and dropped it in a hurry, and now there was something else besides tears lurking in those expressive eyes. Fear.

"I don't want anyone else to get hurt."

"When you say 'anyone'... Could you clarify? If Laurent happened to stumble off the edge of a very tall building, would you be upset?"

"I don't want *you* to get hurt."

Phew. "Oh, I won't."

"But—"

Saved by the demon. Why did women always have to argue? Joseph sauntered in with a cardboard tray of takeout coffee and a carrier bag from Gerard's Boulangerie, but before I could claim my cappuccino, he tossed a car key at me. I caught it one-handed.

"What's this?"

"You told me to source a new vehicle."

"I didn't mean before breakfast. We're starving here."

Wren timidly raised a hand. "Actually, I'm not hungry at all."

Joseph shrugged. "That's okay. I can eat your pain au chocolat. You want the coffee? Or should I drink that too?"

"Is it decaf?"

"Decaf is illegal in this apartment. Trust me; I'm a lawyer."

I checked the key in my hand. "You bought a Nissan?"

"A Nissan Leaf. It's small, it's environmentally friendly, and the salesman assured me it has excellent parking sensors. You're going to love it."

That's what he'd said about the last four vehicles he purchased, and although Joseph couldn't lie to me—as per Clause 137.6 in the Celestial Handbook—I didn't entirely believe him. More than ever, I missed Nevaeh. She'd been only too happy to drive us wherever we needed to go. Often a little too fast, but I'd gladly paid her speeding fines.

"Hurry up with your croissants," I told Joseph. "We need to talk to a man about a murder."

CHAPTER 10
Blane

"This is a gym? Are you certain we're in the right place?"

Joseph mirrored my incredulity and rolled his eyes. "Only in Las Vegas."

Or possibly Ancient Rome. Power Zone occupied a cavernous warehouse whose ambience could best be described as Colosseum meets strip club. Somebody with dubious taste had recreated a gladiatorial arena in East Las Vegas, and it was every bit as horrific as you might imagine. And also historically inaccurate. I'd visited the original version several times back in the day, and sand had covered the floor, not grubby industrial carpet.

The front desk was recessed in a stone archway, lit by pink neon lights. As we waited for the toga-clad receptionist to finish with the customer ahead of us, Joseph knocked on one wall.

"Fibreglass," he commented.

Cheap as well as tacky. Zion wouldn't be winning any design awards. Or hygiene awards—the smell of stale sweat was overpowering. Thank goodness my apartment came with its own gym for those "once in a blue moon" moments when I felt like exercising; otherwise, I might have to put on a pair of sandals and purchase a membership at a place like this.

Or not. I didn't feel inclined to give Zion a cent. After I'd tried researching Power Zone online and found nothing substantial—who didn't have a website in this day and age? —I'd called several acquaintances to ask about the gym and the man who ran it. The general consensus? Zion was loyal to no one, a fixer who'd do everything from selling drugs to sourcing thugs in order to make a quick buck. The thugs were problematic enough on their own, but if Zion was dealing in illegal substances, that took my dislike of the man to a whole new level.

"What can I do for ya?" the receptionist asked. A badge pinned to her toga said "Minerva," and I wasn't sure whether that was her real name or a continuation of the Ancient Rome theme. Her hair was a spectacularly unnatural blonde, almost as white as her teeth, and her breasts were barely contained in her flimsy outfit.

I offered a smile. "Who do we speak to about membership?"

"You want to join this place?" She studied us for a moment, chewing gum loudly at the same time. "*You?*"

Perhaps in hindsight, I should have worn sweats rather than a suit. But sweats were so...*slouchy*. "Excuse the attire— we swung by on our way to work. This place comes highly recommended."

"Uh-huh." Her tone said she didn't believe that for a moment. "What do you do? For work, I mean."

"I'm an entrepreneur, and my friend here is a lawyer."

"Yeah, so they don't allow lawyers in."

"Is that a joke?" Joseph asked.

"The boss hates lawyers." Minerva shrugged. "Ever since

his divorce. His ex-wife was a real pain in the patootie, so I heard."

"I should sue for discrimination."

Oh, sure, that would help.

"How about we just don't mention our occupations to your boss?" I suggested.

"You mean lie on the application form?"

Minerva's tone was disapproving, but she'd said "they" didn't allow lawyers in, not "we" didn't allow lawyers in. No, she didn't feel like an integral part of the business. She wouldn't much care if we said we were astronauts as long as we ticked the right boxes. And in truth, Joseph was more of an astronaut than a lawyer—he'd travelled between worlds with me, but he'd never passed the bar exam. The sum total of his legal expertise came from Google, Netflix, and a dog-eared copy of *Law for Dummies* that my little sister had gifted him. But the human whose body he'd expropriated soon after we arrived in Plane Five had graduated magna cum laude from NYU Law, so Joseph claimed knowledge by association.

"Why don't we say he's a professional hustler?" I asked. Joseph opened his mouth to protest, and I kicked him in the shin. "There isn't much difference."

Minerva giggled. "I guess that would be okay."

"Do you think we could get a tour of the place before committing? It's certainly...unique."

"Isn't it something? It was part of a movie set before Mr. Ziaroni relocated it."

His name was Zion Ziaroni? He sounded like a type of pasta.

Yes, it was "something." An abomination. The former emperor Titus—who'd found himself in Plane Three thanks to his escapades with the Praetorian Guard—was proud that the Colosseum had stood as his legacy for almost two thousand years, but I wasn't sure he'd be quite as thrilled when I told him about the tacky replica in Sin City. No, he'd be horrified. Every member of the Flavian dynasty had taken their construction duties very seriously. Thousands of slaves had toiled over the stonework for years.

Not that I planned on returning to my former role any time soon. Running Plane Three certainly had its enjoyable moments, but wrangling the realm's most troublesome souls had been no walk in the park. Especially when my father began criticising every facet of my management style. Too much carrot and not enough stick, apparently.

"Which movie?" I asked.

"Uh, I think it was called *Ben-Hur Over*."

Joseph snorted a laugh. "That doesn't sound particularly mainstream."

"You have a problem with adult entertainment?"

I kicked him again.

"No, no problem."

"About that tour..." I reminded her.

"Oh, sure. I'll take you through, and Nero can show you around."

Nero? Was I meant to call him Emperor? He was a squat little man with an abundance of hair, not only on his head but also sprouting from his arms, legs, chest, and armpits. I pitied whoever had to clean the drain after he showered. His muscles said steroid abuse, and his flattened nose said he'd been in one too many brawls. And lost.

As Minerva had done, he looked us up and down.

"You take a wrong turn?" he asked.

Plenty of them. A man couldn't live for thousands of years without making a few mistakes. The question was, had I made another today? We rounded the corner into the gladiatorial arena-slash-gym, or rather, half a gladiatorial arena, because Zion appeared to have suffered from space issues when he decided to recreate Ancient Rome in a seedy part of Vegas. Instead of a complete oval, the arena cut off short at a wall, and a full-height mural attempted to recreate the effect. Badly. It didn't help that someone had painted a Hitler moustache on the nearest *rudis*. And instead of the rows of treadmills, stationary bicycles, and weight machines I'd expected to see, we got cages. Four metal cages, plus a motley arrangement of mats and punching bags at the far end. This wasn't a regular gym. In the nearest cage, two half-naked men were beating each other to a pulp. The coppery tang of blood hung in the air, along with the musk of fresh sweat.

"Now I understand the Colosseum thing," Joseph muttered under his breath. "All they need is loincloths and a couple of lions."

"And spears. Don't forget the spears."

I'd never forget the spears. On one particularly gruesome visit to Rome, I'd watched a man get impaled right in front of me. The spear went in one side and out the other. It was all so...barbaric. And to what end? Violence wasn't a sport; it was a tool.

Unless you were in Plane Three, of course. In Plane Three, where pain was a way of life, we held regular sword-fighting contests, boxing matches, and extreme sports competitions. Last century's "So you think you're a warrior?" league had been a high point on the social calendar. And before you call me a bloodthirsty hypocrite, the rounds were judged on style and technique, not the amount of guts spilled, and the losers were already living it up in the Underworld—it wasn't as if the winners could kill them again. The overall victor, a strapping Norseman named Ragnar, had defeated Genghis Khan in a nail-biting final, an outcome Genghis hadn't been at all happy about. I'd been forced to put him on time-out after he threatened to set fire to the judging panel and curse their ashes.

"Can you give these guys a tour?" Minerva asked Nero, ignoring the "wrong turn" comment.

"Sure." He waved a hand at the half-oval full of grunting men. "We got cages, we got weights, we got punching bags. There ya go."

"That's it?" I asked.

"What else d'ya want? A juice bar?"

"Everyone needs vitamin C."

Nero doubled over laughing. "Hey, Zion. This smartass wants a juice bar."

Zion was here?

I followed Nero's gaze to the cage on our left and looked up. And up, and up, and up. Zion was larger than Goliath— I knew that firsthand. Over six feet tall, with shoulders wider than my new Nissan. Zion's arrogant sneer suggested he shared Goliath's attitude too. The Philistine giant might have been defeated by David and a handful of pebbles, but he was still a cocky son of a bitch whose ego was bigger than his oversized body.

Zion threw one final punch that left his sparring partner staggering backward and studied us through the mesh of the cage.

"You're in the wrong place, pretty boy."

Guess again.

Zion didn't know it yet, but I was exactly where I needed to be. And now I was left with a choice. Should I embrace my inner devil or play nice for now?

Joseph and I had achieved our first goal: we knew who Zion was, and we had an idea of the layout of his lair. Should we back off and formulate a plan or push forward and demand answers? Both approaches had their advantages —and disadvantages. If we forced the issue, we'd tip our hand and Zion would know we were digging into Wren's predicament, but we might also get the answers we needed faster. And with Caria's life in peril, time was of the essence. Plus I quite liked the idea of having my apartment back. Wren was the first woman to spend the whole night in my space since I lost my darling Nevaeh, and having her there was...uncomfortable. Not she's-going-to-stab-me-in-my-sleep uncomfortable, more that she stirred up feelings of guilt. Her presence was tarnishing my memories of Nev.

Yes, things would be easier if Wren wasn't around.

If she wasn't in my space, I wouldn't think about her so often.

But there was also something to be said for moving slowly. For stepping back, for watching and waiting. Seeing who Zion associated with. Climbing the tree slowly instead of leaping for the top branch and potentially losing my grip.

I didn't have long to make a decision. The cage door was open, and Zion was already reaching for his towel...

CHAPTER 11

Blane

When Vee and I dealt with the buffoon in Wren's home, we'd taken the cautious approach. Used words rather than fists. So what had changed? Everything. We had Wren now, and she was safely tucked away in my apartment. Club Dead had twenty-four-seven security—guards at every entrance—plus any would-be intruder would have to go through Joseph and me. But if we were taking care of Wren, we couldn't be hunting for Caria at the same time. A tricky problem with an unpalatable solution, made more difficult by the fact that Wren had vetoed police involvement.

"Why are you still standing there, pretty boy?" Zion asked.

He was an industrial diamond of a man—full of flaws but still potentially useful.

"Why? Because I have a business proposition for you."

Joseph sighed while Minerva's eyebrows winged up.

"Huh?" she said. "I thought you wanted a tour of the gym?"

"You've been the perfect hostess, my sweet, but we can take it from here."

Her mouth opened, then closed again, and she turned to Zion. He dismissed her with a flick of his wrist.

"You can go back to the front desk."

Nero didn't leave, and neither did the man Zion had been using as a punching bag a minute previously, even as blood dripped from his nose onto the floor. The two of them formed up as foot soldiers, one on each side of their boss and a pace behind.

"Nice place you have here," I lied.

"What do you want?"

"On Tuesday evening, I bumped into a fellow in a friend's apartment, and he mentioned that you were the man to ask if there was a problem that needed solving."

"What fellow?"

"I didn't catch his name, but he was there to pick up Wren Gillebrand. Big guy, definitely worked out."

Ah, there it was. The slight flicker of shock as Zion found himself on the back foot. That didn't stop him from trying to bluster his way through the conversation, though.

"Uh, yeah, Darryl. Guess he didn't find her. You see where he went?"

"As a matter of fact, I did. I gave him a ride to the state line and strongly advised him against returning to Nevada. But we had a nice chat on the way, and then I got curious. Imagine my surprise when I began asking around and found out Wren wasn't the only woman to go missing this week."

No shock this time. Either Zion had successfully regained control of his poker face, or he already knew about Caria.

"Yeah, well, it's Vegas. Women go missing all the time."

"That doesn't concern you?"

"I got a business to run here. If you wanna talk about whores, go talk to someone else."

"What if the 'whores,' as you so eloquently put it, *are* your business?"

"I don't run whores. Too much trouble. Try the Pink Squirrel—plenty of bitches there."

"I'm not looking for a chance to get my rocks off. I'm looking for Caria Hearst. And I want to hire you to help me."

Zion's snort told me what he thought of that idea.

"I thought you were a man who fixes problems for money?"

"Not that kinda problem. You wanna find a woman, hire a damn PI."

"Oh, I have a reasonable idea where Caria is. She's staying with Laurent. I just need you to identify which of his properties she's at."

The snort turned to laughter. "You want..." He sounded like a distressed donkey. "You want me to start nosing around in Laurent's business?"

If I'd learned one thing during my tenure at Club Dead, it was that insecure men didn't appreciate having their masculinity questioned. And Zion wasn't as tough as he wanted others to believe. The insults, the posturing...

"You're right; what was I thinking? I need a man with balls, not one with a pussy."

"What the fuck?"

He gave a telling glance left and right. No, he didn't want to lose face in front of his henchmen.

"Now that we've met, I realise you're the wrong person for the job. Rest assured, if I ever need a guy to hook me up with tickets to the ballet, I'll think of you."

Although that comparison was somewhat unfair to ballet dancers. Anyone who could leap around in pointe shoes for hours at a time deserved more admiration than a man who carefully selected his sparring partners to be weaker than him. I turned to leave, motioning to Joseph to follow, keeping my wits about me because Zion struck me as the type of coward who'd shoot a man in the back. I didn't need to ruin another suit jacket, not when my favourite tailor had a waitlist.

"Hey, wait a minute…"

"Time is money, my friend."

"How much are you paying?"

"I thought you said you were incapable of doing the job?"

"Incapable? No, no, no, I'm very capable."

"Then what's the problem? You're too friendly with Laurent? Have you told him yet that your man failed to locate Wren?"

His hesitation gave me my answer.

"I thought not."

"It's only a matter of time. I have the best network in Vegas."

Doubtful. "You do? That's terrific. Whatever Laurent's paying you, I'll double it for you to locate Caria."

Another snort. This jackass really needed to work on his negotiation technique.

"As I thought. All hat and no cattle."

Or should that be all loincloth and no bears, seeing as we were in a second-rate replica of the Colosseum? Whatever, I'd finally hit the right button. Zion turned an alarming shade of puce, and if the building hadn't been so stiflingly hot, I'd have seen steam coming out of his ears. He was gloriously mad. In fact, he reminded me of Genghis when Tamerlane ate the last toasted marshmallow.

"All hat and no cattle? Fuck you, man. I'll do your job on one condition."

"Which is?"

The disturbing gleam in his eye told me I probably wasn't going to like the suggestion, but I'd spent years wrangling despots and tyrants into shape. I could deal with a mere thug. As for money, I had plenty of that as well, thanks to the hordes of hidden treasure that my guests in Plane Three had graciously given me directions to. They'd even held a going-away party for me. Whenever I made a rare visit, they invariably asked when I planned to return, right before they began bitching about Decima and her rules, rules, rules. No stoking up the winds of Hell whenever it got a bit hot. No playing skittles with the bones of our enemies. No encouraging Cerberus to chase his tail. And she'd disbanded the male voice choir, an overreaction to Caligula's inability to sing in tune if there ever was one. The simple solution was to stand Caligula next to Ivan the Terrible, and Ivan's volume drowned out the painful parts.

"You gotta fight me first," Zion said.

I raised an eyebrow. "Fight you?"

"In the cage."

Did he have a death wish? I began to rethink this plan—would a man this dumb truly be capable of finding Caria? Zion was all brawn and no brain. But getting the job done with Joseph alone would be challenging. We were unfamiliar with the main players, and if someone in Vegas got wind of us asking questions and Caria turned out to be in, say, California, Laurent could dispatch her to Plane Four before we got there.

"I'm not really dressed for a fight today."

"We can find you a pair of sweatpants." He turned to Nero. "Go find a pair of sweatpants."

"I'm not wearing secondhand sweatpants."

"Knew you were a chicken." Zion's grin was triumphant as he resorted to schoolyard humour, flapping his arms and

ELISE NOBLE

clucking. "You come in here with your big mouth and your fancy suit, but you're not man enough to throw a punch."

Zion had backed himself so neatly into a corner that he couldn't have escaped if his opponent were a toddler. I hid my joy as I gestured toward the cage.

"In that case, after you."

CHAPTER 12

Blane

"You should have worn a black suit today," Joseph muttered as he took my jacket. "The French blue is going to show the bloodstains."

I'd begun wearing blue again after Lola, the four-year-old child I very much suspected was the reincarnation of my dear Nevaeh, told me it was her favourite colour. Nevaeh had loved the cerulean sky, the deep blue of the Pacific, and the turquoise of the Caribbean Sea. Her eyes had been the colour of worn denim, and even now, they were the last thing I saw before I fell asleep and the first thing on my mind when I woke up. When I bought her jewellery, it had always been sapphires. I wore one of them in a ring now.

Nevaeh's return was problematic in so many ways, her age being the most significant issue. All those feelings I'd had for Nev were wrong now that she was a young child. But I couldn't turn off my protective instincts. I'd failed her once, and I wouldn't do so again. Unfortunately, that had led to me putting on a few pounds seeing as Marianna, Lola's mother, had started a small baking business. I was her best customer. I might not be a significant part of Lola's life, but I could ensure her mom wasn't short of money.

And the excess cakes wouldn't prevent me from taking on Zion.

Or winning.

Perhaps I should have cut him a little slack on account of his lack of celestial knowledge, but I couldn't get past the fact that he'd sent a man to kidnap an innocent woman. It wasn't as if Laurent wanted to invite Wren over for coffee and cookies. No, I very much feared that if he got his hands on both ladies, nobody would ever find the bodies.

Joseph watched my back as I climbed into the cage. Zion was so delightfully oblivious as he jogged on the spot and cracked his neck from side to side that I had to suppress a smile. He took his time wrapping his hands while I leaned against the side of the cage, legs crossed at the ankles, and waited.

"Are you ready yet? Time is money, remember?"

"You wanna call the ambulance before or after I pound you into the floor?"

"Let's not waste a valuable medical resource."

Ever watched a pet cat play with a mouse? They rarely go in for the kill right away. No, they prefer to toy with their prey, even giving it false hope of salvation before pouncing. Sometimes, they abandon it altogether. Take Myrtle the Maine Coon, for example. In Plane Two, she spent hours catching mice, crickets, spiders, even small snakes, and letting them go in my parents' home. She also enjoyed snaffling valuable knickknacks and shitting in the bunkers on my father's favourite golf course. Myrtle irritated my parents to no end, but who could blame her? Until my second-cousin Orwell got ahold of Great-Uncle Tiberius's notes and began experimenting, she'd been a perfectly normal—by celestial standards—twelve-year-old girl. Now she only assumed her human form at random moments and spent the rest of the time wreaking havoc.

Anyhow, I digress.

Zion finally got his act together and swung a right hook. Hard. Which was a good thing, because I sidestepped and caught the wince as his fist connected with the wire mesh. By the time he recovered, I was behind him, and my jab to his kidney only riled his temper. The growl he let out was barely human. I should know. In my peripheral vision, I spotted Nero moving toward the cage, and Joseph stepped forward too. He'd run interference while I dealt with this unethical idiot. I had nothing against sin, per se, but there were some lines a man shouldn't cross.

Another growl, and Zion swung again, this time with an uppercut. I blocked, punched him in the stomach, and waited politely while he got his breath back.

"Why do men like you invariably have to do things the hard way?" I asked. "Violence isn't always the answer."

The growl turned into a roar, and a blow glanced off my shoulder as I spun away. Beating me was nothing but a pipe dream, but I didn't want him giving up too soon. Nero was at the cage door now, and Joseph tapped him on the shoulder. When he turned, my demon sidekick felled him with a single punch to the jaw. Zion hadn't hired Nero for his brains, then. The sparring partner hovered in the background, no doubt trying to make up his mind whether he wanted to be next.

Slowly, slowly, Zion began to realise he'd made a monumental error. He'd judged me on my appearance, and supernatural strength and speed were two factors he hadn't considered. Plus his accuracy was terrible. A left jab missed me completely, and when he stumbled forward, I helped him down to the mat. Hard. Blood from his nose speckled the canvas like it was a cut-price Jackson Pollock painting.

"Aargh!"

"You wanted this," I reminded him. "Broken ribs are an occupational hazard."

He garbled something that sounded suspiciously like, "Fuck you," which only served to remind me how long it had been since I'd indulged in pleasures of the flesh. Almost two weeks now. Thank goodness Nevaeh wasn't around to see me turning this fool into ground beef—she'd been a confirmed pacifist.

"Now, let's continue the conversation we started earlier. You're going to locate Caria, and when you do, I'll compensate you for your time." Later, I'd work to tear apart his drug empire, but that could wait for a month or two. "And if you fail, I'll come back and show you a whole new meaning to the term 'spineless.' Do you understand?"

I took the grunt to mean "yes."

"Don't get any cute ideas about tipping off Laurent, either. Not unless you want your Colosseum to go the same way as the Temple of Artemis."

"The...the what?" Zion choked out.

"Look it up." I hadn't come here to give a history lesson. "I'll dismantle your little empire piece by piece, and then I'll dismantle you." When I glanced around, the sparring partner was nowhere to be seen, and Nero was still on the floor. The bigger they were, the harder they fell. I patted Zion on the shoulder. "You have one week. I'll be in touch."

That's how it worked in Plane Three. I gave a punishee a task and a deadline, and they fulfilled their duty. On those rare occasions a resident let me down, I came up with a suitably egregious penalty, and everyone else stayed in line for another year or two. So far, things seemed to work the same way in Plane Five, although I couldn't get quite so creative with my disciplinary measures. Tongues would wag if I conjured up a wall of flame in the middle of Las Vegas.

Once we got outside into the daylight, Joseph looked me up and down and groaned.

"You have blood on your pants. And your shirt."

At least it wasn't *my* blood. I'd sliced my hand open on one of Zion's front teeth, but once I'd picked the piece of broken enamel out of the wound, the flesh had regenerated almost instantly—another advantage of being not entirely human. All I had to show for my trouble was smooth skin.

"Let's pick up lunch from La Nostra Casa on the way back," I suggested. Vee had recommended the restaurant at the end of last year, and I'd eaten there a number of times since. The food was excellent. "You'll have to go inside to collect our order, obviously."

"Can't we get it delivered? Rosetta keeps trying to set me up with her granddaughter."

La Nostra Casa was a real family affair. Rosetta and her husband, Carmelo, owned the place, her son cooked, her daughter looked after the books, and her grandkids waited tables on the weekends. Which was why Joseph and I tended to visit Monday to Friday, although it would be amusing to see him pushed into a date with Giorgia Romano. The woman literally never stopped talking.

"We have to drive right past the place. What does Wren like to eat?"

"How should I know?"

"You're right—just order one of everything."

After all she'd been through, Wren deserved to be thoroughly spoiled.

CHAPTER 13

Blane

"Is that...is that blood?"

Wren was standing in front of the refrigerator when I walked into the kitchen with Joseph, and her expression morphed from confusion to horror, quite unnecessarily.

"Yes, but it's not mine."

That didn't seem to reassure her. "Then whose is it?"

"Zion's."

"What? How?"

"He had a nosebleed."

"A nosebleed? That's all?"

"Some people are prone to them."

Judging by the state of Zion's nose—squashed and not particularly straight—it wasn't the first time the appendage had been broken, and if he kept acting like a murderous thug, it wouldn't be the last either.

"What did Zion say? Does he know where Caria is?"

"No, but I hired him to find out for us."

Ah, now we had shock and possibly a tiny bit of anger.

"You...hired him? As in, you're paying him money? The

man who broke into my apartment and tried to kidnap me?"

Uh-oh. She sounded far from happy, and now she had her hands on her hips. When Nevaeh used to do that, it had been a sign to tread very, very carefully.

"Technically, that wasn't him. It was a man named Darryl."

Ah, now the fire was back in her eyes. "Zion was still responsible."

"Yes, yes he was. And he'll only be helping us temporarily. I'll dismantle his business empire later, but we're in a time-critical situation, and I needed to get him onside fast."

Wren sagged against the counter. Her shoulder-length hair was damp from the shower, and despite the fact that the couch was reasonably comfortable, she didn't appear to have slept well. Those dark circles under her eyes looked as if they'd been drawn on with a Sharpie.

"What if he tells Laurent?" she asked.

"He won't." In my estimation, Zion was crazy, not stupid. In some ways, he reminded me of Akhenaten. And while I wasn't Zion's favourite person, I'd seen the fear lurking in his dark little piggy eyes after I let him scramble to his feet. More importantly, he thought I was crazy too, and he didn't want to wake up minus his spine. "So all you have to do is stay safe until we retrieve Caria, and then life can get back to normal."

"Oh, you think? Laurent's never going to stop searching for us."

"Once Caria's safe, we can get the authorities involved."

"Didn't you listen to anything I said before? Laurent owns the cops. That's the reason Caria was taken in the first place."

"Not *all* the cops. Think about it—if the police didn't

worry him, why go to so much trouble to keep the two of you quiet? Why not let Caria tell whatever stories she wanted to? If he was confident that no cops would act on the evidence, he wouldn't care what she said. No, she got unlucky, that was all. If she'd spoken with a different officer, we wouldn't be having this conversation."

And not only that, I bet Detective Callahan would be interested in finding out the name of the cop who'd betrayed Caria. That bad apple needed to be put through the waste disposal. But any internal investigation would take time, time that Caria didn't have, and Callahan would risk tipping off the wrong person. Or worse, sending a SWAT team full of Laurent's buddies to perform a "rescue," only for Caria to die in the crossfire.

But Wren didn't seem convinced by my reasoning. "I'll have to discuss it with Caria." A sob burst free. "If we can find her."

"We'll get her back."

And once we located the missing woman, Joseph and I could pay a visit to wherever she was being held and flick souls out of bodies left, right, and centre. But first, we needed an address. If we went to the wrong property and one of Laurent's men raised the alarm before I managed to separate him into his constituent parts, then Caria would be in more danger than before. One phone call, and Laurent would move her. Or kill her. My sister Decima could work medical miracles in an emergency—if I grovelled hard enough—but if a soul had departed a body, it was rarely possible to reunite the two.

"How?" Wren asked. "How will you get her back? Laurent will be armed to the teeth."

"Let me worry about that."

"That's it? That's your answer? Maybe you don't understand, but Laurent's a psycho. A rich, mean psycho, even worse than Zion. He acted so charming to Caria, but Kayden's girlfriend grew up in Vegas, and she heard that one time, a drunk teenager peed on the wheel of Laurent's car, and Laurent made two of his men hold the kid down while he lopped his, uh, man part off with a cigar cutter." Wren gave another sniffle. "I wish Kayden had told me that before Caria went missing."

I puzzled over the logistics of the lopping. "It must have been a large cigar cutter. Or a smaller-than-average dick."

"Perhaps it shrivelled?" Joseph suggested. "If he was scared, that could happen."

"Or maybe it was just a tall tale."

Rumours didn't take much to get started around here. Sometimes, I heard stories about myself—that I'd abandoned a man to die in Death Valley after I saw him backhand his girlfriend in Club Dead, that I'd burned a punk's house to the ground after he insulted a homeless person, that I'd broken a fool's jaw when he insulted a server in the VIP area, that I'd once thrown a drug dealer out of an airplane—but only half of those things were true. I mean, I didn't even own an airplane. It was a cliff I'd tossed him off of.

Anyhow, I let the rumours persist because I'd rather be feared than taken advantage of. Perhaps Laurent took the same approach?

"I hate this," Wren said. "I hate it. Laurent gets away with everything."

"Not this time. And as long as you're safe, he has to keep Caria alive, so just relax while Joseph and I deal with the tricky parts."

"Relax? How can I relax?"

"I don't know. What do you usually do to unwind?" As long as drugs weren't involved, I could probably facilitate it.

I recalled the note on the mirror in Wren's apartment. "Yoga?"

Joseph could pick up appropriate clothing and one of those mats if Wren needed it. Hiring a teacher would have to wait—the fewer people who knew Wren was here, the better—but there was bound to be an app available.

"I go to classes at the Fitness Factory, and I signed up for one of those online cooking courses—nothing fancy, just lasagne and risotto, that sort of thing—but I only got through the first two lessons." Wren glanced around the kitchen. "This place is a chef's dream. I thought that maybe I could make a salad for lunch, but the healthiest thing I found was a jar of pickles. You're not a big fan of vegetables?"

Ah, another perk of being immortal. I could eat whatever I wanted without having to worry about clogged arteries.

"They taste okay when they're coated in batter and deep fried." I held up the bag from La Nostra Casa. "Plus we brought calzone. I'm almost certain there are olives in it."

"How do you not have scurvy?" Wren pulled open the refrigerator door. "Look in here—there are four kinds of cake, three kinds of cheese, and a bottle of Chardonnay."

"It's an excellent vintage, from my own vineyard, no less. And you should try the cakes—Marianna delivers them daily."

Lola's mom was a proud woman who hated to take handouts, so instead of giving her cash, which Joseph said would be weird in any case, I supported her fledgling business with regular orders. Usually for cakes, but she made excellent cookies and pastries too.

"That's not the point I was trying to make. I mean, how do you look like that if you live on junk food?"

"Look like what?"

Now Wren's cheeks went quite pink. "Like, uh, like..."

"Like he got airbrushed into an infomercial for an AbTrainer-3000?" Joseph suggested.

Pink turned to scarlet. Interesting.

"Uh, yes. That."

"I have excellent genes." Gently, I steered her away from the refrigerator and closed the door. "But if you want vegetables, I'll buy vegetables. Make a list, and I'll have them delivered. Fruit too. Clothing, books, anything you need."

"You don't have to do that."

"What kind of host would I be if I couldn't provide you with a carrot? Now, just relax and make yourself at home. In a few days, we can forget this ever happened."

I was a born liar, but at that moment, I honestly believed I was telling the truth. If only I'd seen the storm that was brewing, I might have repented my sins, fallen to my knees, and begged Father for my old job back. Because Plane Five was about to become Plane Three on Earth.

But although I had many gifts, foresight wasn't one of them. Crystal balls were nothing more than pretty decorations. So when Wren sighed and opened the bag I'd dumped on the kitchen island, I merely changed my shirt, fetched three plates and the requisite cutlery, took a seat alongside Joseph, and tucked into lunch.

CHAPTER 14
Wren

Everything would get back to normal, Blane said. Well, that was a big fat lie, wasn't it? How could I ever forget what had happened? That a woman was dead, that my best friend was missing, that a man had come to my apartment to kidnap me too, and that now I was holed up in my boss's luxury penthouse. The tall, dark, and handsome boss that maybe, just maybe, I'd secretly had a crush on for months.

Not an "I hope we match on Tinder" crush, more of an "unattainable and therefore safe" crush, the kind of pointless infatuation usually reserved for movie stars and pop singers. And wealthy-but-slightly-dangerous businessmen. As in, one step up from a book boyfriend but a hundred steps down from an actual dating prospect. A man who might say a few words to you every once in a while, but the only place he'd be getting naked was in your dreams. And perhaps I'd had those dreams once or twice. Okay, once or twice a week, but definitely no more than that.

And now I'd accidentally told him he was hot. Well, not

told him, but a picture painted a thousand words, and my cheeks had said them all.

Totally inappropriate.

Caria was missing, Blane was going above and beyond to help me, and even his weird assistant was being supportive. I wasn't quite sure what to make of Joseph Beauregard. I'd seen him around, and he was what Caria called a "little" man. Not in size—he was average height and probably went to the gym a couple of times a week—but in character. A little too slick. A little too watchful. A little too obsequious when it came to Blane. A man who didn't do anything wrong, per se, but there was something off that I couldn't quite put my finger on. Paola in housekeeping had mentioned he was a lawyer, which might have explained a thing or two. I'd dated a lawyer once. Big mistake.

Huge.

After the breakup, I'd vowed that my days of messing up were over, that the move to Vegas to be near Kayden would be a fresh start. And until last week, I'd stayed more or less on track. Found a job I didn't dread going to, earned enough to cover the rent, and made one good friend. Then life fell apart again. This time, the poor judgment was Caria's rather than mine, but it didn't make the fallout any easier to bear.

"You don't like calzone?" Blane asked.

"Huh?" Sugar honey iced tea, I'd zoned out, and now he was looking at me funny. The calzone was a picked-apart mess on my plate. "No. I mean, yes, I do like calzone, but I don't have much of an appetite at the moment."

"Understandable, but you should try to eat. Starving would be suboptimal. Do you want Joseph to run out and pick up something else?"

"More wine?" Beauregard suggested. "Chocolate? Xanax?"

"Xanax isn't food," Blane told him.

"Well, Perla eats it like candy, and she says it changed her life."

Perla, the bartender at Tilt? She knew the ingredients of every cocktail by heart, always wore shoes I'd barely be able to stand in, let alone walk in, and—until recently—had spent half her breaks crying in the bathroom. Boyfriend trouble. Couldn't live with him, didn't want to do the time for killing him. When I'd gently suggested there might be another solution, more of a halfway house, she'd given me a condescending look and told me I just didn't understand.

But apparently, Beauregard did, seeing as she'd confided in him about her medical care.

"This isn't exactly something I can discuss with a physician. What would I say? 'Oh, hi, doctor. I'm feeling kinda down because my best friend was kidnapped by a gangster, so could I get a prescription'?"

"No need. There's a guy who hangs out in the diner next to the Devil's Den, and he can get as many Xanax as you need, no questions asked."

"Isn't that illegal?"

"Only if you get caught."

"Aren't you an attorney?"

"If everyone followed the rules, I'd be out of a job."

A reasonable point, but I still wasn't going to purchase dubiously sourced drugs, and I especially wasn't going to purchase dubiously sourced drugs from the Lucky 7 Grill.

Blane gave him a sharp look. "Wren isn't taking Xanax."

"And there's no way I'm going near the Devil's Den," I told him. Although it had closed almost a year ago, its reputation as Vegas's seediest casino had been well-deserved, and the whole street was a no-go area. I knew that because I used to work there. My boss was okay—he'd given me the opportunity to deal blackjack when no one else would—but

I'd been so nervous walking to the bus stop at night that I'd only stuck it out for six months. "What were you doing there? Trolling for new clients?"

Blane's lips quirked in amusement, but he shook his head. "Joseph only works for me now. But I'm interested in buying the Devil's Den, which means paying a visit or two."

Was he serious? His expression suggested that he was. "But...but you already own Tilt. And Club Dead. Both of those are real nice places, and the Devil's Den..."

"Isn't? Yes, I'm aware of that. But it's in a good location overall, and it has potential."

"Didn't someone get shot right outside?"

"Yes, but if I redevelop the casino, it'll drag the surrounding businesses out of the gutter along with it."

Well, okay then. I figured he knew what he was doing. The tables at Tilt were always packed with high-rollers, tips were great, and there hadn't been a single raid on the place since I started working there. Not like at my first job in Vegas. I'd waited tables at Destiny's Gate—which I always thought sounded more like a cult than a casino—and the staff used to joke that the cops had reserved parking next to the front door.

"I don't know much about the business side of casinos, but I hope it works out. And I'll pass on the prescription medication."

"Suit yourself," Beauregard said.

Blane agreed with me. "Good choice."

"How about a cake instead?" Beauregard suggested. "Marianna's here."

Where? I glanced around, and ten seconds later, the buzzer sounded. Beauregard got up to open the door. Was he psychic or something? How had he known she was outside? My ex used to do spooky stuff like that, and he'd told me we had "a special connection," which I'd thought was cute until I realised he'd installed tracking software on my phone. I suppressed a shudder at the memory.

Marianna was a petite Latina carrying an insulated bag in one hand and a small boy on the opposite hip. A girl followed behind her, three or four years old, and she held a small pink bag of her own.

"*Hola*," Marianna said, beaming at all of us, even Beauregard. "How are you?"

Beauregard shrugged. "Can't complain."

"Oh, he can and frequently does." Blane returned Marianna's smile and rose to kiss her on the cheek. "My day just got better now that you've arrived."

Even with her olive skin, Marianna couldn't hide her blush. "You'd say that about anyone who brought you food."

"I definitely don't say it to Joseph. Or the pizza delivery guy. Or Feng from Wong Fu's, even when he doles out extra fortune cookies."

The little girl had seemed shy when she first walked in, trailing behind her mom and staring at her feet, but when she got near Blane, she suddenly grinned and threw her arms around his legs.

"*Hola*, Lucian. I made cookies."

Lucian? That was his first name? How come the little girl used it when nobody else did?

"What kind of cookies?" He patted her on the shoulder, then lifted her onto one of the high stools at the counter. "Are they chocolate?"

She nodded solemnly. "They're the best kind."

"Are you going to stay and eat one?"

She looked to her mom, who said, "Yes, that's okay. You're our last delivery."

"Excellent. Coffee?"

"Please, that sounds good."

"I want coffee," the little girl announced.

"You don't like coffee, *mi cielito*," Marianna told her. "How about juice?"

"I want coffee."

Blane winked at her. "We'll make your special coffee, *angelito*."

She giggled, and sheesh, Blane even knew how to charm a young child. A grown woman stood no chance.

And maybe the magnetism was contagious? The girl turned to me and smiled. "*Hola*, Wren. You can have a cookie too."

The oddest feeling came over me. A strange familiarity, strong and somehow comforting. As if I'd seen the little girl before, but that was impossible. I'd certainly remember her piercing blue eyes and impish grin. And how did she know my name? She pronounced it "Rin," but it was close enough.

Marianna was looking at me curiously. "Have you met Lola somewhere already?"

"Not that I remember. Uh, I love cookies."

Lola put her bag down on a stool. "I know. Next time, we'll make the peanut butter ones."

My stomach clenched. How did she know that peanut butter cookies were my favourite? Or was it just a lucky guess? Lola couldn't have been out of pre-K, but she unsettled me.

"Can I help with the coffee?" I asked Blane, not only because I owed him a debt of gratitude, but because I needed to gather my thoughts. "I worked as a barista for a while."

"A woman of many skills. But also a guest, so I don't expect you to lift a finger."

"What if I want to?"

He studied me for a moment, and maybe he understood

how awkward I felt here in this beautiful apartment. "Then I won't stop you." A pause. "Marianna, meet Wren. She's staying with me while we iron out a few kinks in her personal life."

Curiosity turned to sympathy. "Man trouble? I know all about that."

Blane answered for me. "In a manner of speaking. Let's make those drinks."

CHAPTER 15

Wren

L ola's "special coffee" turned out to be hot chocolate. While I got to grips with the coffee machine, Blane dumped two spoonfuls of instant powder into a mug, added hot water and plenty of milk, and then frothed it with one of those little electric whisks. This was a side of him I hadn't seen before today—the man who cared enough about a young visitor that he kept a pink Hello Kitty mug in his cupboard.

Who cared enough about an unexpected guest to provide her with fancy toiletries and new clothes. I'd stuffed a few things into a bag before I ran out the door, and I figured I could wash my underwear in the bathroom sink, but when I left my room this morning, I'd found a row of carrier bags outside the door with a note. *We can exchange anything that doesn't fit.* But it did fit, all of it, and whoever he'd sent out shopping had picked the type of clothes I liked —leggings, slouchy sweaters, a pair of fluffy slippers. Shorts for outside, although I couldn't imagine when I'd be able to leave. It was exactly the stuff I'd buy for myself, if my credit card wasn't dangerously close to the limit and I could afford to visit designer stores rather than Target.

The only designer clothing I'd owned in the past had been gifted to me by Dominic. Dresses I had no occasion to wear and shoes I'd twist an ankle in. I say "gifted," but really I'd ended up buying it myself because he still owed me nearly four thousand bucks that I'd loaned him to pay his law school tuition. He'd repay me as soon as he got a job, he'd promised, but what he'd actually done was squander his paycheck on things I didn't want and then fuck an eighteen-year-old named Rebecca. *Call me Becky*, she'd said when he introduced us at the company picnic three weeks before I found her naked beneath my fiancé. I wanted to scratch her pretty green eyes out.

But they were in Wyoming and I was in Vegas, so I forced myself to think of something other than Dominic and Becky and the fact that she was pregnant.

"Does Lola come over often?" I asked Blane quietly as Beauregard produced a box of toys from somewhere.

"A couple of times a week. Marianna is a friend of Vee's, and she's still finding her feet in the city."

"How did Lola know my name?"

Blane's brows drew together. "Honestly, I'm not sure. Marianna drops snacks off for me at Tilt from time to time, and the kids often tag along, so maybe she saw you there?"

It was possible, although I was good with faces and I didn't recall bumping into them.

"I guess."

"Lola's very clever, and she has an excellent memory. Every time I buy her a new book, she reads it overnight and tells me about it the next day."

"She can read already?"

"Okay, so they're mostly full of pictures, but she can read a little."

"How old is she?"

"Four. She just had a birthday."

"You're a good man, Blane."

"There are many who would disagree."

If only I'd known that in less than a week, I would be one of them, then I'd have done things differently. Fled the country with Kayden, or even taken a cab back to the Rest-E-Z Motel and prayed. Although praying wouldn't have done me much good, as it turned out.

But clairvoyance wasn't one of my gifts, so I just finished making the coffee, drew a cat in the foam on Lola's hot chocolate, and took a seat at the table. The cookies were lumpy but delicious all the same, and Marianna cut slices of strawberry shortcake and served those too. How did Blane still have abs?

"I wish I could bake like this," I mumbled around a mouthful of fruity goodness. "I mean, I'm fine with the basics, but..."

"I learned from my mom," Marianna said. "She worked in a hotel in Los Angeles."

My mom had been too busy trying to make ends meet to teach me to cook. Kayden and I had mostly been left to fend for ourselves, locked in the apartment while she went out to work. At the time, it had been normal, having a mom who was barely there. She used to come home in the early hours, send us to school, and then sleep until it was time to pick us up again.

But one morning, when I was eight years old and Kayden was seven, she hadn't come home at all. We'd been terrified when the police broke down the door, more frightened still when we were shipped off to foster homes and expected to adapt to a whole new way of life. Too old for anyone to want to adopt us, too young to understand the details of what was happening. In the beginning, we'd sometimes get placements together for a month or two, but most of the time, we were shuffled around Wyoming alone, fed and clothed but never truly wanted. Email was our lifeline until I followed him to Nevada.

"My mom wasn't that great of a cook."

There, that sounded better than saying she was in prison for dealing drugs, didn't it? Although she swore she'd only been acting as a courier, the jury hadn't believed her. Did I believe her? Honestly, I barely knew her. We'd lost touch over the years, and I had no idea what to think.

The one certainty was that she hadn't been much of a mom.

"If you want, I can show you how to make a cake," Marianna offered.

"Cookies," Lola said. "Peanut butter ones."

"Or cookies."

My heart gave an awkward flip. I'd always struggled to make friends. There'd never seemed much point when I always got moved on again a few weeks later, and if I kept my head down, the bullies mostly left me alone. Caria was the one person who'd seen the real me. Caria, the extrovert who'd insisted on dragging the introverted new girl at yoga out for cocktails and showing her the city. And as for Lola, I had to be reading too much into the situation. She was just a normal little girl who loved peanut butter.

"I'd like that. Cookies or cake, I don't mind which."

Marianna beamed at me. "Great! I'll give you my address, and we can arrange a day. Maybe this weekend? I promised Lola and Pablo that we'd go see the Wildlife Habitat at the Flamingo on Saturday, but we could do Sunday?"

This Sunday? No, no, no, Caria had to take priority. And Marianna wanted me to go to her home? Keeping a low profile was more important than baking. Now I needed to decline, but politely. Darn it, I should have learned. *Keep your head down, Wren.*

"Uh, I'm not sure..."

But Blane interrupted. "Why don't you come over here? I'll provide all the ingredients, and Lola can play with Myrtle. Joseph won't mind watching Pablo."

Beauregard didn't look thrilled at the idea of playing babysitter, but he nodded his agreement. "Anything for cookies."

"What about...you know?" I asked.

"All in hand," Blane assured me, and Marianna didn't seem to pick up on the tension.

"Oh, sure. We can come over, but I'll bring the ingredients."

"Then it's a date." Blane quickly corrected himself. "For the two of you. Well, not a date, more of a... Never mind. We'll see you on Sunday."

Awkward, but I knew how to handle that. *When the conversation gets tough, change the subject.* That philosophy had stood me in good stead through the years, including in my current job. Or at least, the job I should have been doing if I weren't lying low in an apartment to avoid a psychopathic killer and his henchmen. If a guest got too personal, I steered the conversation back toward blackjack. If he suggested some quiet time alone, I asked how his wife was.

"Who's Myrtle?" I asked. It was an unusual name. "Is she a friend of yours?"

"She's a cat. And I also have a cousin named Myrtle—actually, she's my fourth cousin once removed—but cat-Myrtle is around more than girl-Myrtle."

"You own a cat?"

I hadn't imagined Blane as the type of man who'd have a pet. He seemed too...I don't know...not so much self-centred, more focused on other things. But he'd surprised me plenty of times over the past twenty-four hours, so maybe I'd been too quick to judge by appearances?

"She'd dispute the 'own' part, but she mostly lives here."

"Mostly?"

"She comes and goes."

"A mouser, huh?"

Blane spluttered his coffee. "Heavens, no. She likes to sneak into shows on the Strip."

"Really? How do you know?"

"Because I put a tag on her collar, and people keep calling us to collect her. Do you like cats, Wren?"

"I always wanted a pet, but when I was younger, I got moved around too much."

"How about now?"

"Now? I guess...I guess I still dread having to leave at a moment's notice, and it happened, didn't it?"

"We're going to fix that." Blane watched me over the rim of his mug. "You said you got moved around. Who moved you? Your parents?"

Ah, crap. Why didn't I learn to watch my big, stupid mouth?

"Not my parents. My brother and I were both in the foster system."

"I see. Was that a good thing or a bad thing?"

"I...I...I'm not sure." Honestly? I'd missed my mom, but she hadn't been a great parent by any measure; I'd learned that as I got older. What I craved was stability, but it still remained stubbornly out of reach. "There was no point in wishing for what-might-have-beens, because I didn't have the power to change anything."

"But you do now. In the winds of change, find the courage to spread your wings and soar."

Soar? He had me confused with someone else. Survival

was my goal. Survival, occasional flickers of happiness, and chocolate milkshakes from Good Eats. Nobody made milkshakes the way they did, health violations be damned. Caria always told me I should take a chance. And once, I had taken a chance. I'd accepted Dominic Winchester's proposal and moved from Clearmont to Cheyenne, only to find him in bed with a barely legal intern a month before we were due to get married.

I shrugged, non-committal. The thought of getting into a deep and meaningful conversation with my boss, his weird assistant, and a virtual stranger gave me the heebie-jeebies.

Beauregard came to my rescue. "Spread your wings and soar? You got that out of a fortune cookie."

"So? That doesn't mean it's not true."

Marianna giggled. "I got one from Wong Fu's last week that said 'A closed mouth gathers no feet.'"

"Why would you want to gather feet?"

"I have no idea."

"Probably written by someone with a foot fetish," Beauregard said. "It's a thing."

That was true; it was. "One of the girls in my yoga class sells pictures of her feet on the internet. She makes good money. People will pay a fortune for unwashed socks."

"Are you joking?" Marianna asked.

"Swear I'm not. She gets a pedicure every week and writes it off as a business expense."

And we were away from the subject of my past. Phew. Beauregard found a dubious website—toenail clippings for thirty bucks a bag, anyone?—and Marianna eww-ed as she finished her coffee. Lola drank her hot chocolate, and Pablo managed to knock the top off his sippy cup and spill juice everywhere. When Blane wiped up the mess, I found myself slightly surprised he didn't have a housekeeper for that. He'd always struck me as a man who would avoid doing his own dirty work. *Life is full of surprises.* While the three of them chatted, I got back to fretting over Caria. How was she being treated? Was she even still alive? The helplessness of the situation left my stomach churning. This was like being a child again, sitting there on the doorstep with my black plastic bag full of belongings as I waited for the harried lady from CPS to show up with news of my next adventure.

"Have you heard anything from Zion yet?" I asked Blane after Marianna and the kids had trooped into the elevator. Beauregard had departed too, muttering about an issue with scheduling in Club Dead.

"Not yet." Blane's phone rang right at that moment, and he glanced at the screen. "I have to take this."

"Is it...?"

"No, it isn't. Nothing for you to worry about." He flashed me a smile, but there was a tightness in his expression. "Everything is just fine."

CHAPTER 16

Wren

B lane said there was nothing to worry about, but I
watched him pacing on the other side of the room
as I considered my options. He looked stressed.
Preoccupied. He appeared content to let Zion handle the
search for Caria, but was that wise? I didn't trust the man.
Okay, so I'd never actually met him, but he'd sent men to try
and kidnap me, and that had to count for something, right?
He was hardly an upstanding citizen. But Blane said this was
the way it had to work.

Did I trust *him*? I didn't think he'd deliberately set out
to hurt me, or Caria, but his judgment sometimes seemed a
little off. As if he didn't quite understand human nature and
how vile it could be.

Snippets of conversation floated across the room.

"Are you certain? Cédric Voltaire?" Blane muttered
angry words that might have been a curse. "How much is he
offering?"

Who was Cédric Voltaire? Not the magician who used
to work at the Golden Oyster? *The Magnificent Voltaire.* I'd
waited tables there soon after I moved to Vegas, and he'd

gotten fired for groping one too many asses. And before he got fired, he got flattened. Molesting a lady who turned out to be the Nevada ladies' taekwondo champion had been a grave error in judgment.

"Put in a counteroffer," Blane said, then paused. "No, more than that. I don't want to waste time going back and forth."

He hung up and stared out the window for a moment. The view wasn't much, but there was a tiny park down below, just a patch of scrubby grass and a few benches where people hung out with their dogs. A fountain. A statue of a stranger. Objectively speaking, the park near Tilt was nicer. The city actually watered the grass there. Grass in the desert. A small oasis of expense representing man's fight against nature, an exercise in futility. Kayden felt differently, of course, seeing as his life revolved around golf greens, although he was always telling me about new cultivars that required less water.

Blane turned around, and for the first time, I saw him look...troubled. But only for a moment.

"Everything okay?" I asked.

"Yes, everything's fine." A pause. "For the most part. Can I ask you a question? I'd be interested in getting a woman's perspective."

"Okay?"

Did he want advice on a gift for a girlfriend? A sister? I realised I knew nothing personal about the man, other than the fact that he had a cat named Myrtle and took too much sugar in his coffee. And yet, I'd be sharing his apartment for the foreseeable future. Would I ever feel safe enough to go back home? I mean, I couldn't stay here forever, but—

"If you moved halfway across the world to escape your ex, and then it turned out he was trying to buy a business in the city you now called home, would you want to know? Or would you prefer for someone to prevent the purchase while you lived in ignorant bliss?"

I pondered the question. That's what the call had been about, wasn't it? Blane had already put in a counteroffer; he was just deciding whether to enlighten the woman in question. Who was she? He must care about her. A bud of jealousy unfurled because nobody had ever fought for me like that, but I pushed it away.

"This isn't hypothetical, is it?"

Blane shrugged one shoulder, but he didn't elaborate.

How would I feel if Dominic suddenly upped sticks and moved to Vegas? Giving Blane an honest answer was the least I could do, so I considered the question for a long moment.

"Running into an ex would sure make me uncomfortable, but I guess I'd have to consider the chances of that happening. At work, I wouldn't have to worry because he doesn't make enough money to play at Tilt, and where else do I go? He'd never be seen dead in a yoga studio, so that only leaves the grocery store. Okay, sometimes I go out for dinner with Caria or Kayden, but I'd have to be really unlucky to bump into him."

"That isn't hypothetical either, is it?"

I returned his one-shouldered shrug. If I knew Dominic was in town, I'd be watching my back the whole time, always on edge. Was that better or worse than being kept in the dark?

"Do your non-hypothetical friend and her ex run in the same circles? How likely are they to bump into each other?"

"Reasonably likely. She saw him going into a hotel on the Strip last month, but he didn't see her. We figured he was on vacation."

"So she knows he's here; she just doesn't know he's thinking of staying?"

"Exactly."

"Then you should tell her. If there was a super low chance of her finding out he's in town, then I'd say not to worry her unnecessarily, but she's going to find out. And if she realises you knew and kept it a secret, she'll be upset."

"So it's okay to keep a secret as long as there's a negligible chance of the other party discovering the truth?"

Oh, we weren't going there. I wasn't giving him a free pass on withholding information.

"It depends on the secret. If you do something horrible like, say, sleeping with an intern just because you don't think you'll be found out, then no, it's definitely not okay. But if you genuinely have the other person's best interests at heart, and you're simply trying to protect their feelings, then maybe it would be all right in certain circumstances. Like if a friend asks what you thought of their home-cooked dinner, and the pasta was overcooked, you still say it was delicious. Because it doesn't really matter, so there's no point in hurting their feelings, get it?"

"I get it. Your ex slept with an intern?"

Sugar honey iced tea. Even in my head, I replaced the word I actually wanted to say out of habit because Dom hated me cursing. But then I realised... Dom wasn't a part of my life anymore. I didn't give even one shit what he thought.

"Can we just not talk about him?"

Another shrug. "As you wish. But for the record, I don't have an intern. Not unless you count Joseph, and I'm definitely not doing the deed with him." Blane pulled a face. "Not that he wouldn't make an excellent partner for the right man."

"He's gay?"

"He's more...gender fluid."

"And you're not?" I asked before I could stop myself.

Why did this man make me speak before I had a chance to think?

"Definitely not." Wow, Blane was devilishly handsome when he smiled properly. "I'm only into women."

I swallowed hard because at that moment, I very much wondered what it would be like if Blane was into me. And the idea was terrifying. Overwhelming. Delicious.

"Right. I'm glad we got that straight."

His smile grew even wider. "So am I, Wren. So am I."

CHAPTER 17

Blane

When I first moved to Plane Five, it had felt like an extended vacation. A break from the rigours of wrangling unruly souls. But this week, I yearned for the days when my biggest headache was managing Tsar Ivan's temper tantrums.

Joseph arrived beside me. Silently, of course, but I could feel his energy.

"Why have you been staring at the bar staff for the past ten minutes?" he asked. "Is there a problem?"

We were standing on the balcony outside my office above Club Dead. The balcony spanned the width of the building and allowed me to watch over the goings-on without having to elbow inebriated humans out of the way. To our right, the VIP area on the mezzanine provided an endless source of entertainment when the club was open, and down below, the main bar and dance floor were empty save for the staff busy preparing for tonight's influx of guests.

"There are many, many problems."

"So, should I fire them?" Joseph offered a little too enthusiastically.

"The problems aren't connected to the bar staff."

He perched his ass on the chrome railing and studied me. "You mean Wren?"

"She's one of the issues, yes."

"Are you talking about more than just the whole 'bestie's been kidnapped by a psycho' thing?"

"Why would you think that?"

"Because I saw the way you looked at Nevaeh, and now I see the way you look at Wren Gillebrand."

Many times over the past several years, I'd been glad that Joseph had been selected to accompany me to Plane Five. He'd proven to be both loyal and discreet, qualities oh-so necessary for his current role. But he was also reasonably perceptive, which was unfortunate at this particular moment in time.

"I'm helping her through a difficult patch, that's all."

"Aurelia says you have a saviour complex."

"Aurelia reads too much."

My little sister always had a book in her hand. Few people ever ventured into the Celestial Library, a dusty, cavernous building full of ancient texts and occasional words of wisdom from Plane One's past residents, but Aurelia treated it as a second home. Her official job title was Executive Board Trainee, which basically meant that someday, she'd be expected to take over the management of Plane Two when Mom and Dad retired. *If* they retired. Dad spent most of his time playing golf anyway, so few people would be able to tell the difference. For now, Aurelia was in charge of the spirit guides who visited any recently departed souls unlucky enough to be stuck in Plane Five, but the spirit guides more or less organised themselves, so she'd quickly grown bored with her job. In order to fill time, she'd adopted the role of head librarian, and she spent her time squirrelled away between the stacks.

"Aurelia would argue that it's impossible to read too much," Joseph said.

"Of course she would—she's probably been studying Socrates."

"You can't deny that you always go for needy women."

"Wren isn't needy. She's just...been impacted by circumstances beyond her control."

"So are you admitting that you like her?"

"I'm admitting nothing."

"Nevaeh isn't coming back, you know. You wouldn't be betraying her memory if you moved on."

"Nevaeh literally is back." Lola Vasquez had inherited my late girlfriend's soul—I felt it on a cosmic level. "She comes to my apartment every other day for cookies and cocoa."

"I meant in a form that wouldn't get you arrested if you took her out for dinner. I say this as a friend and also as your lawyer—don't go there."

"Of course I'm not going to go there. Do you think I'm an idiot?"

"Sometimes."

Yes, today was definitely one of those days I regretted having Joseph as my earthly assistant.

As for Nevaeh, I'd always love her, but now that she'd been reborn, that love had to take a different form. I'd do everything in my power to protect Lola, to make sure she didn't suffer in this life as she had in the last.

But I also found myself wanting to protect Wren. *Needing* to protect Wren. I felt a pull toward her, a connection I couldn't explain and wasn't sure I should want to. She had no one but Kayden to depend on, and her ex sounded like an asshole. She deserved a little kindness. For someone to show her that she was worth everything her ex had convinced her she wasn't. Maybe I could take *her* out for dinner? Discreetly, because if one of Laurent's people spotted her, I'd have to intervene, and things could get awkward if I was forced to dispatch a man to Plane Four in public.

Hmm. Would she interpret dinner as a date? Perhaps Joseph was right and I *was* an idiot? It was a possibility, but I'd never admit that.

"I'm not even going to dignify that with a response," I said. "Don't you have things to do? I need you to keep an eye on the situation with the Devil's Den."

"Are you planning to tell Vee about the Voltaire issue?"

"Yes, I'm planning to tell her."

"Are you sure that's a good idea?"

Not one hundred percent, no, but if I wanted Wren to trust my judgment, then I had to trust hers in return.

"It's the right thing to do."

"*Putain de merde*, I have to leave the city." Vee began pacing in my office. "No, the country."

"Why don't you take a seat for a moment? I'll open a bottle of wine."

I'd come to Tilt this evening to give her the Voltaire-related news and spill the beans on the Devil's Den, and it was going down about as well as I'd expected. Which was to say, badly.

"Wine? Are you crazy? I need to pack."

"You can't leave town. What about your life here? What about Callahan?"

"If Voltaire finds out I'm with Jack, he'll kill him. We're still *married*, Blane."

"Only on paper. The fact that you've been avoiding the man—sorry, the vampire—for the last century should have told him it's over."

"Voltaire doesn't care about love. He only cares about control."

"And world domination? Conquering Europe wasn't enough?"

"Jack looked into that after we saw Voltaire on the Strip. The *connard* made a rare mistake, and the Parisian police want to speak with him about the disappearance of a backpacker. Usually when he's thirsty, he picks women nobody will miss, but this time, he managed to abduct the granddaughter of a wealthy Italian politician."

"Oops. That's a grave mistake to make."

"She was travelling through Europe on a gap year. Dammit! I don't want to leave Vegas, but if Voltaire stays, I'll have no choice. Why is he even here? He hates places like this. It's too loud for him here, too garish."

"If you have money, you can buy silence. A high-roller suite, entry to a private poker room. Does he enjoy gambling?"

"He did play a lot of *poque*," she admitted, naming an old card game that was a forerunner of poker. "Even when casinos were banned in Paris, he used to run underground games from our home."

Which would explain why he was so interested in owning a casino.

"People change, sometimes for the better, sometimes for the worse. I'll make sure he doesn't get the Devil's Den. Maybe he'll give up and move on? I hear Alaska is nice at this time of year."

"I doubt he'll move on. For whatever reason, he's decided that Vegas is the place he wants to be."

"Don't run yet. Give me a few weeks to buy the Devil's Den, and then we'll reevaluate."

"Do you need money? I have money."

I didn't need Vee's money. If the worst came to the worst, I'd pay another visit to the Caribbean with Joseph to dig up some more gold. Prices were excellent on the black market these days. And I'd also ask Aurelia to have a nose through the library and see what information she could find on vampires. Great-Uncle Tiberius had been cagey when he created them, by all accounts —he wasn't a man who liked to admit to his mistakes—but occasionally he'd left scribbled reminders to himself, and many of his notes got scooped up and archived when he disappeared. If vampires had a weakness, I needed to find out about it.

"Money isn't an issue, but if Callahan's in the mood for looking into things, I'd like a favour."

"What kind of favour?"

"There's a fellow named Laurent causing problems around here, and I could do with some background on him."

"What kind of problems?"

"Oh, nothing you need to worry about."

"Wait, is this about Wren's disappearance?"

Shit. "Why would you say that?"

"Because it's not like you to abandon a damsel in distress to work on something else. You have white knight syndrome."

"Have you been talking to Aurelia?"

"How would I talk to Aurelia? She's in a whole other realm."

"Whole other *plane*. A realm is a totally different concept."

Vee rolled her eyes. "Okay, a whole other *plane*. Stop trying to change the subject. Do you have a lead on Wren?"

Hmm, how should I explain the situation?

Vee might have dismissed the idea of wine, but I rose from my chair and walked over to the drinks cabinet anyway. Picked out an earthy Sangiovese from my vineyard in Tuscany—we grew two varieties of grape there—and took a moment to consider my next move while I removed the cork.

"Try this," I said, handing her a glass.

"Which part of 'stop changing the subject' didn't you understand?"

I had to tell her, didn't I? Vee was smarter than Joseph, and fobbing her off wasn't an option. She'd only start poking around herself, which had the potential to stir up a hornets' nest.

"Wren is safe. I've been in touch with her, and she's fine, but a friend of hers is missing."

"Missing? Has she filed a report?"

"Not yet, but I'll encourage her to do so."

"I could ask Jack to—"

"No. I promised her no cops."

"But—"

"Even if I think it's a bad call on her part, I'm not going back on my word. I told you that Wren was safe to put your mind at ease, but I can't say more than that without breaking a confidence."

Vee opened her mouth, then closed it again. Finally, her expression softened.

"That's what I like about you, Blane. You consider people's feelings and do the right thing. I woke up in the early hours worrying about Wren, and even though I'll toss and turn tonight thanks to Voltaire, knowing she's okay gives me one less thing to lose sleep over."

"I'm sorry I put Voltaire in your head."

"I'm not. I'd rather know than get a nasty surprise later."

She squeezed my hand. "Thank you for telling me. And I'll ask Jack if he has any intel on Laurent. Is that a surname?"

"I'm not sure, but from what I've heard, he's an unsavoury character. Tell Callahan not to ask too many questions. There might be a mole in the police department."

"A mole? Do you know that for sure? Is that why Wren won't go to the police?"

"I can neither confirm nor deny."

"So that's a yes? Sheesh, what did she get involved in?"

"Nothing. She was an innocent bystander."

A woman in the wrong place at the wrong time. Although now that she was in my apartment, it felt as if she was in the right place, just under the worst possible circumstances. My phone rang, and I was about to send the call to voicemail when Vee shook her head.

"Take it. I need to get to work anyway. I'll make sure Callahan treads carefully."

CHAPTER 18
Wren

"Hey, who are you?"

The big fluffy cat stalked toward me, tail in the air, and I closed the refrigerator. Several half-empty Chinese takeout boxes had appeared since yesterday, but there still wasn't much in the way of actual food. I'd gotten out of bed with the idea that I could make Blane breakfast—and make myself useful—but at this rate, he'd be getting coffee and three kinds of cake. What time did he start his day? Closer to lunchtime than breakfast, most probably. He hadn't gotten home until five thirty in the morning. Soft voices in the hallway outside my room had woken me, Blane talking to Beauregard, and it was only eight o'clock now.

Did Beauregard live here? Was that weird, a lawyer living with his boss? Or did he have an apartment? I mean, I understood they were friends, but... Maybe they were more than friends? No. No, Blane had been very clear that he was straight. Plus I was also living with my boss, and we were barely more than acquaintances. Could I even call him a friend, or was I more of an irritation?

This was such a damn mess.

Gah.

Should the cat be on the counter? Probably not, but its confident attitude and the claws that clicked on the granite surface made me hesitate to shoo it away. Was this Blane's cat? I risked checking the diamond-studded name tag. Yes, her name was Myrtle.

"Well, aren't you a pretty thing?"

Was she friendly? I hoped she was friendly.

The cat placed her behind daintily in front of the toaster and examined a paw, then she turned her striking green eyes on me. Her gaze was intense as she sized me up, probing, and I took a step back. Then told myself not to be so stupid. She was only a cat.

"Don't worry, I'm not here to steal your place in Blane's affections. I'm just... Well, I'm having a few issues with a man." Myrtle kept staring. "Not an ex. Okay, so I'm having problems with him too, but the reason I'm here is that an asshole kidnapped my friend, and... Why am I talking to a cat?"

This whole week had been surreal. And awful. Deep down, I still hoped to wake up and find this had all been a bad dream, but I was beginning to accept the reality. Caria was gone. I was living on borrowed time. Living with my hot boss, who assured me he had everything under control, but did he really? He was a businessman. A successful businessman who seemed to think he was invincible, but a businessman nonetheless. His answer to my problem was to march into the lion's den and fix things with the sheer force of his personality, but I'd heard enough whispers about Zion to doubt Blane's solution. Zion was a monster. The wyrm to Laurent's wyvern. But what could I do? Tell Blane the stories I'd heard from my former colleagues at the Devil's Den? Explain that Zion was a sly son of a bitch who might have set fire to a man's car with him inside it? Bystanders had tried to drag the victim free of the flames, Dennis the pit boss among them, but the guy had been handcuffed to the steering wheel. Plus his dog had burned in the trunk. Okay, so Zion's involvement had never been proven, but Kevin who worked in the Lucky 7 Grill swore he'd seen Zion leaving the scene.

If I made a fuss, Blane would kick me out, and then I'd be on my own. Caria would only have a penniless blackjack dealer fighting in her corner. We'd both end up dead, and nobody but Kayden would come to our funerals because Caria didn't have much family either—only a sister, and she was in prison. That was another thing we'd bonded over. We both understood what it was like to have lost loved ones, not to death but to the justice system.

"This is a nightmare," I muttered, and Myrtle tilted her head to one side. "Do you want breakfast? Is that why you keep watching me? Where's your food?"

I hadn't expected her to answer, but she surprised me by jumping off the counter and trotting to the pantry. Maybe her food was kept in there? I was poking around the bags of candy, a liquor store's worth of top-shelf alcohol, and stacks of unopened cookware when Myrtle leapt up to the highest shelf and pushed a box off the edge. It landed at my feet. Waffle mix? Was that a request or merely an accident? I scooped it up and checked the ingredients—flour, sugar, milk powder, and raising agents, whatever those were. I didn't know a whole lot about cats, but back when I lived in Cheyenne with Dominic, I used to feed our neighbour's kitty when she went to visit her daughter in New Hampshire. Trixie the Siamese ate meat out of a can, and the only treats she got were turkey-flavoured.

Then again, Blane lived on junk food, so there was a good chance his pet's diet wasn't much better. Obviously I couldn't give him a lecture, but he did say that he'd buy any groceries I wanted, so maybe I could sneak a more appropriate type of cat food onto the list? Although that wouldn't help right now.

"Let's see if we can find you some chicken, okay? Or fish?"

Perhaps there was something suitable in the freezer behind all the ice cream and fancy gateaux?

"Myrtle doesn't eat chicken or fish," Blane said from behind me, and I squeaked and dropped the waffle mix. Then stumbled backward, tripped over my own feet, and would have landed on my ass if he hadn't caught me. Strong hands hooked under my armpits and hauled me upright, then his arms snaked around my waist to steady me.

Holy hotness, he was hard. His chest, I mean, not other parts that I absolutely wasn't going to think about. I realised this was the first time he'd touched me.

"You okay?" he said, leaning in so close that his breath puffed over my ear.

"Uh, yes, just super clumsy. I'm sorry."

"There's nothing you need to be sorry about. Not unless you try to feed Myrtle chicken, anyway—she's vegetarian."

"A vegetarian cat?" I asked, trying desperately not to focus on his arms. Why wasn't he removing them? "Is that healthy?"

"Healthier than starving. She turns her nose up at cat food."

"What about... I don't know, getting her something from the rotisserie?"

Blane finally released me, and I turned to face him on shaky legs. I'd expected him to look tired after less than three hours of sleep, but he was bright-eyed, clean-shaven, and dressed in another of those perfectly tailored suits. Today's was dark grey.

It matched the circles under my eyes.

We were close, too close, and the generously sized pantry suddenly felt tiny. But I didn't step back, and neither did he. No, he just smiled, a devastatingly beautiful smile that made me forget, for one brief moment, that my whole world had fallen apart.

"Rotisserie chicken would be a waste of money. Myrtle knows what she likes, which is a waffle for breakfast." He nudged the box I'd dropped with a toe. "Joseph usually makes them, but if you want to save him the trouble, the waffle iron is in the cupboard beside the stove."

"The cat...eats waffles?"

"Only one waffle. If you make two, she'll take a bite of the second, but you'll end up throwing most of it away. There's a can of whipped cream in the refrigerator, and the maple syrup is just..." He reached for the shelf behind me, his white shirt stretched taut over well-defined pecs, leaning so close that I could feel the heat rolling off him. His cologne was a subtle mix of cedarwood and citrus. "...here."

"Right," I mumbled into his chest, pulse racing, then raised my head and found him watching me through amber eyes. "Uh, do you want waffles? Or Mr. Beauregard?"

He chuckled softly. "I definitely don't want Mr. Beauregard."

"That wasn't what I meant."

"I have to go out this morning." He tucked my hair behind my ear, and it seemed that now the dam had been broken, he was going to keep touching me. And heavens above, I kind of liked it. "But have dinner with me tonight."

"What?"

"Dinner. It's the meal that comes after lunch."

Now I tried to push him away, but it was like

attempting to move a boulder. He didn't budge an inch. And rather than feeling trapped, I felt relieved because this was the man protecting me. Relieved and a tiny bit sweaty.

"Dinner where? I can't exactly go out, and I'm not having candy for an appetiser, cake for an entrée, and liquor for dessert."

"Here. I'll have food delivered." He ran a finger along my arm. "You'll be safe, I— Fuck."

Blane hopped back, cursing, and I looked down to see claw marks in his pants. Myrtle stared at him through narrowed eyes.

"You little psycho," he grouched. "These pants were new."

Was it possible for a cat to look utterly unapologetic? Because somehow she did. Then she batted the box of waffle mix toward me and miaowed.

"Aw, I think she's hungry." *Don't laugh, don't laugh, don't laugh.* "I should make her breakfast."

"Use DoorDash—order her steak tartare and a dozen oysters."

Myrtle swiped at his ankle again, but this time, he jumped to the side.

"Brat," he growled. "Do that again, and you'll get a one-way ticket to the animal shelter. Coach class."

I gasped. "You can't!"

"You're absolutely correct; I can't. Last time she ended up there, she escaped and came right back."

I poked him in the chest, hard, which hurt me more than it hurt him. "You asshole! You took your cat to the shelter?"

"No, of course I didn't. She removed her collar, and a well-meaning stranger picked her up. One of the staff downstairs spotted her on the shelter's website—she was Cat of the Week, no less—and by the time I arrived to pick her up, she was already on her way over here."

Oh.

"Sorry I poked you."

"Forget it. And don't let Myrtle take advantage—she'll have you running her a bubble bath and blow-drying her fur if you're not careful."

"I thought cats hated water?"

"Myrtle isn't a normal cat."

Surprisingly, she didn't take offence at that, just preened and licked a paw. *Dumb, Wren.* Of course she didn't take offence. She was a cat. A reasonably smart cat, but she couldn't understand human words. Could she?

"I'm beginning to realise that."

Blane flashed me one last smile. "I'll see you tonight."

Then he was gone, leaving me alone with a cat whose IQ was probably higher than mine, a box of waffle mix, and a whole bunch of confused thoughts, some of them inappropriate. When I was with Dominic, I'd secretly wished for a little excitement in my life, but now I'd changed my mind.

CHAPTER 19

Blane

"**I**s everything okay?" No, of course it wasn't. "Forget I asked that. Is there a problem with the food?"

Wren's light had dimmed the moment she walked into the dining room. But before that, there was a second of hesitation in the doorway when I thought she wouldn't come in at all.

It reminded me of the very first time we'd met, in my office at Tilt. Barry McKee had interviewed her first, as he always did, but I insisted on having the final sign-off on every employee in a position of trust. If a dealer colluded with a player, the casino could lose thousands.

Wren had paused in the doorway, a deer in headlights, before taking a tentative step forward. I'd glanced at her résumé again. Technically, she didn't have the amount of experience we were looking for, but Barry said she had the looks and the members would love her. Sweet, innocent little Wren. We could work on a person's skills, but their aura was impossible to manipulate.

That little pause... Nevaeh had done the same thing seven years ago in Carpathia. I'd walked into a hotel courtyard with a struggling, muddy husky in my arms, and her eyes had widened as she exited the dining room. She'd frozen mid-step. A long moment passed. And then she'd begun laughing.

"If you train the dog to walk on a leash, you won't get a mud moustache," she said, and then Joseph started laughing too, the spotless asshole. I'd tried to delegate dog transportation duties to him, but the dog kept growling, probably because we'd been in Plane Five for less than a year at that point, and Joseph hadn't been so good at hiding the darkness back in those days.

"He's not my dog," I told Nevaeh. Wasn't that obvious? We'd found the mutt hopping around on three legs during our hunt for lost werewolves. "Is there a veterinarian around here?"

"Uh... Let me check."

She disappeared back inside, and the dog whined. There was a gate at the entrance to the courtyard, and after Joseph closed it, I set the mutt on the ground. It was surprisingly fast on three legs. I knew that because I'd already had to chase it down once, and the beast had bitten me when I finally caught up. Four neat puncture wounds in my right calf. I'd nearly left the creature on the damn mountain. But then I'd sighed because it clearly had a broken leg, and if Aurelia heard I'd abandoned it there to starve—or become a snack for the werewolves, if they were indeed in the area— she'd either cry or whack me with a library book. Getting bitten again was more palatable than either of those options.

Nevaeh returned a minute later with a wizened gent in tow, five feet nothing of leathery skin, whiskers, and grumpiness. He didn't speak any English, and Nevaeh was struggling with Ukrainian, so I stepped in. Languages were compulsory at the Celestial Academy—all of them, even the obscure ones only spoken by a waning handful of Nepalese elders who weren't fond of strangers anyway.

There was a veterinarian in the next town. The old man had a truck we could borrow—for a fee, of course—but there was a problem. I didn't know how to drive, and neither did Joseph. Why would we need to? We were still using celestial transportation in those days, and on the rare occasions I needed to get somewhere slowly, I hired a chauffeur.

But there were no chauffeurs to be found in this desolate corner of Plane Five, and I couldn't take shortcuts through time and space with the dog. Long-distance Energy Enhanced Physical Relocation, which everyone just called leepering, involved stepping between planes, and dogs weren't allowed in Planes Two and Three without a permit. When they departed Plane Five, they went straight to one of the secondary planes, colloquially known as the Rainbow Bridge, and those in charge there had banned humans from visiting in case we messed up their home. Ditto for pretty much every animal plane, and having seen what humans had done to Plane Five, I honestly couldn't blame the managers of the secondaries. Anyhow, the "no humans" rule peeved the Celestial Council, who introduced a convoluted system of requests and authorisations for animals who wished to be reunited with their humans in Planes Two or Three.

All that was to say, we couldn't get the husky to the veterinarian without help.

"Can I hire you to drive?" I asked the old man.

"No, no, I'm waiting for a chicken."

"I'm sorry?"

"My friend Balázs, he is bringing a chicken. For dinner."

"He couldn't just leave the chicken somewhere for you?"

"No, no, I have to wait."

I turned to Nevaeh. "I don't suppose you have a driver's licence?"

She did, and a love of speed that would have scared a mere mortal. Somehow, we made it to the veterinarian in one piece, although the smell of smoke coming from the truck's engine suggested it wasn't long for this world.

From there, we had to go to the city because the local veterinarian wasn't equipped to pin the dog's leg back together. I'd toyed with the idea of trying Decima, but firstly, she didn't have much experience with healing animals, and secondly, she hadn't been fond of dogs since Lord Byron's Newfoundland chewed up her favourite purse and then snapped at her when she tried to retrieve it.

The truck wheezed its last on the outskirts of Ivano-Frankivsk, and I dispatched Joseph to procure alternative transportation for our return while a kindly cab driver drove Nevaeh, me, and the husky to the animal hospital. That had been a long night. Someone found us blankets, and I tried to get comfortable on a hard plastic seat as we waited for news. Nev pushed a row of chairs together and stretched out, her head resting on my thigh as I gently probed for information. Why on earth was this sweet, beautiful woman festering on a Carpathian hillside?

The answer?

She'd been sent there by her family as a punishment. Nevaeh was meant to be proselytising to the locals, but instead, she'd abandoned her mission and holed up in the worst hotel in the history of Tripadvisor. From Oklahoma to Ukraine via rehab—quite the journey.

"Dad's a pastor," she explained. "You know the kind on TV with the 900 numbers? And I'm the black sheep of the family. I didn't live up to *expectations*."

"And what did he expect from you?"

"For me to toe the line. Join him in the family grift—

sorry, the family *business*—and at least pretend to be following the word of God."

It was tempting to explain that the man she thought of as God was probably sitting in the clubhouse at his favourite golf course, sipping a good aged Scotch and grumbling that Opus Vi weren't sending the grifting televangelists to Plane Three where they belonged. But she'd think I'd lost my mind, so I just made one of those sympathetic *mm-hmm* noises that didn't mean much.

"The Bible doesn't do it for you?" I asked.

"It was more the hypocrisy. Men like my dad acting all pious and telling people how to live their lives, but then doing the exact opposite. I mean, he cheats on my mom constantly, but she just carries on keeping house and walking two steps behind him as if none of that matters."

"Maybe she doesn't know?"

"He isn't subtle about it. She must know. One time, a local reporter caught him in a strip club, and he swore he was only there to minister to those poor unfortunate souls who took off their clothes for a living."

"And people believed him?"

"People always believe him. He has a degree in psychology, and he knows how to use it. Even my older sister falls for his bullshit."

"But you don't?"

Nevaeh gave a tiny, sweet smile, and that was the moment I realised the true purpose behind my trip to the Carpathian Mountains. I'd been destined to meet her.

"I decided that I prefer sin."

After a widely publicised search, the husky had gone home to its Polish owners, who'd lost the mutt when it ran off after a deer while they were on vacation, and Nevaeh had come home with me.

Unfortunately, so had her demons, and I didn't mean Joseph's relatives.

Now she was gone, and instead, Wren Gillebrand was in my life. The day we met, I hadn't intended to hire her. Her résumé was filled with low-level positions, and she never seemed to last long in any job. But she'd gingerly sat in my visitor chair and bitten her lip, and I'd done what I had to do. I'd split her souls from her body and basked in the beautiful rainbow shimmer of her subconscious. Then, once I'd put her back together, I'd offered her a glass of water and a job.

And she'd proven to be the best blackjack dealer I'd ever employed.

But now I was beginning to suspect that she was so, so much more. There was something about her...

Which brought us to the present moment, Wren inching toward me, staring at the flickering candles on the dining table as if they were the fires of Plane Three itself. At least she hadn't seen me light them. The fact that I'd simply thought the flames into existence rather than using matches would probably have alarmed her.

"I...I didn't realise... I thought Mr. Beauregard would be here."

"Someone has to ensure Tilt is running smoothly." When she didn't move, I added, "Do you want me to bring him back?"

Her gaze dropped to the table. "Why are there candles?"

Ah, she was upset by the ambience? I'd asked Joseph to arrange a cosy dinner for two, and perhaps he'd gone slightly overboard on the romance. The last thing I wanted to do was make Wren uncomfortable.

"We've had a few issues with the lighting lately."

"The lighting?"

"Flickering, turning off, unexplained buzzing."

"Really?"

The words came out sceptical, and as she tilted her head to one side and narrowed her eyes, the gesture was so...so *Nev* that my heart lurched. Wren couldn't be Nevaeh. *Lola* was Nevaeh, I was quite confident of that. Yes, occasionally souls got cleaved in half, but they became twins. Wren and Nev had been alive at the same time, leading totally different lives. If Nev's soul had been cleaved in Plane Four, Lola would have a sister.

So why did I get that *feeling* whenever Wren looked at me?

I didn't know the answer, but I did know that Nev and I had promised never to lie to each other. Obviously, I'd left some things out, like the fact that I was immortal, but I'd never lied outright. Yes, yes, I realise I should have come clean about my origins, but thanks to her parents, she'd had a strong hatred of all things metaphysical, and I'd been terrified that she'd walk away.

"No." I sighed. "The electrics are fine. I just thought women were fond of candles. Around the tub, at dinner, fancy ones sitting on the shelf. Did you know there are whole stores devoted to scented candles?"

Nevaeh had patronised most of them. She used to spend hours in the tub, a glass of wine on the side, candles all around. That was where I'd found her. Floating, her pale blonde hair spread in the water like a halo. I'd been too late. Too late to catch her soul as it departed for Plane Four and beg Decima to fix her body. Too late to keep the woman I'd loved with my whole heart.

"One of my foster moms had an asthma attack from a scented candle. She got taken away in an ambulance."

"Was she okay?"

"I'm not sure. When she didn't come back from the hospital after a day, I got moved somewhere else."

My heart ached for young Wren. Which was surprising. I hadn't known it could do that.

"Want me to get rid of the candles?"

She thought for a moment. "No, leave them."

Wren took a seat opposite me at the dining table. Joseph had chosen it, a long mahogany behemoth that seated sixteen. Once, I'd thought that a bistro set would have been big enough, but over the past few months, we'd hosted Vee and Callahan, Marianna, Lola, and Pablo. Myrtle joined us for dinner when she was in human form, and Aurelia leepered in occasionally too. I enjoyed the company.

"Are more people joining us?" Wren asked. "I mean, there are only two plates, but enough food to feed an army."

"Joseph may have gotten carried away with the ordering."

"I have no idea how I'm going to repay you for all of this."

"Repay me?"

"For the food I'm eating? Room and board?"

"Why on earth would you think you have to repay me?"

"Because...isn't that usually how it works?"

No, not in my world.

"What skinflint made you pay for your own dinner?"

Her cheeks reddened. Yes, I'd hit the nail on the head. She'd dated a man who insisted on splitting the check instead of treating his woman like a queen. When she didn't answer, I pushed a little harder.

"Did he tot up the cost of every item, or did he order the expensive stuff and then split the bill down the middle?"

Now her cheeks turned scarlet, and I knew he'd done the latter.

"You're worth more than that, Wren. I hope you ditched him after the first date."

"We were engaged," she said, so softly I almost missed the words. And I'd been blessed with excellent hearing.

"Then I'd say you dodged a bullet."

And the man who'd taken advantage of her had been a fool.

I wasn't going to take advantage of Wren, and I was no fool. I was just very confused. There was something strange about this woman, and I was determined to get to the bottom of the mystery.

CHAPTER 20

Wren

I t should have been awkward.

More awkward, I mean. Of course it was weird—I was having a candlelit dinner with my freaking boss, my *hot* freaking boss—but it could have been so much worse. I could have been squirming in my seat.

Instead, all I felt was a mild sense of unease as Blane chatted about the gambling industry and asked me how I liked living in Las Vegas.

"In a normal month, I mean," he clarified. "Obviously, things are difficult at the moment."

"It's better than Wyoming."

"In what way?"

"I guess...I guess it's easier to slide by unnoticed."

"You don't want to be noticed?"

Instinctively, I shuddered. After Dominic cheated on me, it hadn't taken long for the whispers to spread through the neighbourhood in Cheyenne, probably because he'd begun parading Becky around like some kind of prize. Everyone knew he'd done me dirty. And even though it was him who cheated, him who schemed and lied, somehow it was my reputation that had ended up in tatters. *Poor little Wren Gillebrand, not good enough to keep a man.* Not pretty enough. Not smart enough. Not ambitious enough. Everywhere I went, the pitying looks had followed.

"Better to stay anonymous than to be noticed for the wrong reasons." I forced a smile and nudged the conversation in a better direction. "Plus there's so much vibrance here. So much positive energy. Where else can you go with a handful of quarters and turn it into a million bucks?"

"Atlantic City."

At first, I thought he was being flippant, trying to put me down the way Dominic always used to. Reminding me that he was the knowledgeable one. But then I realised there was no snark in Blane's tone. No, it was another of those weird cultural missteps he seemed to make on occasion. He genuinely thought I'd asked a question, and he was offering the answer he assumed I wanted.

"Right. Atlantic City."

"Or Macau, if you want to travel farther afield."

"Have you been to Macau?"

"A few times."

Of course he had. Men like Blane travelled the world. Girls like me took the bus from flyover country to Sin City when there was nothing left for us at home.

"How about Atlantic City?"

"A few times," he said again, but this time, he pulled a face.

"You don't like it there?"

"The locals leave something to be desired."

"The locals? Do you mean the Mob or New Jerseyans in general?"

Blane crinkled his nose. "Now that I think about it, I suppose there might have been Mob involvement."

He *supposed*?

"Are we talking about a particular incident here?"

"Joseph and I were on the Boardwalk two or three years ago, and a woman got upset with him."

"Why did she get upset?"

"She accused him of staring at her breasts."

Yikes. "And...was he doing that?"

"Not staring, exactly. But the way they defied gravity was fascinating. And she seemed quite proud of them, judging by her choice of outfit."

"What was she wearing?"

"A rhinestone-spangled bikini. It did draw the eye somewhat. Anyhow, she threw her soda at Joseph, and then her boyfriend pulled a gun and told us to get out of town if we knew what was good for us. After that, we never went back."

"Did you report him?"

Blane shook his head, which was odd, seeing as he'd encouraged me to go to the police about Zion. But what would the authorities have done? Probably nothing. If criminals owned cops in Vegas, they sure as heck owned more in Atlantic City.

"There was no need," Blane said. "Karma took care of the problem."

"Karma?"

He ate a forkful of caramelised cauliflower. Tonight's menu was nouvelle cuisine, plate after plate of prettily presented morsels that took us on a culinary tour of Europe. Possibly the most delicious meal I'd ever eaten, but undoubtedly standard fare for a man like Blane.

"The funniest thing happened—his pants caught on fire. And he must have missed the 'stop, drop, and roll' lesson because he danced around for a while and then ran into the ocean."

"His pants just...caught on fire?"

How could that even happen?

"His lady friend flicked her cigarette end at me, and I guess there was a spark. The big man moves in mysterious ways. Anyhow, I prefer Vegas over Atlantic City, so I can't say I was devastated when we had to leave." Blane pointed to my wine glass. "Top up?"

Before we sat down for dinner, I'd vowed to keep my wits about me. I barely knew Blane, and in my experience, no man was this nice without having an angle. He'd said I didn't need to pay him money for room and board, but what if he expected another type of compensation? The thought should have horrified me, but to my shock, I found I didn't hate the idea. Not that Blane would ever be interested in a woman like me for more than a quick roll in the sack. A few mindless hours in that enormous bed I'd glimpsed, naked and sweaty and— *Stop*. What was wrong with me? Blane was my *boss*. I should be grateful he was acting professional, not wondering if he looked as good out of his suit as he did in it.

"Wren?" He was staring at me expectantly.

"Uh, no. No, thanks. No more wine." Definitely no more wine. I'd already drunk too much. "Have you always lived in Vegas?"

"No, I moved here six years ago. Coming up to seven soon."

"Where did you live before?"

He paused to take a mouthful of steamed lemon sole. "I moved around. Vegas is the first place I've really felt at home."

"I guess I can understand that." Once, I'd hoped Cheyenne might become home, but now that I looked back, I saw I'd only ever been a guest there. No, not a guest. More of an accessory. A small part of Dominic's life to be taken advantage of until I was no longer useful. The apartment in Vegas might have been small, but it was mine—as long as I paid the rent, anyway—and I hated the idea that I might be forced to leave. "Did you hear anything from Zion yet?"

"No, but I gave him a week to find Caria. I'll check in with him in the morning. Give him some gentle encouragement."

A week. So much could happen in a week. Caria could be dead, I could be homeless, and the corrupt cops could sweep it under the carpet.

"I hate the waiting. Can't you call him tonight?"

"Patience is a virtue, my dad always says, but I view it as more of a necessary evil. And I doubt Zion will have spent much time on the matter so far. He had to get his nose reset, and by all accounts, there's a multitude of possible locations he needs to check for Caria."

"I thought you said he just had a nosebleed?"

"Cause and effect."

"How did his nose get broken?"

"He tripped and ran into my fist."

I put my head in my hands, and a groan escaped. Making a man like Zion angry definitely wasn't the smart thing to do.

"What's wrong?" Blane asked. "You don't like fish?"

How could he be so dense? "The food is fine. I'm just not sure..." I trailed off because I couldn't afford to alienate this man, not when he was providing my income, my food, and a roof over my head. And what if he was right and I was wrong? Instinct told me Zion was a loose cannon, but what did I really know about the criminal underworld? Maybe not as much as Blane. Not that I thought he was a criminal or anything, but he had a greyness around the edges.

And perhaps that was why I didn't push him to act

differently... Because if we found Caria, we'd need every bit of that murkiness to set her free.

"No, there's no problem." I made an effort to smile. "The food is delicious. You mentioned your dad—are the two of you close?"

"My parents live in a retirement community not too far from here."

"I meant close as in...close. Like, do you have a good relationship?"

"Right, I see." He took a sip of wine and considered the question. That alone told me their relationship wasn't the best. "We've had some differences of opinion over the years, but he's family."

So was my mom, but I never spoke to her anymore. She hadn't even put me on her visitor list.

"Do you have any brothers or sisters?"

"Two sisters, one older, one younger. Decima is the bane of my existence, but Aurelia's a darling. You'll love her."

He wanted me to meet his sister? That was...weird.

"Does she live around here?"

"Not too far away—she likes to drop in on occasion. How about you—is Kayden your only sibling?"

"Yup, it's just the two of us. I haven't seen my mom in years, and I don't even know who my dad was." That was the wine talking because I never normally discussed my screwed-up past. "I guess that's why Caria means so much to me. Because I'm mostly alone, and she was the first..."—I sniffed back tears—"the first real friend I made."

Caria was the busiest person I knew. She worked as a waitress in a fancy bar—that was where she'd had the misfortune to meet Laurent—and she studied interior design at college during the day. Part-time, but she'd almost earned her degree now. Plus she went to yoga classes at the Fitness Factory, she jogged in the mornings, and in the pre-

Laurent days, she'd ventured out on several dates a week. Despite all that, she'd *still* found time for me.

She messaged every day, and when I was feeling down, which was often, she always cheered me up.

Her loss was one I'd never get over.

"We'll find her, I promise. Whatever it takes."

Blane sounded so confident that I wanted to believe him. Later, I'd look back on that statement and realise it was the one time he didn't skirt around the truth. *Whatever it takes.* Would I have acted differently if I'd known what was to come? Would I have run screaming from the building and jumped into the Grand freaking Canyon?

Quite possibly.

"I miss her."

I struggled to hold back my emotions, and that night, I saw Blane's sweet side. He dried my cheeks with a handkerchief, then appeared perplexed when the tears kept coming. Finally, he crouched at my side, a little awkwardly, it appeared.

"Aurelia tells me that hugs are the best medicine. Which seems bizarre when you consider that hospitals exist, but if it would help, I'm open to the idea."

"Caria was a hugger," I said miserably.

"Caria *is* a hugger. Think positive."

"I'm trying," I whispered.

That was the moment everything changed. When Blane's arms wrapped around me, I stiffened for a second, then relaxed as the strangest warmth spread through every atom in me. My head fell against his shoulder. His arms tightened, and I'd never felt so safe, so protected, so calm as I did in his embrace. Even with chaos all around, Blane's aura soothed my senses.

"Aurelia is right," I mumbled against his shirt.

"So she always tells me."

Was this normal? To feel so utterly at peace in a man's arms? With Dom, all I'd experienced was an unpleasant sense of trepidation because his hugs were usually accompanied by a request to iron his shirts or pick up a slice of pecan pie from the diner.

"I feel weird," I murmured.

"I feel...confused."

Confused? I leaned back to look at Blane, to gaze into amber eyes that had lost their usual sharpness. He brushed the hair away from my damp cheeks, and for the briefest moment, I thought he might kiss me. But he only sighed.

"You should get some sleep."

I didn't say a word when he picked me up and carried me to the guest room. By rights, I shouldn't have slept a wink, but when Blane laid me on the thousand-thread-count sheets, my eyelids were so heavy that I couldn't keep them open.

Maybe I imagined him kissing me on the forehead before he left the room?

Maybe I imagined the brush of his fingertips across my cheek?

Maybe I imagined his whispered words?

Who are you?

CHAPTER 21
Blane

"Put me through to Zion."

"Mr. Ziaroni doesn't take calls."

I recognised Minerva's voice, and she sounded fed up.

"Tell him it's his sparring partner." Then curiosity got the better of me. "Is his name really Zion Ziaroni?"

"The Zion part comes from his surname." Her next words were a whisper. "His first name is Peace, but he said it doesn't fit his image."

"Peace? As in the opposite of war?"

"His mom was one of those hippie types."

Well, she'd certainly failed as a parent.

Unsurprisingly, Zion managed to find his way to the phone reasonably quickly after Minerva explained who was calling, and the next voice I heard was his. He sounded slightly nasal, probably thanks to the swelling.

"What do you want?"

"Is that any way to speak to a client? I'm calling for a progress report."

"You know how hard it is to find a woman who a man like Laurent doesn't want to be found?"

"Yes, which is why I hired a professional."

"Yeah, well, I'm a Vegas guy. The girl ain't in Vegas; I got that on good authority. Now I gotta check all the other places she might be. It's like lookin' for a speck of flour in a brick of coke."

"And that's something you have experience with?"

"Flour in coke? Nah, man, my nose candy gets cut with creatine and vitamin powder. Got the healthiest buyers in Sin City."

Zion seemed oddly proud of that little incongruence. Me? My blood only boiled hotter.

"Oh, really?"

"Swear. Everyone knows if you want the good stuff, you come to Zion. You interested?"

"In drugs? Certainly not. The clock's ticking, and I suggest you focus on finding Caria."

"Laurent's a late riser. There ain't nothing I can do while the sun's shining."

"Then I suggest you get some sleep because you have a busy evening ahead of you."

I hung up, turned off the burner phone, and tossed it into my desk drawer. No way would I be giving that intolerable scumbag my actual number. Joseph watched me from the office couch, drink in hand.

"Bad news?"

"No news, which is almost as disappointing. Caria's not in Vegas, apparently, but beyond that, the fool has no idea. And I suspect he's too busy feeding addictions to care."

"You think we should hire someone else?"

"Like another investigator?"

"When the soul who previously inhabited this bag of

bones did lawyer stuff, he used investigators. I saw the notes in his files."

"Tempting, but if we need to bend a few earthly rules in order to retrieve Caria, I don't need external scrutiny."

"No questions about dead bodies?"

"Mortals get strangely attached to flesh and blood, what with their carved headstones and decorative urns and murder investigations."

Years ago, I'd struggled with the concept of human feelings, but now that I'd spent time in Plane Five, I understood. Humans loved harder and deeper because their time was limited. Friendships ranged from fleeting to lifelong, but there was an intensity to them not found in the other realms. I'd experienced it myself with Nev.

And last night, I'd felt that connection again with Wren.

Entwined souls found their way back to each other, Aurelia always said, and that had been true with Lola. But how did Wren fit in?

I'd peeped into her room this morning to check she was still breathing, then left her to sleep. She'd felt it too, the connection between us; I knew she had. And it had surprised her. Maybe even shocked her the way it had shocked me, but for a different reason. She was shocked because she'd felt the power of the aetherbond for the first time. I was shocked because I'd felt it for the second.

There had been much speculation about the aetherbond through time. Aurelia found it a fascinating topic, so much so that she'd absorbed every mention she could find in the Celestial Library and loved to regurgitate the snippets over dinner. *Did you know that when a celestial bonds with a human soul, they're bound for eternity? Please could somebody pass the salt?*

Not every soul was bonded, and with the way they got shuffled around in Plane Four, few on Earth were lucky enough to find their soulmate, although air travel had made things easier. And it was perfectly possible to fall in love with another without being bound. But the aetherbond amplified every emotion, leading to a deeper connection, a familiarity that stretched across the ages. Legend said that bonded souls were always linked, even across long distances, a cosmic thread that helped them to find each other through the ages.

The way I'd found Nev.

And Wren.

How could I be bonded to two women? They'd walked Plane Five at the same time, so it wasn't a simple case of soul recycling.

"You want me to give Zion a kick up the ass?" Joseph asked. He'd put down the drink and stretched out, his feet resting on the arm of the couch.

"Not yet. We'll save that treat for another day. If he's in the hospital having his bones screwed back together, he won't be out looking for Caria."

"You're no fun anymore."

"We still have fun; it's just a different—"

The door cracked against the wall, and Myrtle stomped in. Girl-Myrtle, not cat-Myrtle. Celestial beings matured more slowly than mortals, so she was in the equivalent of her early teens now, a delightful ball of angst and whining.

"You need to tell the new girl to put more syrup on my waffles. Like, a teaspoon is *not* enough."

"She's probably thinking of your health."

"Seriously? I'm freaking immortal."

"Yes, but Wren doesn't know that. You forgot to take off your collar."

"Gah." Myrtle's fingers flew to her throat, and the tags jingled as she tossed the offending article onto my desk. "I hate that thing."

"Some women in the club wear collars by choice."

"But those are cool, edgy collars with spikes, not pink glitter."

"You want a spiky collar?"

"Decima told me it would look dumb with the fur."

"That's one of the rare instances where I have to agree with her."

"Can you take me home? I've seen every show on the Strip, and I'm soooo bored. Plus I haven't hung out with Aurelia for ages."

At least if I took Myrtle home, she'd stop complaining. Or if she didn't, she'd be someone else's problem. I was about to answer in the affirmative when Joseph cut in.

"Would your desire to visit Aurelia have anything to do with the fact that Orwell's birthday celebration is happening tonight?"

"Is it?" she asked, going for innocent but missing the mark by a mile.

"Myrtle, Myrtle, Myrtle... You need to learn to lie better than that." I put an arm around her shoulders. No way was her timing coincidental. "What's your plan?"

Silence.

"Myrtle?"

"Okay, okay, I was going to shit on the cake."

"And then you changed back into human form? Awkward."

On the plus side, at least she hadn't needed to claw at my pants to request a trip back home this time.

"I mean, I still could."

Good grief. Even Joseph looked faintly disgusted.

"Let's not go there. I'll drop you off in Plane Three, and you can collect an assortment of slugs from Sawney Bean's vegetable garden. Cut the cake in half and put the slugs in the middle."

"Slugs?"

"Did you forget Orwell has molluscophobia? Add a few snails for a bit of a crunch, then smooth the icing over afterward."

Her eyes lit up. "Oh my gosh, you're a genius. We need to leave, like, right now."

I smiled to myself. Myrtle was a pain in everyone's behind, but at heart, she wasn't a bad kid. I'd been a little surprised when she showed up with Aurelia one day and announced she wanted to move to Plane Five, but I understood the sentiment, which was why I'd offered her a home. Meanwhile, Aurelia spent her spare time scouring the library for a way to reverse the hex Orwell had put on Myrtle, but with no luck so far.

Travel between planes was severely restricted, and the rules were complex. We couldn't have folks sliding back and forth to wreak havoc. Only senior members of a celestial house had the ability to leeper freely, and we were able to bring other celestial beings with us if we chose. Not humans, though. I could take Myrtle to Plane Three, Decima could leeper her to Plane Two, and Aurelia could bring her back to Vegas again—she'd be going to the party.

All I had to do was visualise a portal, take Myrtle's hand, and step through to a new dimension.

After checking carefully for witnesses, of course.

She gave Joseph a finger wave, and a moment later, we were back in the pits of Plane Three. Right in the middle of a fight. Cleopatra and Marcus Antonius again. One of the Electi had quite rightly dumped the pair of them into Plane Three, and now they were destined to bicker forever after. The only thing that could make it worse would be if Julius Caesar— Oh, there he was. Right on time.

"I'm just saying that if you hadn't hired a celestial

assassin as your messenger, we wouldn't be in this predicament," Marcus Antonius whined in Ancient Greek.

"How was I supposed to know he'd betray both of us?"

"You didn't get suspicious when he just happened to have an asp?"

"Well, if you hadn't asked him to stab you in the stomach because you were too cowardly to do it yourself..."

"He offered!"

"Serves you right for stealing my wife, *stultissime*," Caesar put in.

"You were already dead, *matula*."

"And you didn't have a hand in that? The Electi just happened to appear in the Senate?"

Then Decima steamed in. "This is your final warning. The final final warning! If you disturb the peace one more time, there's a cave on Mount Malum with your name on it."

Final final warning? You didn't give warnings. You simply acted, and people got the message. But this wasn't my circus anymore. These weren't my monkeys.

"Have you considered a three-way?" I asked. "It's a great way to relieve sexual tension."

"I do *not* have sexual tension," Cleopatra snapped.

"Sure you don't, queenie. That's why you flush every time Marcus stares at your cleavage, and everyone's seen you checking out Julius's package. I'm just saying a three-way would be a win-win for everyone. A win-win-win," I corrected.

"It's not the worst idea Lord Blane has ever had," Caesar admitted.

"No, that was the archery contest with live targets."

Ah, yes. When the prey started hurling the flaming arrows back at us like kiddie-sized javelins, I'd realised the error of my ways.

"What are you doing here?" Decima demanded. "You can't just walk back into this plane and undermine me."

"Relax, sister. I'm not here to stay. Myrtle merely needs to collect some slugs for a project, and if you could just drop her in— Actually, I'll take her myself. It looks as if you've got your hands full."

"Then collect your slugs and stop interfering."

"One more tip before we go—if there's no peace, you can't charge people with disturbing it."

"He makes an excellent point," Marcus Antonius said.

Decima pointed toward the garden full of rotting vegetables. "Get out of here."

"Blane!"

In stark contrast to Decima, Aurelia greeted me with a squeal and a hug, the latter of which I returned gladly. If I had one regret about leaving celestial life, it was that I rarely saw Aurelia anymore. But I couldn't complain about her staying in Plane One. Aurelia had the most vibrant of rainbow souls, and better for her to be sheltered from the evils of the other planes than to have that light dim.

"I didn't know you were coming," she muttered against my chest as I blew her fine blonde hair away from my face. "I would have made cookies."

"Myrtle wanted to attend Orwell's birthday celebration."

"Oh." Aurelia looked up at me. "Oh dear."

"I also want to pick your brain." As Plane One's librarian, Aurelia had access to aeons of information. "And of course I've missed you."

"I'll make coffee." She crinkled her nose. "Such that it is."

Decaf. Plane One had decaf. Father insisted the pure souls of Planes One and Two had no need for artificial stimulants and had deemed them unwelcome. There was caffeine-free coffee, alcohol-free wine, and dairy-free ice cream. Cigarettes were banned completely because my mother hated the smell. They'd even sucked all the fun out of chocolate.

Aurelia made us mugs of the mildly flavoured water that passed for coffee, cut us each a slice of bland cake—because sugar was also considered unhealthy—and curled up in her favourite overstuffed armchair. Although she was entitled to digs at the palace in Plane Two, she chose to live in a cosy cottage near the library in Plane One, opposite the park and close to the beach. Mount Olympus rose in the background.

"Don't you ever get a craving for proper food?" I asked. "We're immortal. Candy can't hurt us."

She just shrugged and said, "Dad."

He always had been a stick-in-the-mud, and things had only gotten worse after Orwell slipped a particularly interesting variety of mushroom into his birthday dinner a couple of decades ago. He'd lost his mind after a remarkably accurate painting of him doing the funky chicken at the nineteenth hole found its way into his favourite art gallery. The prankster was never identified, and Dad hadn't seen the funny side. Thankfully, Mum had talked him out of banning birthday celebrations altogether, but he'd tightened up on the rules around banned substances after that. I pulled a candy bar out of my pocket.

"Want to split this?" Leepering with small inanimate objects was possible. Clothes, for example. Nobody wanted us to show up naked, not unless we dropped into the nicest colony at the Garden of Eden.

"You shouldn't have that," Aurelia said.

"What does it matter? I'm already the black sheep of the family."

"No, you're not. Cynthia is the black sheep."

Ah, yes. Another of Orwell's "experiments."

"Do you want half or not?"

"Of course I do."

She broke off a square of chocolate and stuffed it into her mouth. "What do you want help with?" she asked around chewing. "Are you struggling with the whole 'sin is fun' thing again?"

"Always, but that's not why I'm here today." I told her about the mess with Caria, the fact that Wren was sleeping in my guest room, and the strange connection I'd experienced last night. "I thought the aetherbond was a one-time-only deal. One found their soulmate, and that was it. Nev's soul is in Lola, I'm confident of that. So how can I be feeling the same thing with Wren?"

"That's a question I can't answer." Which annoyed Aurelia; I knew it did. "But it's not entirely unknown."

"It isn't?"

"Great-Uncle Tiberius did a research study on the aetherbond several thousand years ago, and three participants reported experiencing a connection with more than one person."

"The study involved celestials?"

Aurelia nodded. "A footnote said there was also anecdotal evidence from mortals in Plane Five, but he didn't run a formal study there. And besides, celestials have stronger reactions to the aetherbond than humans, so it stands to reason that they'd provide a more conclusive response. Humans often get love and lust confused."

And money. "So, the dual connection... A sister? A half-sister?"

Nevaeh did have a sister, but Esther was firmly

ensconced in the family firm. With no brother, she'd become their father's designated heir. One day, the five campuses of the Fellowship of the Sacred Way in Tulsa, Oklahoma, would all be hers, along with the church's TV channel, its airplane, and the twelve-bedroom mansion Pastor Michaels had bought to use as his "parsonage."

But a half-sister wasn't beyond the realm of possibility. Pastor Michaels was fond of visiting strip clubs in his spare time, and I knew all too well what went on in the VIP rooms.

Could Nev and Wren be related? I wasn't sure how I felt about that.

"Oh, no, the aetherbond specifically can't work with siblings or even half-siblings. Not when they're born in the same cycle, anyway—there's a genetic component of the bond that doesn't allow such things." She glanced out the window in the direction of her beloved library, a behemoth of a stone building that contained millions of books, notes, and papers and a very poor cataloguing system. "Let me look into it."

"If anyone can solve the mystery, it's you."

"Or maybe finding the answer isn't important?" Aurelia smiled softly. "Just let your heart guide you."

CHAPTER 22

Wren

"Something smells delicious."

Blane's voice made me jump. How did he creep up behind me so silently?

"I-I thought I'd make dinner. Mr. Beauregard picked up the ingredients."

"Call him Joseph—we don't stand on ceremony around here. What are you making?"

"Nothing fancy, only a stir fry. I really, really craved bok choy and beansprouts."

When I was six, I'd thought a diet of cakes and candy would be the best thing ever, but now that I'd tried living the reality—with the addition of potato chips and alcohol— I finally understood the attraction of the produce section.

"Do you want a glass of wine to go with that?"

"Just a small one? I figured I'd make Myrtle dinner as well, but I can't find her. Cat-Myrtle, I mean." Girl-Myrtle had dropped by for coffee earlier while Blane was out, and she was a little strange. One minute, she was sipping a cappuccino, the next, she was scratching like crazy. Then she stuttered a bit and literally ran out the door because she'd forgotten to turn off her curling iron at home. Doubly weird because her hair was straight with a hint of frizz. "Do you think she's gotten lost on the Strip again?"

"No, she's at a friend's place."

Huh? "Your cat has playdates?"

"Something like that. And this isn't a criticism, but could you put more syrup on her waffles in the mornings?"

"More syrup? I used half the bottle. Is syrup good for cats?"

"Probably not, but Myrtle wants what Myrtle wants."

"How do you even know what she wants?"

Blane pulled the cork out of a bottle of white with a quiet *pop*. "I can tell by her general attitude."

That was weird, but at least Blane cared about his pet. Too many cats ended up in the shelter. *Permanently* in the shelter.

"Maybe there's some kind of cat-friendly syrup we could get?"

We. It was a slip of the tongue, but Blane's lips just quirked in a lopsided smile that made my stomach flip-flop.

"We could, but she won't like it. I'll ask Joseph to check the pet store. Or Vee might know—she also has a cat."

Blane set a glass of wine beside me and leaned against the granite-topped island, framed by a vase of fresh flowers and a bowl of fruit. Roses and peonies, and the bowl—an ornate creation made from silver spirals—cost more than I earned in a month. I knew that for certain because I'd gotten curious and googled it.

Today's suit was charcoal, his dress shirt open at the collar. A perfect specimen of a man, if you went for the smart, uptight type. Which I never had, but I'd tried the disorganised, pedantic, personality-of-a-cockroach type, and where had that gotten me? Laughed out of Cheyenne, that's where. Dom had worn suits, but he'd never looked good in them. No, he'd had the aesthetic of a used car salesman, and he constantly fiddled with his collar as if it were choking him.

If only it had.

Still, he was Becky's problem now, and I had a whole new set of challenges to deal with. Starting with the way my emotions ratcheted into overdrive whenever Blane came too close. Four feet between us, and I was already beginning to sweat.

"How was your day? Did you hear anything about Caria?"

"She's not in Vegas. Zion is still trying to locate her."

"But that's only the beginning, isn't it? Even if he finds her, how can we get her back?"

"I'll go with Joseph."

"Go and what? Knock on the door and politely ask Laurent to hand her over?"

"We'll come up with a plan when we know where she is."

"Did you miss the part where I said Laurent is a murderer?"

"No, I'm a good listener. Is something burning?"

Dammit. The chicken was beginning to blacken around the edges. My cooking was more "avoid starvation" than gourmet, but I'd found instructions on the internet, and as long as the chicken was cooked all the way through, we wouldn't die. I tossed the vegetables into the wok, and— Oh hell... Maybe I'd been wrong about the dying part? Flames roared toward the ceiling, and I leapt back with a panicked scream and stepped on Blane's foot.

"Shit! I'm sorry."

Water. I needed water. There was no handy bucket, so I dumped the roses and peonies onto the floor and hefted the vase. In one smooth motion, I turned and threw the remaining contents at the wok, except what I actually did was soak Blane because the flames were gone and he was standing in the way.

Suddenly, dying didn't seem like such a bad option after all.

"Please, just kill me now," I said with a groan.

"Wouldn't that be counterproductive? Aren't you staying here because you want to remain alive? And for future reference, throwing water on a grease fire is a spectacularly bad idea. Next time, just put the lid on the pan."

Next time? Boy, he really had a lot of confidence in me. And danger aside, the water had served a purpose. Blane's shirt had gone translucent, plastered against taut abs and a hard chest, a happy trail of dark hair leading past his hips to a part of his anatomy I definitely shouldn't be thinking about. What the hell was wrong with me?

"Next time, I'm cooking goldfish crackers with a side of potato chips."

"Goldfish crackers are a snack, not a meal. Tomorrow, I'll pick up dinner on my way home." He lifted the lid and peered into the wok. "This is salvageable. Good thing I like my bok choy chargrilled."

He flipped the contents expertly and adjusted the heat, and I stared. "You can cook?"

"When the need arises. Why don't you take the weight off your feet?"

"I..." I was a failure. Even the simplest thing ended up in disaster.

"You what?"

"I wanted to make dinner as a thank-you. For letting me sleep here, you know? And I can't even manage not to ruin that."

"The flames only lasted a moment."

"And now you're wearing a wet shirt."

He stared at me for a beat, then shucked his jacket. When he began unbuttoning the shirt, I realised what he was planning.

"No, no, no."

The shirt joined the jacket on a stool, and I was forced to look at my boss in all his semi-naked glory. Smooth, tanned skin. Muscles that would make a superhero weep. Two perfect grooves leading from his hips and disappearing under his leather belt.

"Problem solved," he announced, picking up the spatula and prying the chicken from the bottom of the wok. "Any other complaints?"

Absolutely not.

I was forced to sit on a stool and watch the muscles rippling in Blane's back as he finished making dinner. The man was an enigma. He could cook, and yet he chose not to. He was wealthy, but he still treated mere mortals like human beings. He had a business empire to run, yet he was spending the evening here with me. And perhaps most puzzling of all, he looked like a living god, but I'd seen no evidence of a woman here, unless you counted the two Myrtles, and I couldn't imagine he was into incest or bestiality. *Was* sleeping with a fourth cousin incest? I mean, she looked about fourteen, and he wouldn't, would he?

"Do you have a girlfriend?" I blurted, then closed my eyes in embarrassment when he slowly turned, one eyebrow raised.

"Why do you ask?"

"Uh...uh... I just don't want to get in the way. Make anyone uncomfortable by being here, I mean."

"No, Wren, I don't have a girlfriend."

My name on his lips sent a flash of heat through me, and

this was all kinds of wrong. His smirk said he knew that, but he was going to keep standing there shirtless anyway.

"Shouldn't you put more clothes on? What if the oil spits?"

"I'll be fine."

Oh, so freaking fine.

"I could get you a fresh shirt."

"Feel free, if it makes you more comfortable."

The smirk was still there. He was enjoying this, wasn't he, this little game of verbal chicken? And he thought I'd blink first and get the shirt. Well, the joke was on him. I swallowed half the glass of wine, smiled, and shrugged.

"No, I think I'll just sit here and enjoy the view."

While trying to hide the panic rising inside me. This was starting to feel dangerously like flirting. Dangerous because when this was over, I'd still need a job, or at the very least, a good reference. But I just couldn't quit. That strange pull I'd experienced last night was back, tethering me to this spot. To this moment.

To this man.

CHAPTER 23

Wren

B lane slid a plate in front of me and took a seat opposite. There would be no escape from the glorious view. Tentatively, I took a nibble of chicken. A little dry, but that was probably due to my efforts.

"What do you think?" he asked.

"I think that shirts should be made illegal." *What?* I dropped the fork and clapped both hands over my mouth. "Sorry! I'm so sorry. I don't know where that came from." When Blane didn't speak, I kept babbling. "These past few days, I've been feeling out of sorts. Off-kilter. And then I find myself waffling and doing things I wouldn't normally dream of." Such as hugging my boss. "I don't quite understand why."

"I don't understand why either."

"I can only apologise."

"You have nothing to be sorry for. I'm the one sitting here without a shirt on."

"Which is also my fault."

Blane took another mouthful of assorted green stuff and

chewed slowly. "How about we agree that this is an unprecedented situation, and due to the unusual circumstances, either one of us might inadvertently do something indecorous."

"Indecorous? Do you secretly moonlight as a dictionary?"

"Too formal? Okay, strike out 'do something indecorous' and replace it with 'act like an asshole.' Better?"

"I guess."

"And let's also agree that if one of us should act like the aforementioned asshole, the other will raise the issue and permit the offender to rectify the position."

"Okay." That would give me some breathing space.

"I assume that suggesting you remove your shirt as well would fall into 'asshole' territory?"

My eyes rolled of their own accord, and so did my stomach. "Duh, yes."

And also: holy hell.

My hotter-than-sin, wealthier-than-a-small-country boss was definitely flirting. I channelled Chandler from *Friends*. Could this *be* more inappropriate? Yes, it certainly could if I did as he suggested and removed said garment, and the fact that I was actually considering it made me facepalm.

"Then I apologise for being an asshole," Blane said, although he didn't sound sorry at all.

"It's fine. Eat your vegetables."

"Yes, Mom."

Add "bizarrely adorable" to Blane's list of qualities, or maybe that was the wine's opinion? I tried desperately to change the subject.

"So, do you own any clothes that aren't suits or dress shirts?"

Oh, well done, Wren. That was brilliant.

"Do boxer briefs count?"

Heaven help me.

"Let's skip the underwear."

"Skip it as in, take it off?"

"No!" I thunked my head on the counter. "Keep all of your clothes on. I just meant, do you own a pair of jeans? A T-shirt? Sweats? What do you wear when you kick back and watch TV?"

"I don't watch much TV. The real world is far more fascinating."

"You're totally missing the point of my question."

"I do have shorts, and possibly a pair of jeans somewhere. But what's wrong with the suits? I thought women liked men in suits."

"Women do. They also like hot lumberjacks, men in grey sweatpants, and cowboys."

"So you're saying I should chop down trees and ride a horse in grey sweatpants?"

A vision popped into my head. "A horse in grey sweatpants? I guess you'd have to make sure it didn't kick you when you helped it to dress."

His forehead creased into a frown. "Why would I...? Oh. Right. Ambiguous phrasing, yes."

"I'm just saying that casual pants might be more comfortable when you're chilling at home. Or not. I mean, it's up to you. Shirtless also works."

Mental note: next time, change the subject to anything other than Blane's clothing. Or the lack of it. Sheesh, the man could have his own calendar. Twelve months of suits. Winter through fall. Snowsuits, bathing suits, suit-suits...

"You want me to dress like a stripper? Cuffs, a bow tie, and Velcroed-on pants?"

"Can we stop talking about your clothing now?"

"You started it."

"I freaking know that. But a woman reserves the right to change her mind."

"Yes, I've heard that before."

"From one of your sisters?"

The atmosphere changed. Relaxed, jokey Blane disappeared, and his smile dropped.

"From my former girlfriend. She used to say it all the time."

"I'm so sorry." What was I meant to say in this situation? "Uh, was it a bad breakup?"

Yikes, now I was just being nosy.

"The worst."

I forced a smile. "Well, I hope she doesn't still live in Vegas."

"She does, in a manner of speaking. At the Woodlawn Cemetery."

Oh *hell*. All the life had been sucked out of the room, and Blane... Blane looked like death himself. This whole time, I'd assumed he was merely another douchebag player. I mean, I'd heard rumours of beautiful women following him into a suite at Tilt, only to re-emerge three hours later looking thoroughly dishevelled.

But underneath it all, he was grieving?

Pleasures of the flesh but not of the mind, Vee had once murmured in response to one of those rumours. At the time, I hadn't understood what she meant, but now I thought I might. Blane was a red-blooded male who enjoyed sex, but his heart still belonged to the woman he'd lost. Was that the reason he never spent the night with any of his bed buddies?

My fork clattered to the plate. This time, it was my turn to offer a hug. I walked around the counter and wrapped him up in my arms, and there was that connection again. That strange, fuzzy thread of energy that made everything seem right. Did he feel it as well? I hoped he did. I wanted him to.

"I'm so, so sorry. Was it... Did it happen a long time ago?"

"Just over five years." His voice came out croaky. "Seems like the blink of an eye."

Five years ago, I'd still been making mistakes with Dom in Cheyenne, and it seemed as if a lifetime had passed since then. But the bereaved worked to remember their loved ones. I'd done my best to scrub Dom's smug face from my brain, but on a bad night, his scrawny ass thrusting away on top of his intern still haunted my dreams. I'd have gladly kicked him into hell if I could.

But there was no shrine in Blane's apartment, not that I'd seen anyway. No pictures, no mementoes.

"I didn't realise," I murmured.

"How could you?"

"The staff usually gossip," I said, and then wished I'd bitten my tongue.

"My relationship with Nevaeh was private. We had a place in the Arts District as well as this apartment, and she rarely came to work with me."

Nevaeh. Blane's voice had cracked on her name, and my heart broke too. What was I supposed to do in a situation like this? I'd experienced plenty of heartbreak, but not death. My losses had come with a different kind of hurt.

"Do you want me to give you some space?" I whispered.

He shook his head. "Having you here is a balm to my soul."

"You feel it too?"

Blane knew exactly what I was talking about. "Yes, and I can't explain it."

Well, that made two of us. Blane lifted me to straddle his lap, and I tucked my head against his shoulder. My heart beat wildly against my ribcage, and I felt the answering thud from his in return. How could something be so wrong and yet so right at the same time?

"What happens now?" I asked, and I wasn't sure whether the question was directed at myself or at Blane.

"What do you want to happen?"

His amber eyes fixed on mine, dark fire flashing in their depths. I couldn't tell him what I wanted. My head was a mess, my thoughts jumbled. And I was ashamed to admit that while he was confessing heartfelt truths about his late girlfriend, heat was pooling between my thighs.

"I don't know. I've never been in this position before."

And his cock was *right there*. Thick and long and...wait, was it hardening?

Blane managed half a smirk. "Really? Then you've been missing out."

His usual cockiness was missing, as if the innuendo came from habit rather than the heart. And it was true—I was in new territory. Not just sitting on a man's lap, but on my boss's lap. The boss I was staying with because my best friend had been kidnapped. His thumb stroked my back lightly, and the gesture was strangely comforting. There was heat between us, a smouldering flame that threatened to erupt, but he wasn't acting like a horny jerk.

"This is inappropriate," I blurted as I resisted the urge to squirm. Or grind. Semantics.

"Highly inappropriate," he agreed, glancing down.

I followed his gaze, and if I'd been embarrassed before, now I was mortified. There was no hiding the damp patch on my yoga pants.

"Maybe I spilled something?"

Half a smirk turned into a tired smile. "That's really the line you're going with?"

I made one last attempt to put the brakes on my

runaway brain. To stop the boulder from careening through my common sense.

"I'm not going to be another one of your three-hour girls."

"Wren..." Blane's hands moved from my waist to my upper arms. He held me gently. "That's not what this is."

"Then what is it?"

"It's...evolving. I thought I was just going to help you find your friend, but..."

"But what?"

"But then I felt it."

"Felt what?"

"*Everything*. You were right under my nose the whole time, and I didn't even realise."

"I don't—"

Blane's lips brushed across mine. And suddenly, I did. I *did* understand. Those smouldering coals flared into life, and a burst of heat surged through me. One touch of his lips —*one*—and my future flashed before my eyes. Blane was front and centre. The Lord of freaking Fire.

"Okay, I do. I do get it."

CHAPTER 24

Wren

This time, his kiss was deeper, and my arms found their way around his neck. Making out with Blane was like mainlining a chocolate fudge sundae. Delicious, moreish, and undoubtedly bad for me. His tongue stroked against mine, and I was keenly aware of the moan I let out. Every sense was heightened, every nerve ending singing with electricity. His bare chest pressed against nipples begging to be released from the confines of my bra, and all the doubt inside me turned to desire. I wanted him. No, I *needed* him, and the feeling must have been mutual because now his cock had the girth and length of a utility pole. My damp patch was probably the size of a dinner plate.

"More," I gasped when he pulled away.

But Blane only shook his head and lifted me effortlessly onto my feet. Tears prickled at my eyes in a heartbeat. Why were my emotions so intense around him?

"Did I do something wrong?"

"Of course not. But you're not a three-hour girl, Wren Gillebrand, and dinner's getting cold."

"You want me to...eat?"

"I want you to keep your strength up because I have plans for you later."

My thighs clenched. "You don't have to work?"

"Joseph can handle it."

This time when I took a seat opposite Blane, I was shaking. In the space of ten minutes, my world had been rocked to its core, and that core was molten, a puddle of lava sloshing in my belly. I pushed my food around my plate, suddenly too fraught with nerves to eat.

"I thought you liked vegetables?" Blane asked.

"I do."

"Should I order something else? La Nostra Casa delivers."

"It's not the food that's the problem." I took a deep breath and decided to be honest. "It's you, going hot and then cold."

Blane's forehead creased in puzzlement. "No, I'm still hot."

Oh, he was. Incendiary.

"I meant that one minute you're kissing me, and the next you're dumping me off your lap and telling me to eat my stir-fried salad."

"That wasn't me going cold. That was me desperately trying to act like a gentleman when what I want to do is bend you over this counter, tear off those stretchy pants, and fuck you until walking is nothing but a distant memory. And it's still an option, but I thought you might need a moment to digest the next step in our relationship."

"Our relationship?"

Our one-week stand or whatever this was? Weird connection or no weird connection, this couldn't be a long-term thing. Blane was a living god, and I was...not. There was a fifty-fifty chance I'd have to leave Vegas anyway, so maybe it was worth the risk to experience his monster cock in the interim, but a *relationship*?

"You felt the bond. What else do you think this is?"

"Uh, an ill-advised womanly reaction to good genes?"

"I'm not wearing jeans; we've already established that."

A giggle burst from my lips, and then I realised he was actually serious.

"Genes as in genetics? Never mind, just forget the food and bend me over the freaking counter, okay?"

Blane moved at dizzying speed. One moment, I was staring at that handsome face, and the next, my cheek was pressed against icy granite. All the reasons why this was a terrible idea flashed through my mind as he kept his word and shredded my yoga pants.

He was my boss.

He was hung up on the past.

He held all the power.

But tonight, I didn't care.

Every time I tried to permanently exorcise the ghost of Dom's dick from my psyche, my chosen partner fell woefully short of the mark. Dating apps were a minefield. Either I attracted a forty-year-old sleaze who'd fabricated his entire profile, or I got a man with serial killer vibes. Caria had stepped in to rescue me more than once. And now I had to rescue her. Blane was my best hope for that.

Blane, who was currently fiddling with my bra strap.

"It's hooked behind—" I started. "Okay, you got it."

Why was there a weird burning smell in the air? I forgot to worry about it when he cupped my breasts in his hands, rolling my nipples in a way that sent sparks shooting downward. He was in the driver's seat tonight. I was just along for the ride.

"So sweet and delicate," he murmured into my ear as he

nudged my legs farther apart. "I'm going to ruin you for mere mortals."

I didn't doubt that promise.

"Tell me you have protection? And I'm not talking about a gun," I added to clarify.

"I don't own a gun." Was he serious? He was tangling with Zion and Laurent, and he didn't have a single firearm? "But I do have plenty of condoms." Good to know where his priorities lay. He dragged one finger through my slick folds. "And lube is irrelevant tonight."

That finger skated over my clit, and a shudder ran through me. He'd barely touched me, and I was already ready to detonate.

"Hurry up."

"I thought women liked it when men took their time?"

"Okay, so usually that's true, but rules are made to be broken."

Lords above, that finger was magic. It worked its way in maddeningly slow circles, pressing and releasing, teasing as Blane swept my hair to one side and peppered kisses across the back of my neck. It was over in roughly two minutes. The orgasm tore through me, and if he hadn't pinned me to the counter with his hips, I would have sunk to the floor. My legs were as wobbly as a baby fawn's. I slumped onto the granite and relished the refreshing coolness.

"Angels above," I muttered.

"Not quite. I'm the other guy. Don't move."

"I can't. I literally can't."

He walked away, and I felt that bond stretching, stretching, even though he was still in the apartment. And I hated that. I needed him close. I just...needed him. Footsteps, the rip of foil, and he pressed against me again.

"Spread your legs wider, my little succubus." He ran a fingertip down my spine as I obliged, and that one little touch sent tentacles of heat through me. This was like nothing I'd ever experienced. Sex had always been me lying on the back seat of a car or later a bed, and even though Dom had been the best of my past lovers, I could count the number of times he'd left me satisfied on one hand.

Blane could leave me satisfied *with* one hand.

"Look at me, Wren." He fisted his hand in my hair and turned my head to the side. "Are you okay?"

"Define 'okay.'"

Oh, hell, he'd taken his pants off, his underwear too, and that cock was enormous.

"Do you want me to stop?"

"Absolutely not. I want you to hurry up and keep your promise. Ruin me."

First, he kissed me again, nipping at my lower lip. Pain mingled with pleasure, and I gasped as the sensation travelled through my body. All my life, I'd wished for gentle hands and rose petals, for sweetness and love, but it turned out that what my body really needed was a dirty devil who took control.

Blane pushed me down on the counter again, and that filthy cock nudged at my entrance. He gave me an inch. Two inches.

"More. I want all of it."

He slid in on a groan, and I gritted my teeth as I adjusted to his size. Who would have guessed he was hiding that beast beneath those tailored suits? I mean, the three-hour girls had always left smiling, but I'd also heard rumours that payment was involved, so... Yowzers! He slammed into me, and I cried out.

"Oh my—"

"Blane. I'm Lucian Blane, and that's what you'll call me."

He gripped my hips and thrust again. I had to stand on

tiptoes, and my calves burned as he pumped into me with a punishing rhythm. Or at least, it should have been punishing, and there was pain around the edges, but that was nothing compared to the orgasm barrelling toward me like a freight train. So wrong, yet so good. My whole body stiffened as I clenched around him, and when he released a moment later, a wildly different kind of heat spread through me.

"Angel..." Sweet Blane was back again. He leaned over my spent, sweat-slicked body, his breath puffing against my ear. "You're beautiful. You're perfect. You're mine."

"Yours," I mumbled back, too shattered to say anything else.

Then I found myself in his arms, my limbs limp as he carried me to his bedroom. To his gargantuan bed with views over Vegas. I'd never been inside before, only caught glimpses from the doorway, and I realised there was a roof terrace to the side that I never knew existed. A private sanctuary in the middle of the city buzz.

"The glass is one-way," he said when he caught me looking. "Nobody can see us."

At that moment, I didn't care about the glass. All I cared about was the connection. He laid me gently on silky sheets, and when he settled next to me, I curled against his side.

"That was so...so...unexpected."

"I knew last night that it would happen. It was just a question of when."

"I meant the intensity."

He brushed damp hair back from my face. "That's what happens when you meet the person you're meant to be with."

Blane was actually serious, wasn't he? This wasn't simply some line he was spinning to get me into bed. After those orgasms, I'd get naked with him any time he wanted, so there really was no need to lie.

"Talk to me, Wren," he ordered.

"I...I don't know what to say. I guess I'm a bit dazed right now."

"You're not the only one."

"You don't look dazed."

"Looks can be deceiving." A long pause. "I thought Nevaeh was it for me. That I'd met my soulmate and lost her, and I'd never again experience that bond. Then you came into my life and tilted my world on its axis. So now I have to adjust to the fact that my understanding was flawed, and that's going to take a few days. I imagine it'll take you time to get used to the idea as well."

Blane stroked my back, the gesture comforting rather than sexual.

"I'm scared," I confessed. "Of what I'm feeling, of what's happening. My life is out of control, and you have all the power."

"No, no, no. Wren, you're the one with the power here."

"How do you figure that?"

"You hold my heart in your hands, my darling, and you could crush it if you chose."

I put a hand on his chest and felt those heartbeats, strong and steady, and they calmed my rising sense of panic.

"This is getting kinda heavy for a first date, Blane."

"I don't mean for it to feel that way. It's just a simple fact. But if you'd prefer to hold my cock in your hands tonight, that would also be acceptable."

The smirk was back, a relief because horny Blane was easier to deal with. Horny Blane didn't send my emotions bungee jumping off the Golden Gate Bridge.

"I'd rather taste you."

He gestured toward his rapidly hardening utility pole. "Feast away."

CHAPTER 25

Wren

"You look tired."

Marianna set a bag of cookie ingredients on the counter and then put Pablo down in a playpen that had appeared at one end of the kitchen while I was in a lust-induced coma. Had Blane set that up before he left this morning? Or was Joseph lurking somewhere? I'd worked out he didn't live here, but he sometimes stayed in a spare bedroom.

"I didn't get much sleep last night," I confessed.

"Are you still having trouble with a man?"

"It never seems to end."

"Blane will fix it. He's one of the good ones."

"You really think so? This past week has messed with my mind, and then I found myself here, but I barely know him."

And he barely knew me, but from the way he was talking, now he thought I was tethered to him for all eternity. Which had to be a line, right? I mean, Dom had told me that we'd be together forever, but those declarations had only lasted until his tuition was paid.

Blane hadn't asked me for money or anything else, so what was his game?

It was a puzzle I couldn't work out.

"He's helped me so much since we met, and Vee has too," Marianna said. "Without the two of them, I don't know where I'd be."

Lola held up her arms, and I lifted her to sit on the counter. The counter I'd been bent over last night as Blane fucked me into another dimension. Shit, had anyone sanitised it?

"Let me just wipe the surfaces before we start. It's so kind of you to come over like this."

"We have peanut butter," Lola announced. "The crunchy kind."

"That's my favourite."

"I know."

Huh? "How do you know, sweetie?"

"From before. Your hair is pretty."

I'd piled it into a messy bun and secured it with a chopstick. Sex hair chic.

"Uh, thank you?"

"You should put flowers in it. The ones that Mommy has in our kitchen."

"She means orchids," Marianna supplied, and a chill ran through me. I loved orchids. They were my favourite plant. The little girl had wormed her way into my heart the way she had into Blane's, but there was also something not quite right about her.

"Orchids," Lola echoed. "Pink ones. Can I have juice? The orange kind?"

"Sure, sweetie."

I poured OJ into a plastic cup, and she sipped, watching me as I dug around in cupboards for a mixing bowl. Lola disturbed me, but at the same time, I felt weirdly protective toward her. Was that the sound of my biological clock ticking in the background? I was twenty-seven, and although I'd always assumed I'd have kids someday, I figured thirty was a good time to start worrying about finding a suitable father. How would Blane fit in with that plan? He obviously doted on Lola and Pablo, but did he want kids of his own?

Wait, why was I even thinking that way? Me and Blane, we wouldn't last that long. He'd get bored with me in a week.

Once Lola had finished her juice, she slithered off the counter and went to help Pablo with his plastic blocks, leaving me a moment to talk to her mom.

"What did she mean, 'from before'?" I asked quietly.

"Lola just says those things sometimes."

"Really?"

"Often to Blane. And if we'd met him in the past, I'd certainly remember. A woman doesn't forget a man like him."

Perhaps I was puzzling over nothing? Kids said funny things all the time. Back in Wyoming, my neighbour's little boy thought he was a frog, and for six months or so, he'd spoken in croaks with the occasional ribbit. He'd also insisted on frog-hopping everywhere until one sunny weekend when his mom's back was turned. She'd taken him to visit a friend, and he'd jumped into the lady's pond and nearly drowned. That was the end of the hopping.

And Marianna was right about Blane being unforgettable.

"That's true." An image of Blane's O-face was permanently burned into my retinas. I'd spent half the night riding him like an X-rated cowgirl, and when I complained that my thighs were getting chafed, he'd offered to buy me a pair of chaps. "Although I can't forget the douches either, no matter how hard I try."

"My abuela used to say, 'You have to kiss a few frogs to find your prince.'"

I had an unwelcome flashback to my ex-neighbour's kid and his green facepaint. Yeuch.

"So far, all I've kissed is a snake and a bunch of slugs."

Marianna pulled a face. "I also found a snake."

"I like snakes," Lola piped up from the playpen.

"She loves every animal," Marianna explained. "She keeps asking for a dog, but we live in an apartment."

"The only way a dog will break your heart is by leaving this world. I wish I could adopt one someday."

Someday, when my future wasn't a clusterfuck of calamities just waiting to happen.

Marianna knew her way around Blane's kitchen, and once Lola was settled with her "special coffee" and Pablo was happily stacking his plastic blocks, she walked me through making the best peanut butter cookies I'd ever tasted. Chewy in the middle, crunchy around the edges, half dipped in chocolate. I began to understand how Blane lived on junk food.

"These are so good. I don't suppose you have any tips on making actual meals? I tried to cook for Blane last night and accidentally set the pan on fire."

"What were you cooking?"

"A stir fry. Nothing too complicated, or so I thought."

"Were the leaves wet when you put them in the pan?"

"Uh, maybe? Does that matter?"

"The water causes the flames when it hits the oil."

Wasn't water supposed to put flames out? My online cooking course hadn't mentioned a thing about fire hazards. The teacher had gone into a lot of detail about her travels around Italy on a Vespa, chopped up the ingredients real quick, and then glossed over the methodology part.

"So I just need to blot the leaves on a piece of paper towel?"

"Exactly. If you want, I can show you how to make some meals? Do you like Mexican food?"

"I love Mexican food."

"So, how about I come over on Wednesday evening?"

"Does Blane like Mexican food?"

"You want to cook for Blane too?"

"I kind of owe him."

For coming to my rescue, for the roof over my head, for orgasms past and future.

"Blane loves Mexican food."

Lola appeared by my side, a cookie in one hand and her fingers covered in chocolate. She slipped the other arm around my legs.

"Churros are my favourite."

"We can make churros," Marianna promised her daughter.

"Dinner won't be too late for her?" I asked.

The romantic dinner for two would have to wait because if Marianna was helping to cook the food, I could hardly ask her to leave. And she was probably used to sharing dinner with Blane and Joseph. Okay, a meal with friends—that wouldn't be so bad. My aching thighs would appreciate the recovery time.

"As long as she has a nap in the afternoon, she can stay up. Pablo sleeps in the small guest room."

I crouched to Lola's level. Her eyes were the same colour as mine. Strange—I'd never noticed that before.

"Then it's a date. We'll make you all the churros you want."

CHAPTER 26
Blane

"My patience is wearing thin, Mr. Ziaroni."

Two days until the deadline I'd set, and I'd decided to pay him a visit in person. His nose was still slightly swollen, and his black eyes were turning from purple to a greenish yellow. So far, he hadn't challenged me to another duel, although Joseph had acquired suitable attire for both of us should we need to step into the ring again. No need to ruin another suit.

"You think you can do a better job, man? Find the bitch yourself. And it's Zion, not Ziaroni."

"Watch your language."

I was beginning to think I might have to take on a more active role. Zion leaned back in his desk chair, then hurriedly righted himself when it nearly tipped over.

"She's not at the beach house. So maybe she's on the boat? Raph took it down to Huntington Beach, but it's on the way back now."

"Who's Raph?"

"You know, Laurent. Raph Laurent."

Raph Laurent? He sounded more like a fashion label than a gangster.

"So Caria could have been left in Huntington Beach?"

Or worse, encased in concrete shoes and dropped into the Pacific.

"Nah, man, he doesn't have a place there."

"Do we even know if she's still alive?"

Zion nodded, then winced at the motion. "Yesterday, she was."

"How can you be sure?"

"There's a picture."

"A picture?"

He pulled a phone from the pocket of his sweatpants. The screen was cracked, and the back of the case said "Gangstas don't cry," which was a lie because I'd definitely seen a tear or two last Thursday. After a moment of scrolling, he handed it over.

"There she is."

"Is that Laurent with her?"

"Yeah, man."

It was the same woman I'd seen smiling in the photo on Wren's phone. Caria was sitting on Laurent's lap, and judging by the mascara streaked down her cheeks, she was far from happy to be there. He was grinning with an arm clamped around her waist. I peered closer and saw her dress was torn, as if someone had clawed it off her and then forced her to put the tattered remains back on.

It was the first picture I'd seen of Laurent, and he wasn't quite what I'd been expecting. In my head, I'd pictured him as more like me, a businessman with a dark side. In reality, he was a hirsute fireplug of a man in Bermuda shorts. He had a man bun, for crying out loud.

"Where did you get this?"

"From a guy who knows a guy. He wanted to check that this is the woman you're looking for. It's her, right?"

"Yes, it's her."

"That look like a boat to you?"

I studied the background. Laurent was sitting in a velvet club chair in front of a polished walnut bar. Another scantily dressed female was pouring a drink, but she looked bored rather than distressed. There were no windows. A statuesque blonde sat on a stool sipping from a martini glass, her hair styled in a poker-straight bob, but she was wearing a billowy emerald-green dress with long sleeves and ruffled edging. Not the hired help. A girlfriend? Was her expression of faint disgust there because Laurent was still dallying with Caria?

"I can't tell from the picture, but it's possible it's a boat."

"I got a man watching the marina. If they unload her when they get back from LA tomorrow, he'll follow."

"Keep me updated. The clock is ticking."

"Sure thing, boss."

"How is Wren doing?" Vee asked when I swung by to check in at Tilt. Her hair was purple today. "Is she okay? We haven't seen much of you over the past week."

No. No, they hadn't, because I'd been reacquainting myself with the pleasures of the female mind. Go with your heart, Aurelia had said, and I'd decided to take her advice. There were still so many things about the planes that I didn't understand, that nobody truly did, and there was no point in dwelling on life's mysteries when Wren was with me in the here and now.

"She's hanging in there."

"And is there any news on her missing friend?" Vee asked as she settled onto the edge of my desk and helped herself to one of the candies I kept in a glass bowl. The bowl had been a gift from Aurelia, one of her thrift-store finds.

"I'm hoping we'll have some news soon."

I'd wanted a confirmed location by now, but Zion wasn't as competent as he liked to think he was. At least he'd made a modicum of progress. And I'd been able to tell my angel that Caria was still breathing, which was better than nothing.

"I asked Jack about that guy. Laurent? He's bad news."

"That's what I'm hearing too."

"A few years ago, he was on the East Coast—New York and New Jersey. Jack thinks he had a falling-out with the Mob, although the details are hazy. And before that, he ran the biggest call-girl operation in the South of France. He used to brag about having 'a bitch for every budget.'"

"A true businessman."

Vee shuddered. "Apparently, he manages the logistics side of things, and his sister runs the girls. Jack thinks they're doing the same in Vegas, but nobody's been able to pin anything on him yet."

A family business? This was news. "Nobody's mentioned a sister."

"Her name is Delphine, and she stays out of the public eye. Rumour says that she can be more vicious than him when the chips are down."

My mind wandered back to the woman in Zion's picture, the snooty blonde. I'd assumed she was a girlfriend, but maybe she was Laurent's sister?

"The consultant I engaged to assist with the search for the missing girl is hopeful we'll have news by tomorrow, but I'll bear it in mind."

"That's great news, but if there's anything I can do to help, just let me know. I always liked Wren."

"She's a very special lady."

Vee stared at me for a beat, and then her mouth dropped open. "Oh my gosh! You hooked up with Wren."

"How on earth did you reach that conclusion from 'she's a very special lady'?"

"It wasn't your words, it was the look in your eyes. Kind of dreamy. Is she staying with you?"

What? I really had to work on that. "Dreamy" hadn't been an issue in Plane Three. "Nightmarey" had been more appropriate. I blew out a breath and poured myself a glass of Scotch from the carafe on my desk. Thankfully, alcohol didn't impact me the way it did humans—all I got was a pleasant buzz, none of the uncoordinated retching.

"Yes, she's staying with me, but 'hooking up' trivialises the situation."

"Glazing the donut? Letting her ride the baloney pony? Buttering her biscuit? Oh, wait, wait..." Vee's eyes twinkled. "Doing the devil's dance?"

"You're fired."

She tossed a piece of candy at my head. "You love me really."

I sort of did, in a purely platonic way, of course. "The connection with Wren reminds me so much of my time with Nevaeh. And no, I haven't told her that. I believe humans find that sort of thing creepy."

"Promise you won't hurt her, okay? If I have to kick your ass, that would be unpleasant for both of us."

"How would that even work? I can't suck out your soul because, technically, you don't have one, and your 'superior speed and strength' schtick won't work on me."

"That's a good point." Vee pondered for a moment, her cheeks going hollow as she sucked on a piece of candy.

"Maybe I'd just cut the seat out of every single pair of your pants."

Ouch. "That's dirty."

"Girls stick together. I take it you haven't told Wren about the whole 'Lord of the Underworld' thing?"

I spluttered a mouthful of Scotch. "She has quite enough on her plate right now."

"If this is more than a hookup, you can't keep it a secret forever."

"I managed with Nevaeh. And I don't want Wren to run screaming to New Mexico."

"Jack didn't run screaming when he found out about my special diet."

"The next time someone tells me miracles don't exist, I'm going to use you two as an example." I frowned at the staff schedule on my desk. "Were you serious about helping?"

"Of course."

"Latisha's on vacation and Carlene's sick. There's a bug going around, and Pandora's struggling to fill the gaps. Would you work at Club Dead tomorrow night? We could put you in a mask." The serving staff wore costumes, so a mask wouldn't be out of place. When Vee didn't answer right away, I continued, "I don't think Voltaire is in town at the moment."

Her eyes narrowed. "How do you know that?"

"Joseph heard it on the lawyer grapevine."

"Voltaire isn't a lawyer."

"No, he isn't, but negotiations are ongoing with regard to the Devil's Den. I outbid him, but the vendor wanted to allow time for Voltaire to make a counteroffer. Apparently, he went on a wellness retreat and is currently uncontactable."

"A wellness retreat? No way. He probably went on a

murder spree and left his phone at home so the cops couldn't place him at the scene."

"I'll agree that seems a more likely scenario. Anyhow, the vendor's lawyer wanted until Thursday, so I put a time limit on my offer."

"When does it expire?"

"Midnight tonight." Today was Tuesday.

Vee blew out a long breath. "I hate the thought of Voltaire staying here. Hate it. This is my home now."

"And I hate seeing you unhappy. My offer was excessive."

She reached out to squeeze my hand. "You're a good friend."

"At least I've mastered one part of being human."

A tiny smile flickered at the corners of her lips. "I'll work at the club tomorrow as long as I can hide in the VIP area."

"That won't be a problem."

CHAPTER 27
Wren

"How many people are coming tonight?" I asked Marianna. "I thought it was just me, you, Blane, Joseph, and Lola?"

Pablo was asleep in Blane's guest room, and he'd already eaten dinner. Cat-Myrtle was around too, and she might help out with the mountain of food—Blane said she loved tacos, but they weren't good for cats so we couldn't give her too much.

"Vee said she'd drop by on her break."

Aw, it would be good to see her. She was a real night owl —a while ago, she'd confided that a skin condition left her with blisters if she was exposed to UV light—so we'd never socialised outside of work, but she'd always been kind to me. I surveyed the array of dishes laid out on the counters. Tacos, burritos, enchiladas, tamales. A vat of pozole. Bowls of guac and sour cream. Marianna was getting ready to fry the churros, and Lola was watching with rapt attention, her face covered in chocolate sauce.

"We could feed everyone downstairs in the club and still have food left over."

Marianna scrunched her mouth to the side. "Maybe I did get a little carried away."

"A little?"

Her regret turned into a cunning smile. "Well, you do need the extra calories this week."

"What's that supposed to mean?"

"Uh, you and Blane?"

"What about me and Blane?"

"Every time I see him, he's wearing a self-satisfied grin, and you're smiling a lot and walking funny."

Please, somebody shoot me.

"Uh, I..."

"Don't worry; I won't tell anyone. It's good to see him happy after— Never mind."

"After his girlfriend passed away?"

"He told you about that?"

I nodded as I shredded cheese to go with the tacos. Blane and Joseph better not have eaten much for lunch. Ten to eight, and I'd hoped they'd be back by now, not just because I missed Blane but because he'd told me they planned to visit Zion this evening. With every day that passed, my sense of unease grew stronger. Perhaps I *should* have gone to the police? Yesterday, Blane had not-so-casually dropped Vee's detective boyfriend's name into conversation—again—and I wondered how much she knew about Caria's disappearance. Had Blane shared my secret? If it were only Jack Callahan I had to worry about, I'd spill the beans, but detectives didn't work in a vacuum. He'd have a partner, plus he'd have to file reports—one whisper in the wrong ear, and Caria would be in big trouble.

But if Zion didn't come through with the answers, maybe we'd have to take that risk?

Lola held out a churro dripping with chocolate sauce. "This is for you."

"Thank you, sweetie."

"When is Blane coming back?"

"Soon, I think."

"I miss him."

"I do too. Why don't you help me to put the cutlery on the table?"

"Okay."

She skipped off carrying a single knife and fork, leaving me to bring the rest.

"She's usually so shy," Marianna said, glancing at the baby monitor, where Pablo slept soundly on the tiny screen. "When she's here, she comes to life."

"She's adorable." I watched her carefully set the knife and fork at the seat Blane always sat in. "But so full of energy. Honestly, I have no idea how moms get everything done."

Marianna gave a musical laugh. "Through love, willpower, and sometimes sheer desperation. Could you text Blane and see how long he's going to be?"

"Of course."

I'd typed out half a message when the elevator dinged. My heart lifted along with it, but when I glanced toward the hallway, it wasn't Blane and Joseph who walked through the door. No, a statuesque blonde was striding toward me as if she belonged here, but I was certain I hadn't seen her around. Unless she was one of the three-hour girls here in the hope of a repeat?

The thought made my blood boil.

"Can I help you?"

"Oh, you sure can." Her accent wasn't American. Was it French? Or Italian? She looked polished in a European way. Chic. Her hair was cut into a short bob, pale compared to her deeply tanned skin.

"Do we know each—" The words died in my throat

when she pointed a gun at me. It might have been small, but her hand didn't waver, and I had no doubt she knew how to use it. My heart threatened to give out when I saw the men behind her, three of them, and their hard expressions said they hadn't come over for tacos.

"You should have kept your mouth shut, Wren Gillebrand."

My knees buckled, and I clutched at the counter for support. This was about Caria, wasn't it? I'd bet everything I owned—which admittedly wasn't much—that Zion had double-crossed Blane and sold us out.

"Bring them," the woman ordered.

"The kid too?" a man with a scar slicing down one cheek asked, and I realised with ever-growing horror that Lola was standing in full view of the intruders. Thank goodness Pablo was safe in the guest room, for now at least. *Please don't wake up.*

"Do I have to repeat myself?"

Where was security? There were doormen at every entrance to the club, including one by the alley door Blane occasionally used to come and go, and another in the small parking lot. Maybe the intruders had posed as guests and walked right past the velvet rope? But if that was true, they couldn't march the rest of us across the dance floor, so how were they planning to escape? Would they shoot their way out? The men had guns too—I could see the bulges under their jackets.

"Please, just leave my daughter," Marianna begged. "I'll come with you."

"You're in no position to be making demands."

The men advanced toward us. I wanted to yell at Lola to run, but where would she go? To the bedrooms? The men would soon catch her, and worse, they'd find Pablo.

That was when I spotted the knife on the counter. Eight

inches of gleaming steel next to a pile of chopped lettuce. I dove for it.

An earsplitting scream came from the other side of the room, quickly followed by another, deeper yell as Marianna hurled the pan of boiling water—plus several half-cooked tamales—at the man reaching out to grab her.

Then all hell broke loose.

CHAPTER 28
Wren

I lashed out with the knife, catching the man nearest to me in the arm. He leapt back and fumbled for his gun, but it seemed to be stuck in his waistband. When I glanced behind me, Lola was gone. Hiding? I hoped she was hiding.

The burned man was writhing on the floor, and Scarface ran for Marianna, slamming her into the counter with a sickening *crunch*. But I couldn't help because a fist was flying in my direction. I ducked, then slashed with the knife again, but this time I missed.

"Subdue them!" the blonde woman yelled.

Strangely, she seemed reluctant to wade into the fray, a talker not a doer. She'd thought this would be easy, hadn't she? She'd figured we'd just meekly give in. Well, she figured wrong. I threw the fruit bowl at my attacker, and he shielded himself with his arms as apples and oranges bounced everywhere. A bullet whizzed past my ear. Shit! The woman had decided to get involved after all.

An almighty *whoosh* and a flash of heat made my heart seize. Flames flared as the oil from the churros ignited, and now there was a wall of fire between Marianna and her assailant, protecting her from his advance but a danger in itself. Sweat prickled at my skin as I looked around frantically.

Where was Lola?

I spotted her crouching on the far side of the table, but I couldn't get to her. The man intent on snatching me lunged again, this time holding up a wooden chopping board like a shield.

I jumped back, but then there were two of them. Scarface had given up on Marianna, and now he was coming for me too. And it was me they wanted. I was Caria's friend. I was the one with the secrets. But...but I'd told Blane, and Zion knew that, which meant he was in danger too. Everyone around me was in danger.

The second thug had managed to draw his gun, but before he could aim properly, I leapt at him. I was a dead woman anyway. Better to meet my maker on my own terms rather than through Laurent's slow torture. I didn't doubt that he'd draw out my pain as a punishment, not when I'd caused him so much trouble. The pistol fired as I clawed at the man's arm, and a window behind me shattered, but I hung on, stabbing at the man's thigh with the knife.

Were there arteries in a thigh? I was almost certain there were.

Maybe I'd get lucky?

Or maybe not.

Strong arms wrapped around my waist and tore me away, and all I could do was turn my head and sink my teeth into the flesh of my attacker's shoulder. Scarface cursed, and I lost the knife as he wrestled me toward the blonde and the door.

"Hurry up," she snapped.

"What about Todd and Louis?"

"Leave them."

Shit, shit, shit!

I struggled, but Scarface's arms were like steel bands, and I could barely breathe. Half of the kitchen was on fire now, flames licking their way across the dining area, the placemats alight. The smoke thickened. I saw the outline of Marianna through the blaze, but where had Lola gone? If the two of them could get to the bedrooms, they stood a chance. There was a door to the terrace beside Blane's bed, beside the bed we'd shared, the bed where he'd given me a glimpse of real happiness for the first time in my life.

Another screech, but this time it came from...the blonde woman? My captor spun at the noise, and I almost laughed as I saw Myrtle wrapped around her head, raking her face with needlelike claws.

Almost laughed.

But not quite, because she began firing wildly, and Scarface grunted as a bullet slammed into his shoulder.

"You stupid fucking bitch!" he cried, and his grip loosened.

A chance.

I had a chance.

I stomped on his foot, then froze as a blur whipped past me. Suddenly, the arms were gone.

I was free.

My assailant was flying across the room.

Literally flying.

He landed in the flames, and I shrank back as Vee dove at the next man, Todd or Louis, I wasn't sure which. He'd finally managed to get his gun out of his pants, and he sneered as he fired at her once, twice, three times.

She laughed, a high-pitched giggle that sent a chill through me. The colour drained out of Todd-Louis's face, and I didn't know what he saw, but the terror in his eyes caused my heart to stutter.

The gun fell from his fingers as she wrapped a hand around his throat and lifted him clean off the floor.

What the hell?

Hell.

This was Hell.

I was dead, and this was Hell.

The *click-click-click* of stilettos on tile made me turn. The blonde was running for the elevator like the coward she was, and I saw red. Fire, blood, death. I ran after her, ready to scratch her freaking eyes out. The elevator doors were already opening. If I could just catch her before they closed...

She stopped in a hurry, backing up as Blane stepped out.

He was okay.

He was okay!

Joseph was with Blane, and he took one look at the situation and hurried past me. As for Blane, he flicked his gaze in my direction, but his expression didn't change.

"You made a big mistake," he told the blonde.

"The mistake was all yours," she spat. "You have no idea who you're dealing with."

"Delphine, I presume?"

"Think of me as a representative of Laurent Enterprises."

"Blane!"

For the first time ever, I heard something in Joseph's voice that wasn't arrogance or sarcasm. No, it was fear.

In a heartbeat, Blane was running past me.

Gloom fell over the room. I turned, and the flames were gone.

Just...gone.

Smoke curled in the air, but the fire was out. My mind

struggled to process what was happening—it had to be a nightmare, didn't it? Only my worst fears come to life could explain the charred kitchen and the bodies lying on the floor. Three men, two of them decidedly scorched, and Lola.

Lola!

Now I was running after Blane, the lump in my throat making every breath an effort. Marianna was on her knees beside her daughter, and I didn't have to be a doctor to know the blood bubbling from the little girl's chest was bad news. Her eyes were open, her sobs soft yet agonising.

"Mommy, it hurts."

"I'll call an ambulance," I choked out. "I lost my phone. Does anyone have a phone?"

"An ambulance can't fix that," Joseph said. "It looks as if a bullet nicked her heart."

Oh hell, oh hell, oh hell.

Blane was just staring, his face contorted into a mix of shock and misery. I knew how much he cared for Lola. The "special coffee," the sweet gifts, the way he bought cakes from her mom every day to ensure she never went without.

"Fuck," he muttered.

"We need a decision," Joseph told him.

"I know."

"Quickly."

Vee approached, hauling a struggling Delphine.

"You should do it," she said. "Maybe they'll understand, and things will be okay. If you don't act, the only certainty is that you'll lose her again."

"Understand what?" I whispered. "What's happening?"

Blane didn't answer. No, he just nodded once, and Marianna let out a wail as Lola took one last shallow breath and went still.

"No," I whispered. This was my fault. This was all my fault. I should never have come here. I was the reason

Blane's apartment had been destroyed. I was the reason Marianna was slumped over the lifeless body of her daughter, sobbing as if she'd never stop.

"How does it feel to be on the losing team?" the blonde asked as Vee pushed her forward.

"Goodbye, Delphine. See you in the next life."

Blane flicked his hand, and a shadow as black as night separated from her body and hovered beside us for a few moments before scattering. What the...? I froze, the breath turned to ice in my chest. Delphine began crumpling to the floor, but Vee caught her and held her still.

Now would be a real good time to wake up, Wren.

I couldn't tear my gaze away as Blane's hands moved again, and this time, a beautiful rainbow rose from Lola, lighting up the room. The rainbow disappeared into Delphine. What was I even witnessing?

Had someone slipped LSD into the churros?

"It's okay," Vee soothed, stroking the woman's hair. "You're okay."

Her eyes flickered open, filled with confusion and the same horror I was experiencing.

"Well, this should be interesting," Joseph muttered.

I turned to Blane for answers, to beg for reassurance that this was all a trick of my mind.

But he was gone.

He'd vanished into thin air.

CHAPTER 29

Wren

"What happened?" I demanded. "What just happened?"

Vee shook her head. "Wait a moment."

"Wait for what? People are freaking dead. Lola..." A sob hitched in my throat. "Lola is dead."

"Blane's trying to fix that."

"Have you lost your mind? I know I have."

Myrtle rubbed against my leg, purring, then jumped onto the table and began licking soot off her paws. Honestly, I wasn't sure whether to kiss her or throw her out the window. Yes, she'd saved me from being dragged out of the apartment, but there was also a good chance she'd caused Delphine to fire the bullet that killed Lola.

This was all such a freaking mess.

A huge, giant—

I lurched forward as someone stumbled into me. Joseph stopped me from falling, and I did a double take at the pretty blonde in pyjamas who'd appeared out of nowhere. Blane was holding her collar in a death grip with one hand, and he pointed at Lola with the other.

Her eyes widened. "Oh, poop."

"Just hold them."

"Okay, okay," she grumbled. "I'm still half-asleep."

Marianna had gone still. And silent. What was wrong with her?

"Is she...is she...?" I reached for her, but Joseph held me back.

"Don't."

"Will somebody tell me what's going on?" Panic was rising through me now, fizzing in my veins like firecrackers. I considered running for the door, but I'd seen how fast Vee moved earlier. I didn't stand a chance of escape. "*Please.*"

Finally, Blane looked at me. My boss. My boyfriend. The man I'd been falling in love with far too fast. The one man who'd given me a sense of belonging. The man who'd treated me as if I meant something rather than using me as a maid-slash-sex-doll.

And I realised I didn't know him at all.

I was standing there in tatters, my clothes torn, my skin stained with soot, tears rolling down my cheeks. Apart from a smudge of dirt on his dress shirt, he didn't look any different than usual.

"Who are you?" I whispered.

"I'm Blane, my darling. You know that."

I sucked much-needed air into my lungs. "Okay, fine. Wrong question. *What* are you?" My voice turned shrill as I waved my arms around. "Because none of *this* is normal."

"Now, that's a more difficult question to answer."

"No freaking kidding."

"I want to know too," Delphine said, and her accent had changed. Gone was the French or Italian or whatever. Now she sounded American.

"Quite understandable. So, prior to moving to Las Vegas, I was employed in a managerial capacity in a place officially known as Dimension Seventeen, Realm Eighty-Six, Plane Three. Which basically means that—"

"He was the Lord of the Underworld," Joseph interjected. "But he got fired."

Blane glared at him. "I'm doing the talking."

"You're waffling."

"I...I don't understand. Isn't the Underworld a club in Reno?"

"Different Underworld," Joseph said, and Blane huffed at him.

"Make yourself useful and start cleaning up."

"Always so bossy."

But Joseph did pick up a chair. The whole apartment was wrecked, but the worst part was the smell. The aroma of grilled meat permeated throughout.

I desperately tried to cling on to the remainder of my sanity. "Lord of the Underworld?"

"That's more of a human concept. Technically, the planes are more parallel."

"Am I even awake?"

"Unfortunately, yes. Things would be so much easier if you weren't."

"Because you could pretend none of this ever happened?"

He grimaced. "Yes?"

"At least he's being honest," the newcomer said, shrugging.

"Honest? Honest? He's lied about *everything*. Who are you, anyway?"

"She's Aurelia," Delphine said, then her forehead creased into a frown. "Wait, how do I know that?"

"Through a peculiar manifestation of subconscious memory," Aurelia said. "Occasionally, there's a glitch in the soul recycling process, which is why some humans recall snippets of their past lives."

What? "This...this makes no sense."

"Actually, it makes perfect sense. It's just not a concept that most humans are familiar with, so it takes a while for them to get their heads around the details."

"I didn't lie about anything," Blane said. "I was very careful not to do that."

Was he serious? I put my hands on my hips. "Well, you left a heck of a lot of stuff out! And what was that shadow-rainbow thing? What happened to Lola?" Another hysterical sob burst out of me. "And Marianna?"

Blane sighed. "Where to start..."

"Lola died," Vee said simply. "But her soul once belonged to a woman who was very dear to Blane, so he caught it before it disappeared and stuffed it into this bitch's body."

I sat down with a bump, grateful for the chair Joseph had placed behind me. "Are you serious?"

"I know it sounds hard to believe, but yes."

"Are you part of this too? One of these underworld people?"

Joseph snorted. "Heavens, no. Vee is a vampire."

"A v-v-vampire?"

"Honestly, it's not as bad as it sounds. I just can't go out in the daytime, but I've learned to work around that."

"Don't you need to drink blood?"

I couldn't believe I'd even asked that.

"Yes, but only in small quantities, and it's not as if I have to kill anyone to get it."

"So how do you— Actually, forget it. I don't want to know."

She shrugged. "My boyfriend is also my food source."

My pulse ratcheted up a notch. Lord of the Underworld? A vampire? I *had* died and gone to Hell.

"And what are you?" I asked Joseph. "A freaking werewolf?"

He looked faintly disgusted at the prospect. "One of those beasts? I am house trained, you know."

"Joseph is a demon," Blane explained.

Denial was definitely the way to go here. *This is a nightmare. I'll wake up soon.* I studied Joseph, and his eyes weren't glowing red or anything, although if he really was a demon, he'd made the perfect career choice here on Earth.

"So when you're not here doing lawyer stuff or complaining about the temperature of your coffee, you spend your days tormenting condemned souls?"

"I was more on the admin side."

"There's admin in Hell?"

Was I being punk'd? If a camera crew jumped out, I was gonna smash their freaking lenses, I swear.

"Admin is a necessary evil," Blane said.

Sheesh. "This is too much. Way too much." And wasn't Vee dating a cop? I glanced at Marianna. "Why isn't she moving? Is she dead too?"

Blane shook his head. "She's just on pause."

"On pause?"

"Members of my family are bestowed with certain gifts. Aurelia is able to warp time, so Marianna and Lola are currently suspended in the past. They'll remain that way until Aurelia releases them."

I stared at the cute blonde. She barely looked old enough to have finished college. "Is this a joke?"

"No joke."

Blane picked up an apple from the floor and tossed it. When it got within three feet of Marianna, it just stopped. Hung there in midair, unmoving.

This was *insane*.

"So what's your trick? The soul thing?"

"That and the fire thing." He snapped his fingers, and a ball of flames appeared in his palm. The ball stretched out into a rope, then curved into a donut and disappeared completely. "Neither skill is particularly useful in Plane Five, but today was a rare exception."

"This is Plane Five," Vee added. "Earth. There are whole worlds out there that we know nothing about." She glanced toward the bedrooms. "Is Pablo here? I should check on him."

How could she stay so calm?

When Caria disappeared, I'd thought things couldn't possibly get any worse, but I'd been wrong. Totally wrong. Blane had built me up into the woman I'd always dreamed of becoming, and now he'd ripped the rug out from under my feet. The ache in my chest, that was what it felt like to have my heart shattered. And right now, it felt...unrecoverable.

"You could kill everyone in the world," I whispered to the man I'd been losing my heart to. "Steal all their souls and wipe out the human race."

"That could never happen."

I snorted. "Because you're just not that kind of psycho?"

"Well, yes, but there are also fail-safes built into the process. I can only manipulate a person's soul if I have direct visual contact. I can't simply wish a person dead from the other side of the planet."

So if I got the hell away from Club Dead, he couldn't kill me? That was...good. All I had to do was figure out a way to escape from a bunch of supernatural weirdos who were stronger, faster, and deadlier than me, and I might live to see tomorrow.

"So what happens next? Now that I know your secrets, are you planning to kill me too?"

To give Blane credit, he did look absolutely horrified by the suggestion.

"Of course not. Our souls are connected; it would be like killing a part of myself. No, we're going to clean up this mess, and then life can get back to normal."

"Normal?"

Maybe it wasn't me who was delusional. Maybe it was him?

"The kitchen needed a refresh anyway. You can help to pick out the new units."

"Did you hit your head when you got out of the elevator?"

"No, why?"

Now I understood his missteps. Those moments when Blane forgot how to human. Who knew Occam's razor could apply in a situation like this? Blane was some otherworldly being, his home was the scene of a massacre, and he was talking about the decor. He was crazy. *Crazy.* And even if he didn't kill me, I was still dead. A day, a week, a month... Laurent would find me and finish what Delphine had failed at.

"Blane, whatever there was between us is over. Our relationship was based on something that didn't exist."

"The aetherbond is very real, I can assure you."

"The what?"

"The aetherbond," Aurelia said, enunciating clearly as if she were speaking to a first-grader. "Its origins are unclear, but it links certain souls and entwines them for all eternity. Did you ever wonder why you felt so complete around Blane? You're the missing piece of each other." Aurelia glanced at Delphine. "Although Blane is an unusual case. It's rare for one soul to bond with multiple others. Quite fascinating, really. Once I'm finished here, I'd love to sit down and chat about your family tree."

The horrors just kept coming, didn't they?

It took a moment for her words to filter in, but suddenly the pieces clicked together. The way Blane doted on Lola. Her strange familiarity with him. Her age. Souls being "recycled." The woman he'd loved had died a little over five years ago, and Lola had recently turned four.

Lola and Nevaeh had been one and the same person, and now...now...she was still here.

CHAPTER 30

Wren

"That's her, isn't it?" I pointed at the woman who'd tried to kill me. "That's Nevaeh?"

Blane nodded once. "Yes."

"I don't get it," Delphine said. Lola. I should call her Lola. She clearly wasn't that murderous witch anymore.

"That's because you're a four-year-old in a thirty-something body," Aurelia explained. "It'll take time to adjust."

Vee tried to comfort her. "I had to adjust to a new body as well, kind of. It gets easier."

"These shoes hurt, but everything else is good." Lola grinned, which was totally inappropriate given the circumstances. "We're together again. Me and Blane, me and Wren. Can we wake up Mom and make more churros?"

"At least she's not traumatised," Vee murmured, returning to my side.

No, but I was. I'd slept with the Lord of the freaking Underworld. No wonder he'd been superhuman in bed. The first man to treat me well in my whole life, and it turned out he was the devil in disguise. If the charred remains of this apartment weren't a metaphor for my life, I didn't know what was.

"Is Pablo okay?" I asked Vee.

"Still asleep. A miracle."

"I need to get out of here."

"That's not happening," Joseph sang from across the room.

"The hell it's not. Are you gonna stop me?"

"Wren..." Blane reached for my hand, and I snatched it away. "There are people out there trying to kill you."

"You know what? I think I'll take my chances."

But I'd probably fail. I'd failed at everything so far. Saving Caria, finding a boyfriend who wasn't a psycho, making tamales.

"At least wait until we've solved the Laurent problem."

"Oh, please. Are you going to ask Zion to help again?" I asked snarkily. I should have been terrified, I knew I should, but I was just too damn angry. Fury had suppressed the "flight" part of my "fight or flight" response, and I had to squeeze my hands together to stop myself from punching Blane's perfectly straight nose. Fairy tales always cast the devil as an ugly monster. Such lies. He was hot as Hades. Wait, *was* he Hades?

"I can't ask Zion anything anymore."

Deep breaths, Wren. "What did you do, suck out his soul?"

"Disembowelling him would have taken too long. He put a tracking device on my car; can you believe that?"

"Yes, I absolutely can believe that. And it's ridiculous that you didn't preempt him doing it."

"Preeeee-empt." Lola rolled the word around in her mouth. "What's that mean?"

"It means he should have known Zion was a double-crossing asshole," Vee told her. "And he should have taken measures to stop him."

Lola gasped. "You said a bad word."

"I'll fix this," Blane promised. "All I need to do is fetch Decima, get her to repair Lola's body, and then find Caria. Zion said she might be on a boat."

"And you think he told you the truth?" I snapped.

Silence.

"You have to stop trusting jackasses." Even as the words left my mouth, I realised I was being a hypocrite. "If Zion said Caria was on a boat, she's anywhere but on a boat."

"In my brother's defence, he's used to people doing as he orders," Aurelia said. "All this human deceit takes some getting used to. The first time I visited Vegas, a fine-looking man told me Fremont Street was the best part of the city, and when we went there, he grabbed my purse and ran off."

"Did you get it back?" Vee asked.

"Of course. I just followed him to a nice dark spot and paused him. Then I left with my purse, plus his pants, underwear, and shoes."

A giggle escaped before I could stop it. Aurelia left the man's wiener swinging in the breeze? *Good going, girlfriend.* Under different circumstances—meaning circumstances where she wasn't Satan's little sister—I would have liked her.

Blane's phone rang. And after a quick glance at the screen, he answered it. Didn't he understand we were in the middle of a crisis here?

"Pandora, my darling. Is everything okay downstairs?" A pause. "Fire? No, there's no fire here. Maybe the TV was reflecting off the windows? ... Of course I'm sure. Vee? Yes, Vee's helping me out with something in the kitchen. If Kristy can cover, I'll pay her time and a half."

"Where did Zion tell you Caria wasn't?" Vee asked him when he hung up.

"He said he'd checked all the other properties, starting in Vegas, and the boat was the only one left."

"Then she's in Vegas."

"Wouldn't that be too obvious?"

"Not really. Laurent thinks you're a dumbass."

"Which is true," I muttered. "You can't fix this. Did you miss the part where Lola Mark One got shot through the heart?"

"It's true I can't fix that part, but Decima can. Her gift is healing. All I have to do is sweet-talk her into helping out." He rolled his eyes. "That's the hard part."

Aurelia raised a hand. "Uh, Decima isn't available right now."

"What do you mean, she isn't available?"

"She's at the Correction and Control symposium in Realm Fifty-Four, remember? She won't be back until the day after tomorrow."

"That symposium is just an excuse to have fun with whips and chains."

"Exactly, so there's no way she'll leave early."

"Who's looking after Plane Three?"

"Grimalda."

Blane snorted. "Great planes, they'll be having a riot."

The words were English, but the language was foreign. While Blane rattled on about expedited permits and celestial leaping, I stooped to pick up the gun one of the men had dropped. Nobody even noticed. One time, a friend of Kayden's, a gun nut who my brother said had more weapons than brain cells, had driven us out to the desert with a cooler of beer and enough ammo to fight a war against a small country. We'd spent the afternoon plinking at the empty cans before I drove the truck back to Vegas because Kayden's buddy was blind drunk. That was the first

—and last—time I'd tried hanging out with my brother's friends.

Anyhow, I remembered how to remove the magazine, and when I checked, there were eight bullets left.

Would that be enough for Laurent? I had to hope so.

I had to hope that I could get him before he got me.

Time to stop being a coward, Wren. Time to stop waiting for others to do your dirty work.

The spare key for Blane's car was in the little silver dish on the sideboard, blessedly unscorched, and I quickly pocketed it as I passed. I had a driver's licence; I just couldn't afford a car. Lending me a vehicle was the least Blane could do after...after *this*. And I had my phone. Although I didn't have Laurent's address, everyone knew he lived north of Iron Mountain. Okay, maybe not everyone. I glanced back at Blane. How could he be the literal devil and know so little about the sinners in Las Vegas?

In happier times, Caria had giggled as she told me the compound was far enough into the desert that nobody could hear Laurent's sex noises—he was a grunter, apparently—plus it used to belong to a rock star, and he'd themed the place around music. If I couldn't pick out the fancy guitar-shaped swimming pool on Google Maps, all I had to do was drive around the neighbourhood until I saw the big wrought-iron gates modelled on the sheet music of the former owner's first Billboard number one.

I inched toward the elevator as the others carried on talking. Never again would I trust a man. Blane had basically told me to sit down and eat fancy food while Caria suffered, and worse, he'd wormed his way into my heart under false pretences. Okay, so he hadn't explicitly said he wasn't human, but who even asked that? What dating site had a drop-down that went *male, female, non-binary, supernatural being*?

Nobody looked in my direction as I slipped through the door that led to the stairs. They were too busy arguing about Blane's sister. His *other* sister, the one who wasn't holding a mother and child in suspended animation in the room I'd just left.

She'd *stopped time*.

Until now, I'd assumed the plot masterminded by Zion and Laurent was the number-one horror story in Vegas, but then Blane said "hold my Dom Perignon" and flung me into a new nightmare. I was going to die; I knew that. I'd seen things I should never have seen, heard things I should never have heard. There was no way Blane could leave me alive.

Now my only goal was to depart this earth—plane, whatever the heck it was called—on my own terms.

And take Laurent with me.

He was the one who'd set me off on this dark path. Who'd put me on a collision course with the devil and his minions. If Laurent hadn't decided to murder a woman, I'd still have been dealing blackjack in blissful ignorance.

For a heart-stopping moment, I thought the guard stationed at the rear door would prevent me from leaving, but when he stood, I held up the key and kept walking.

"I'm just going to meet a friend. Blane said I could borrow his car."

"He didn't tell me—"

I forced a giggle. "He was a little distracted."

That stopped any more questions, but I noticed Myrtle sitting on a lawn chair next to the guard, watching us, her posture regal and her tail flicking. She must have followed me down the stairs. I imagined she'd been terrified by all the noise and flames, but her expression was judgey rather than fearful. Yes, yes, I knew she was a cat and she didn't have human emotions, but she still managed to peer down her nose.

"Don't look at me like that," I said, then caught myself.

The guard chuckled. "She looks at everyone like that."

Blane's tiny car was parked in its assigned space beside the door, and I quickly slid behind the wheel. The last car I'd driven was Caria's. She'd been so generous—she'd have given you her last nickel if you needed it—and whenever I'd needed to pick up groceries or whatever, she used to lend me her car. And...and...I was thinking about her in the past tense. A sob welled up in my throat when I realised.

The car started almost silently, and I pulled away on my final journey. I had so many regrets in life, but really, only two of them mattered—that I hadn't saved Caria, and that I wouldn't get to say goodbye to my brother. Briefly, I considered calling him, but that was a bad idea. Kayden would panic and alert the cops. If I got unlucky, one of Laurent's moles would tip him off, and his henchmen would be waiting at the gates for me to arrive. Or would Laurent do his own dirty work? Maybe it would be better if he did—I only had eight chances to kill him, and if I had to go through his minions first...

Eight chances to kill him.

Two weeks ago, my biggest problem had been making enough tips to cover the rent each month.

Now?

Now I'd lost everything, including my humanity.

I put my foot on the gas.

CHAPTER 31

Blane

"Just forget Decima for now," Aurelia said. "You could debate with her for an hour and end up right back where you started."

"She's right." Vee took my sister's side, and it was impossible to argue with both of them. "We should go and find Laurent. Not Aurelia, obviously, because she has to stay here with Marianna and the children. But you, me, and Beauregard."

"And me," Lola piped up. "If you're going on a adventure, I wanna come too."

"Absolutely not," I told her.

"But I *want* to."

"Planes above," I muttered, raising my gaze to the ceiling. "She has the mind of a four-year-old and Nev's devil-may-care attitude."

"I'm nearly four and a quarter."

"Sweetie, you have to stay here," Vee told her.

Joseph scratched his chin. "You know, bringing her along wouldn't be the worst idea."

I glared at him. "Yes, it would."

"Think about it—Laurent's expecting Delphine to arrive with Wren. If we send in the two of them, they can distract Laurent while we look for Caria."

"I hate to point out the obvious, but the soul currently inhabiting Delphine's body is (a) a juvenile, and (b) not French."

"Couldn't we swap somebody else into Delphine's body?" Vee suggested. "How about Beauregard?"

"Not a good idea. Joseph wasn't designed to be bound by mortal constraints, and every time he gets a new body, he twitches like crazy for a week or so." I glanced at Lola. "Plus he'd get distracted by the breasts."

"That's true," Joseph agreed. "What if we swapped Wren?"

Had he lost his mind? Wren wasn't going anywhere near Laurent. "Absolutely not."

"Where is Wren, anyway?"

"What do you mean, where's Wren? She's right—" I spun around and scanned my ruined apartment. "Where *is* Wren?"

"She went," Lola said.

"Went where?"

Lola shrugged in answer.

Vee stared at the door beside the elevator, the one that led to the stairs. "Oh no."

"Wait, you think she left? Why would she do that?"

"At a guess? Because she found out her boss-slash-boyfriend is actually the King of Hell?"

"There is no King of Hell. I oversaw the tortured souls department, but now I'm just a regular businessman."

"I think it was the whole 'sucking out people's souls' thing that upset her," Joseph muttered.

"Or maybe the fact that your ex is back on the scene?" Aurelia suggested. "In a manner of speaking."

She felt threatened by Nevaeh? Well, that was just ridiculous. I still loved Nev, of course I did, but love took different forms, as did souls here in Plane Five. What I felt for Nev now was more like fatherly affection. She was four years old, for heaven's sake. I glanced at her. Okay, four years old with D-cups, but that was very much temporary.

And Wren... It had taken a tragedy for me to see what had been right under my nose the whole time. For the raw pain of her emotions to awaken the aetherbond and fill the chasm in my psyche torn open when I lost Nev. It had taken an angel to make me whole again.

And now she was running.

Running, the way I always feared Nev would if she found out who and what I truly was.

Oh, the irony. Lola seemed quite relaxed about the idea.

"I should go after her," I said. "She can't have gone far on foot."

"Who can't have gone far?" Myrtle asked, strolling in on two legs rather than four. "Wren? What in Plane Three happened, anyway? I mean, obviously I know the basics, but who are all these dead people? Where did they come from?"

"The madman who abducted Wren's friend sent them," Joseph explained. "The blonde was his sister, but Blane had to borrow her body to house Lola's soul for the time being."

Lola waved to Myrtle. "I feel weird."

"And when Blane began switching souls around, Wren freaked out and took off."

"Cool. Does that mean I don't have to listen to sex noises all night?"

For the most part, I liked Myrtle, but there were times I wanted to toss her headfirst into an active volcano.

"Wear earplugs," I snapped. "We have bigger concerns than your sleeping habits. Wren's wandering around the city alone, and Laurent is trying to kill her. And next time, could you *not* cause a deranged woman to start shooting wildly inside my apartment?"

"I was trying to help."

"Well, you didn't."

"It stinks in here. You should open a window or something."

"I have more important things on my mind right now. Finding Wren, for example."

"We should split up," Joseph decided. "If Myrtle helps, the four of us can head north, south, east, and west. Wren's only human. Even an Olympic athlete couldn't have made it more than a mile."

"You think?" Myrtle fiddled with her collar. "An athlete can run a mile in four minutes, and you've probably been talking for that long."

My fingers twitched. *Don't throttle the adolescent.* "Then we need to get a move on."

"What about Caria?" Vee asked.

"Wren takes precedence."

I'd lost Nevaeh; I wasn't about to lose another soulmate. And when I retrieved Wren, we'd be having words about priorities. How were we meant to find Caria if we were running around Las Vegas looking for somebody else?

"I don't have a car," Myrtle said.

"Neither does Wren." Although she was wearing sneakers and no doubt fuelled by adrenaline. "We need to get going."

"Oh, she does. She took your Nissan and turned left out of the parking lot."

"She did what?"

"I mean, she might survive? She had a gun tucked into her waistband."

"A gun? Where did she get a gun? I don't even own a gun."

Had she brought it with her? No, no, no, she'd arrived with barely a thing, and Joseph had remarked on her pitiful belongings after he unpacked them into her closet. Which wasn't something I condoned, by the way. He wouldn't be invading her privacy again.

"At a guess?" Vee poked one of the chargrilled douchebags with a toe. "She probably picked it up off the floor."

"That could be a good thing?" Aurelia suggested, staying positive as she always did. "If she has a gun and Laurent sends more henchmen—or women—after her, then she can just shoot them."

Did Wren have a good aim? Had she ever fired a gun before? I realised how little we knew about each other. Wren didn't like to talk about her past, and I'd avoided discussing mine for obvious reasons, so we'd both been living in the present. And even then, we'd stuck to safe subjects—food, pets, work—because any mention of Caria left her upset.

When I got her back, things would have to change. No more skirting around the difficult topics. And I *would* get her back. I'd crawl on my knees and grovel if I had to. Kiss her damn feet and pray she saw beyond the monster she now thought I was.

"We need transport." Yes, I could move fast, but leepering my way around Vegas was a risk I couldn't take. I loved Wren, but I also had to protect my family and our secrets. My father had warned me that if I stayed in Plane Five, I'd just be replacing my old problems with new ones, and at the time, I'd brushed off his warning. But now I had to concede he was right, an admission that irked me to no end. "Joseph, find us vehicles. Myrtle will have to ride shotgun with one of us."

"At least if Wren's in your car, she'll be easier to spot,"

Aurelia said. "I mean, it's harder to hide a hunk of metal than a person."

"Blane's car is mostly made from plastic," Joseph pointed out.

Myrtle rolled her eyes. "Whatever. Stop being so pedantic and find us wheels."

"My car is downstairs," Vee said to me. "The three of us could start out in that while we wait for Beauregard?"

But where would we start? "She could have gone anywhere."

"Doesn't she have a brother?"

"He's on vacation."

"Maybe she borrowed his apartment? We found a hidden key at her place—what if Kayden leaves a key for emergencies too? Do you know where he lives?"

"Yes, over in Mesquite."

"So let's head there. If we hurry, we can get back before sunrise."

"Wouldn't she have turned right out of the parking lot if she was going to Mesquite?" Joseph asked.

Vee huffed out a sigh. "Dammit, you're right."

"Never thought you'd say that, did you?" Myrtle put in, and I held up a hand to stop Joseph's retort before they began bickering.

"What's to the left?" Aurelia asked. "California? Does Wren know anyone in California?"

With startling clarity, I realised that my entire relationship with Wren was upside down. With Nev, I'd built a base of friendship first, and we'd laughed, cried, and grouched together. We'd sipped coffee in Paris, we'd relaxed on the beach in Crete, and we'd hiked in the Carpathian Mountains—although I never did find that werewolf. She'd confided in me about her past, about her dreams of becoming an artist and the problems with her family. About her damaging relationship with drugs and the dark depression that came crashing down when she least expected it. The sex had evolved out of love. The aetherbond had slowly made its presence known, and its exploration had been an adventure we shared.

With Wren, I'd started out more concerned with her abilities as a blackjack dealer than her qualities as a woman. So I'd taken the easy way out and hired Zion, and boy, had that turned out to be a mistake. My only regret was that there hadn't been a handy member of the Electi standing by to send him straight to Plane Three. Decima would have had a field day with him.

Anyhow, with Wren, the aetherbond had hit me like a fully laden semi, and I'd understood right away what it meant. Nev had taught me that much. She'd also taught me that human lives were far too short, so when I'd been gifted a second chance at love, I'd jumped in feet first, unwilling to miss out on even a second of time with the woman fate had brought to my door.

And now I was drowning.

Wren was gone, and with every new revelation, I found it harder to breathe.

Life in Plane Five was so much more challenging than I'd ever imagined.

"She never mentioned an acquaintance in California, but we didn't talk as much as we should have."

"Does she have money with her?" Aurelia asked.

"There's five hundred bucks in the glove compartment," Joseph offered.

"Well, as long as she holes up somewhere safe for the night and doesn't do anything dumb like trying to shoot Laurent, I'm sure she'll be just fine."

We all stared at each other.

No.

No, she wouldn't.

Would she?

Wren had always seemed nonconfrontational, but in the past week, I'd begun to notice the quiet strength she kept hidden. And then there was the link to Nev, whose impetuous streak had run wild and deep.

Lola bounced on her toes. "But you said Laurent was the bad guy? So she should shoot him. I hate these shoes."

See?

If Wren had even a fraction of Nev's impulsiveness, we were in deep trouble.

"Does she know where Laurent lives?" Vee asked.

"I have no idea." I racked my brain, but I couldn't remember her ever mentioning an address. "That particular subject never came up."

"What on earth have you been doing all week?"

Myrtle opened her mouth, and I clapped a hand over it. "Don't."

Vee put her hands on her hips. Uh-oh. "Do *you* know where he lives?"

"Not exactly."

"Define 'not exactly.'"

"Vegas is all I've got."

She tore her hands through her hair. "For Pete's sake. Who would know? This Zion guy? He's definitely dead?"

I thought back to the men I'd left neatly lined up on the floor in the Colosseum with barely a mark on them. If Wren hadn't been in mortal danger, I'd have ruined another suit and enjoyed every second of it.

"He bragged about keeping me occupied while Delphine came to collect Wren. What was I supposed to do?"

Joseph huffed. "I told you we should have tortured him."

"We didn't have time," I said through clenched teeth.

"We could try Google?" Myrtle suggested.

"What's Google?" Aurelia wanted to know.

This was a disaster.

"It's like a library, except you have nearly all the information in the world at your fingertips. Plus a lot of stuff that people have made up, and the challenge is sorting fact from fiction."

Aurelia looked more energised than I'd seen her all day. "Where is this Google library?"

"On the coffee table."

"Where?"

"That grey box."

"No way."

"Yes way, but we'll have to talk about that later. I doubt Laurent broadcasts his address on the internet."

Why would he? Unless he'd opened his doors for a "Homes of the rich and murderous" feature, there'd be no need for him to advertise his whereabouts.

Vee blew out a long breath. "I'll have to ask Jack, won't I? If Laurent is as big an asshole as you say, I bet the cops know where he lives. Is Laurent a first name or a last name?"

"A last name, I believe. Zion referred to him as Raph once."

What were the consequences of involving Jack Callahan? He'd ask questions, but at this moment, saving Wren was more important than anything.

"So they were on first-name terms?"

"Yes?" Dammit, why hadn't I picked up on that? "Call Jack. Just don't invite him over here, whatever you do."

Callahan turned a blind eye to many things, but even he might get tetchy if he saw the bodies littering my apartment.

Vee stepped away, phone to her ear, and began talking softly. I strained to hear, and the fact that I couldn't was a sore point. My hearing might have been above average when compared to a human's, but it wasn't as good as Vee's or Joseph's. The mixed abilities were another fail-safe. The Celestial Council had ensured that no one being had too much power lest they get any big ideas. Nobody wanted a coup. We had the appropriate gifts to do our jobs, no more, no less.

"Well?" I asked the instant she hung up.

"So, Jack wasn't keen on giving us the address, mainly because he thinks we might do something stupid."

"I mean, it's a fair point," Myrtle said.

"But he did say Raphael Laurent lives near Iron Mountain, and if we head over in that direction, he'll join us as soon as he can and ask Laurent some questions."

"No, no, no. Callahan is *not* coming with us," I said.

"Not right now, he isn't. He picked up a new murder case." Vee raised an eyebrow. "Does six bodies in a gym sound familiar?"

"What was I meant to do? Let them go?"

"Why don't we head over to Iron Mountain and listen for the screams?" Joseph suggested, and Myrtle's eyes suddenly widened.

"Wait, did you say Raphael Laurent? Raphael like the ninja turtle?"

"The what?"

"It's a cartoon on the Retro Channel with four— Never mind. I might know where Raphael Laurent lives."

"Where? And how?" I demanded.

"Okay, so I don't have an exact address, but I know he has a guitar-shaped swimming pool."

"Explain."

"I like to sneak into shows at the Cube, right?" Yes, I was well aware of that. I'd had to retrieve her from there in cat form three times. Luckily, the theatre staff thought she was cute. "So I found a new place to hide. A gantry above one of the VIP boxes. It's nice and dark, so if I accidentally turn into the real me at the wrong moment, nobody will notice."

Thanks to the itching, Myrtle got enough notice of an impending shift to skedaddle if she was in company, but she hated to miss a show.

"Lovely, but what does this have to do with Laurent?"

"A couple of months ago, there were a bunch of realtors in the box, and they were talking about their creepy clients. And guess who's the biggest creep of all?"

"Laurent?"

"Right. Raphael Laurent, like the ninja turtle. He kept hitting on his realtor even though he knew she was married, but she had to put up with it because of the commission. The huge commission. She said he bought a mansion from some old rocker, and the place had a pool shaped like a guitar and a pathway that played music when you walked on it."

Perhaps Google would give us the answer after all? I grabbed my laptop and loaded Google Earth. Zoomed in on Iron Mountain.

And there it was.

"Let's go."

CHAPTER 32

Wren

What in the world was I doing here?

The walls were ten feet high and topped with spikes. The lots on either side were empty, and I crept all the way around the perimeter of the sprawling estate, but the only way in was through the ridiculously ornate front gates. Which were guarded by a swarthy man in a small stucco building. Every so often, he looked up from the TV he was watching and glanced around, presumably checking whether there were any idiots he needed to shoot.

Even if I got inside, how would I find Caria? There were so many buildings. A huge main house, plus a detached garage, a pool complex, and what looked like a second, smaller home to the rear. She'd told me Laurent liked his space, but when I saw the residence for myself, my stomach sank. I could search there for a week and still not find her. While I considered my options, I huddled under the branches of a small, shrubby tree next to the gates, one that Laurent undoubtedly paid a fortune to keep alive. His priorities were whacked.

Stay or go? Stay or go?

I'd spent the drive over here trying to come up with a better solution, one that didn't end in tragedy. But there was none. People had died already tonight—Lola, all those people in Blane's apartment, probably Zion too—and the man I'd fallen for had scared me half to death. Was what he said true? That souls didn't die, they got reincarnated? Because if it was, maybe death wouldn't be so bad. Perhaps I'd have better luck the next time around?

A vehicle sounded in the distance, and I stilled. This road was quiet, with the home opposite Laurent's in darkness—empty, judging by the foreclosure notice attached to the gates—and just a handful of properties farther into the desert. Was this why he'd chosen the place? For its isolation? So his dastardly deeds would go unnoticed and therefore unpunished?

Headlights hit me full in the face, and I screwed my eyes shut, praying the driver hadn't seen me through the curtain of green. *Please carry on, please carry on...*

The sleek black car slowed.

Stopped.

The door opened, and my heart hammered so hard that I thought my ribcage would crumble.

Why?

Why was the driver getting out?

Oh hell.

Oh hell, oh hell, oh hell.

He was walking in my direction, backlit by the glow from the guard building. A tall white man with slicked-back dark hair, dressed in dark jeans and a fine knit sweater that might have been cashmere and probably cost more than my rent. He stopped right in front of me, his bearing confident.

"Are you okay in there, *chérie*?"

Shit!

"Uh, yes?" I squeaked.

He tilted his head to one side, questioning, and as I tended to do in these situations, I began babbling. So much for marching through the gates to put a bullet through Laurent's head.

"Okay, so I was on my way to visit a friend, and now that I got here, I'm not certain I have the right address. I was just trying to, you know, check? On my phone, I mean. The internet."

"You walked here?" he asked, and he wasn't American. French, maybe?

"No, my car, uh, broke down." I jerked a thumb along the road, toward the centre of the city. "Back there."

"I see. Well, it's not safe to be out here on your own at night."

No freaking kidding. And now I was kicking myself for not saying that a friend had dropped me off. A witness to my whereabouts.

"You're right. You're absolutely right. I should leave."

Or at least pretend to. I couldn't get cold feet. For Caria's sake, I *couldn't*.

"You're one of Laurent's girls?"

This man knew Laurent? Double shit. And also, girls? Plural? Several months ago, Caria had found a smear of red on his collar that she thought was lipstick, and he'd sworn blind that she was the only woman for him. Plus he'd claimed that the smear was blood, which now that I thought about it, was entirely possible. But from a shaving cut? Yeah, right. More likely he'd murdered someone, another poor, innocent woman who'd fallen for his dubious charms. But at the time, Caria had believed him, mainly because his facial hair grew weirdly fast and he always shaved twice a day.

"Laurent's girls?" I asked.

The stranger smiled, and if he thought it was strange

that I was skulking around in the undergrowth, he didn't show it. If anything, he was looking at me as if I were lunch. He clearly thought I was here for one reason and one reason only, and although my heart ached all over again for Caria, at this moment, I had to be grateful that Laurent liked to stick his dick in things he shouldn't. It gave me a plausible excuse.

"Come on—I'll take you up to the house," the stranger offered. "It's only natural to be nervous on your first visit."

Wait, he was offering to take me inside? All the way to Laurent?

Instinct screamed at me to run, but logic overrode my fears. I had to do this. Nobody else was going to save Caria.

"Really? I'd appreciate that."

The gun weighed heavy in my pocket as I climbed into the shiny black Mercedes. It had Nevada vanity plates—ALPHA–so he lived locally and no doubt had an overinflated sense of self-importance. Classical music played softly, and the heavy scent of cologne accompanied the stranger as he slid back behind the wheel. Eight bullets. I was no hero, but I had eight bullets to end this, and no matter how friendly this man seemed, I'd shoot him too if he stood between me and Caria.

He gave a delicate sniff. "What's that smell?"

"What smell?"

"That smoky, meaty aroma." He glanced around. "Is one of the neighbours having a barbecue?"

Hell, it was me, wasn't it? "Uh, I burned dinner before I left. Honestly, I didn't realise the smell was clinging."

And now I felt sick. I'd wiped the worst of the soot off my face with a handkerchief I found in the glove compartment, and my ripped clothes would hopefully pass as fashion, but there was nothing I could do about the stink.

"It's making me hungry," he said. Gross. "What's your name?"

"Uh..." Dammit! This scenario hadn't figured in my thoughts at all when I was brainstorming on the drive over. "Renata."

He leaned over and took my hand, and my stomach flipped when he brought my knuckles to his lips. Why did hot men always have to act so sleazy? Okay, Blane hadn't overstepped, but he didn't count. He'd just lied about everything instead.

"Call me Rick. How long have you known Laurent?"

"Barely any time at all."

"Where did you meet him?"

A hysterical giggle burst out of me because this was terrifying.

"Through a friend." I mean, it wasn't a total lie. In an effort to avoid an interrogation, I turned the tables back on my chauffeur. "Where did *you* meet him?"

"In Paris. We moved in the same circles there."

"That's where you're from?"

"Did the accent give it away?"

"Uh, maybe? Are you here on vacation?"

"It's more of a business trip. I'm diversifying my investments."

Investments? This guy was definitely rich, not that I hadn't already worked that out from the clothes and the car. And the fact that he was hanging out with Laurent. So, a wealthy, handsome psycho, then.

"Like, you're buying companies?"

"Exactly."

"What's the last company you bought?" I asked, desperate to keep the conversation from turning toward me.

"The last company? A hotel in Italy, but now I'm planning to purchase a casino and a spa in California."

"I thought California only had Native American casinos?"

"The casino is here. The spa is in California," he said. A moment later, the car drew to a stop outside the main residence, and my stomach lurched as Rick came to open my door. A *gentleman* psycho. "After you."

The house was dark. Not literally dark—Laurent obviously didn't care about his electricity bill—but the pale grey facade turned to graphite inside. The chandelier hanging in the entrance hall was a gothic monstrosity of twisted iron, and the light spilling from its fake candles glinted off the silver snakes writhing from the rails of the grand staircase ahead of me. They were made from metal, thank goodness, but still creepy as hell.

Rick waved me ahead of him and shepherded me into the bowels of the house, through a vast living room with a grand piano on a platform at one end. The macabre theme continued—a feature wall was painted blood red, the face of a horned beast hung above the giant TV, and a skull-shaped vase on the coffee table held half a dozen long-stemmed silver roses, their metal petals gleaming under another ornate chandelier. Caria had told me Laurent's home was "a bit weird," and that had to be the understatement of the century.

"Laurent likes the creepy stuff, huh?" I said to Rick. Anything to break the tension that threatened to seize up my lungs.

"His sister chose the decor."

Delphine? I shuddered, both at the decor and at the memory of her soul being sucked out of her body. This place came straight out of a nightmare. I mean, Blane was the literal Lord of Hell, and he preferred peonies and paintings of dramatic sunsets.

"She lives here too?"

"Laurent and Delphine are very close."

"Don't you need to call Laurent? We just kind of walked right in."

"No need. He's expecting you, isn't he?"

"Uh, yes? Yes, absolutely."

As we neared the rear of the house, I heard a familiar metallic *clunk*—a stack of weights falling into place on one of those machines you find in gyms. Dom always used to drop the weights like that—he said it gave him a sense of satisfaction, but his red-faced grimace gave the game away. He kept trying to bite off more than he could chew, and he just couldn't hold the stack any longer.

I wrapped my hand around the butt of the gun in my pocket, ready, but what was I meant to do about Rick? I'd hoped to be alone with Laurent for the next part. What if Rick hung around? He seemed like a nice guy, and could I really shoot him in cold blood when all he'd done was give me a ride to the house?

And where was Caria? Okay, so I hadn't expected to see her shackled to a couch, but there was no sign of her whatsoever in this immaculate monstrosity of a home. Was she in one of the outbuildings? Google had given me a rough layout of the property, and I'd glimpsed roofs over the wall when I did my circuit of the property earlier.

"Raph, I found this evening's entertainment lurking outside. You should tell the girls to buzz the intercom."

Laurent's gaze landed on me, and it felt like a physical thud. Oof. His brows knit in confusion, and I nearly pulled the gun then and there. All I had to do was demand answers, and if he refused to give them, send him to meet his maker. Wait, was that Blane's father? He'd been hazy about that part.

I inched the gun out of my pocket, then froze when a

sickening thought hit me. Did this gun have a safety? If so, was it on or off?

I edged away from Rick, trying to put space between us, and someone up there must have granted a miracle because he helped me out.

"You've left sweat all over the leg press again." Rick strode toward a stack of fluffy white towels sitting on top of a glass-fronted refrigerator in the far corner, and I realised Laurent had been lifting nearly the whole weight stack. Uh-oh. "Is it really too difficult to use a towel?"

"It's my damn house. If I don't want to use a towel, I won't."

Rick threw a towel in Laurent's direction, but the hairy little sleazebag just batted it out of the way.

"What do you care?" he grumbled. "You don't even—"

I saw the moment of recognition. Caria must have shown him a photo. His head swivelled back to me, and he did a double take.

"*You.*"

I drew the gun in an instant, beyond relieved when it didn't catch on the edge of my pocket. Where was the safety? I glanced quickly, but there was no obvious button, and I couldn't afford to take my eyes off Laurent for too long.

"Where's Caria?"

"How the fuck did you get here?"

"Wait, which one is Caria?" Rick asked. "The blonde with the attitude problem? Or the brunette with the big—"

"The brunette is Carla," Laurent snapped.

"Tell me where she is!" Hell, my hand was shaking, and the tremors ran all the way down my arm when his mouth curved into a sickening grin.

"*Mais oui*, this evening is going to be *very* entertaining," Rick said, chuckling.

Laurent took a step toward me, and I jerked the gun. "Don't! Don't come any closer!"

"Or what? You're going to shoot me?"

"Yes, exactly."

"That won't happen."

"You think? You kidnapped Caria, and you tried to kidnap me, so why wouldn't I put a bullet in your head?"

"Because the safety is on."

Shit.

I finally spotted the button and clicked it, but Laurent used my distraction to close the gap between us. When I looked up, he was barely three feet away.

I panicked.

Adrenaline took over, I panicked, and I fired.

Blood blossomed on Laurent's chest, and he stared down in shock. "You shot me."

"Like I said I would."

"You little bitch."

Then suddenly, I didn't have the gun anymore. One blink, and it was gone. My hand was still out in front of me, but it was empty.

"That wasn't very friendly, *chérie*," Rick said, and I realised *he* had the gun now. He was on the other side of the room, and I hadn't even seen him move, but the gun was in his hand. How was the gun in his hand?

"Shoot her," Laurent instructed.

"Where's the fun in that?"

Why wasn't Laurent on the floor? I'd shot him in the chest, but he was still standing. He'd barely even stumbled. He was bleeding, but I was the one whose knees were threatening to give way.

"Fine, I'll—" Bad rap music interrupted him, and he angrily fished his phone out of his pocket and stabbed at the screen. The music stopped. "Fine, I'll deal with her myself."

He reached for my throat, hairy hands outstretched, short stubby fingers ready to choke the life out of me. He was grinning. The sick bastard was actually grinning. Grinning and breathing rather than groaning in agony.

I...I didn't understand.

And then with a sickening realisation, I did.

Blane wasn't the only non-human who'd decided to make Vegas his home.

Who was Laurent?

What was Laurent?

The only thing I knew for sure was that I was going to die if I didn't come up with a plan fast. Did Blane know Laurent's secret? Had they come from the same place? And more importantly, could Blane kill him?

"We have Delphine," I blurted. It was the only card I had left to play.

And for an all-too-brief moment, I thought it might have worked. Laurent froze.

But only for a second.

"Nice try, but you're lying. Your nightclub boyfriend might be able to knock out an arrogant fool like Zion with a lucky punch, but Delphine has a team of armed men. Did *you* get lucky this time? What did you do, sneak down the fire escape?"

I couldn't even recall seeing a fire escape, not from Blane's apartment. Guess he didn't consider it a priority when he could control fire.

"If I'm lying, then where is she?"

That gave him pause, and I could almost hear the cogs turning. Slowly, because although he had the ability to heal from a bullet wound, intelligence perhaps wasn't his superpower. He appeared to rely on brute force instead of finesse.

But Rick... Rick seemed more calculating. I'd seen men

like him at the blackjack table a thousand times over, and while they took risks, they also knew when to cut their losses. And while Rick might have been here with Laurent, the slick Frenchman didn't seem to have much respect for his friend. No, he looked more amused by the situation than anything, and apart from taking my gun, he'd done little to help.

"Call her," Laurent ordered him.

Was that an eye roll? I thought it was, but Rick still obeyed and held his phone to his ear. Nobody answered. From the length of time we waited, the phone was ringing rather than dead, and I pictured the scene in Blane's apartment. The Hellions were probably still standing around, bickering over whether or not they should answer.

Rick hung up and shrugged.

"You don't have Delphine," Laurent said, but he didn't sound quite so certain this time. "She didn't go alone."

"Is that you admitting you sent an armed team to my boss's home to abduct me?" Dammit, I should have thought to record this conversation.

"They came to *talk* to you."

"The only thing she said was 'You should have kept your mouth shut,' and then she ordered her men to grab me. Which clearly didn't play out the way she hoped." Wow, I sounded strangely confident, possibly because I had nothing left to lose. "Maybe next time, you shouldn't send someone else to do your dirty work."

"Delphine enjoys her job. And she's good at it," he added, and a little more confidence had ebbed away. "You're just a whore who made a big mistake."

More than one, if we were counting, but I couldn't turn back the clock.

"You can call me all the names you want, but unless I

walk out of here with Caria, you won't be seeing Delphine again."

"You're bluffing."

At Tilt, I'd occasionally helped out serving drinks when a shift needed filling—I'd had plenty of experience of bar work back in Cheyenne—and one evening, a slightly drunk high-roller had begun talking to me. Mostly about his marriage woes, but he'd also been celebrating a big win at the poker table, a game where he'd come back from the dead. When I'd congratulated him, he told me that when a man had little left to lose, fear took a back seat.

Now, I realised that applied to women too.

I met Laurent's hard stare with one of my own. "Bluffing? Am I?"

Delphine was never going to answer her phone. Or if she did, she'd probably ask for crayons and a cookie.

"Call Delphine again," Laurent told Rick.

But before Rick could dial, his phone rang, and a smug smile spread over Laurent's face. He thought his sister was calling. Guess again.

"Yes... No, he's tied up at the moment. ... Uh-huh. ... Okay, I'll tell him." Rick hung up. "You have a visitor at the gates."

"That wasn't Delphine?"

"Would I describe Delphine as a visitor?"

"Then who the fuck is at the gates?"

"He says his name is Lucian Blane, and he wants his girlfriend back."

Oh. Shit.

CHAPTER 33

Blane

Where did Laurent find his sentry? The man glowered at me from inside the squat little building beside the front gates, and honestly, was a smile really too much to ask?

Maybe it was.

After all, I'd be separating his soul from his body as soon as his master made an appearance. My bet was on it being a shade of darkish grey. The man worked for a monster, but in a menial capacity. He wasn't out performing general thuggery.

My phone buzzed with a message. Joseph, Vee, and Myrtle had hopped over the wall at the rear, ready to start the search as soon as I gave the all clear. What was taking so long? Wren was inside, I was almost certain of it. We'd passed my car a quarter mile away, tucked in at the side of the road, abandoned. A minute spent with Laurent was sixty seconds too long, and it was all I could do to stop myself from marching up the driveway and burning down the front door. Only the need to get Laurent away from the building stopped me. If he was with me at the end of the driveway, the others would have a clear run at the house while I chose whether to suck out his soul right away or ask him a few questions first.

Killing him on sight was tempting, but I knew what Wren would ask me to do. She'd come to find Caria, and I had to adhere to that plan.

"He's not answering," the guard said.

"Call him again."

"I don't take orders from you."

"You'll be taking orders from the devil himself if you don't do as I ask."

I held his stare, and when he didn't immediately dial, I conjured up a softball-sized sphere of flames. Bounced it in my hand. Waited.

He swallowed with an audible gulp. "I'll call him."

"I'd appreciate that."

Laurent clearly wasn't a man who understood priorities. Several minutes passed before the front door opened and he stepped out into the porte cochère. Alone. Where was Wren? I'd half expected him to bring her along with a gun to her head. Hoped he would, if I was honest. Not because I wanted her to be terrified, but because I could remove her from his clutches far faster that way. A little focus, and his soul would be on its way to Plane Four. By rights, it should have been in Plane Three, but the Electi had only just resumed work after a near hiatus that had lasted several centuries.

I said goodbye to the guard, and I'd been absolutely right. His soul was the colour of a thundercloud. It drifted skyward, then scattered for its journey to the next plane. A moment later, I'd signalled to the others.

And I heard a sound that struck dread into my immortal heart.

"Luuuuuucian, I'm bored."

I whirled to see Lola stumbling toward me barefoot, totally unaware of the danger approaching. Fuck. Joseph swore he'd engaged the child locks. How the hell had she escaped from Vee's Porsche?

"Go back to the car."

"I don't wanna."

"You promised you wouldn't get out."

"But it's dark and I'm scared."

Planes above and below, was anything going to go right today? Lola wasn't supposed to be with us at all, but right after I'd given in and let Myrtle ride shotgun alongside Vee, Lola had burst out the rear door and stumbled toward us in Delphine's stupid stilettos yelling, "Don't forget meeeeeee!" When I tried to take her back inside, she'd started crying, and the parking lot wasn't empty. People had begun staring. The easiest thing to do had been to bundle her into the vehicle, and then Joseph had pointed out that it didn't matter if Delphine's body got damaged because I could just stuff Nev's soul into a substitute until Decima deigned to join us. Then Lola had promised to wait in the back seat, and now here we were.

Screwed.

I loved this flawed soul, I truly did, but damn, she could be exasperating at times. Laurent was already halfway down the driveway as I weighed up the options. Lola was in the shadows, but what were the chances of her staying there? Not good. If I dispatched Laurent right away, and the others didn't find Caria, then Wren wouldn't get the answers she so badly needed.

Which left me to lean through the window and hurriedly free the slumped guard's pistol from its shoulder holster.

"Forgive me," I muttered as I clamped a hand over Lola's mouth and pressed the gun to her temple. "Shhh."

She mumbled angrily as I pulled her into view and faced Laurent. If looks could kill, then forget immortality—I'd be dead. He hesitated for the briefest moment, then resumed his march.

"That's far enough," I told him. "I think you have something of mine."

Laurent didn't stop. "You're dead."

"That's wishful thinking."

"It's a fact."

"I said, stay where you are."

"No."

This man was either very brave or very stupid. I had a gun and a hostage, and his hands were empty. So I gave his soul a tug. If I separated his parts temporarily, then I could send Lola back to the car and deal with this fool on my own terms.

But his soul didn't shift.

What the hell?

I tried again, focusing harder the way I'd done a million times in the past, but the black wall of his psyche was firmly stuck. He was ten feet away when I turned the gun on him.

Six feet away when I fired.

Three feet away when I discovered the bullets had no impact whatsoever.

Who was this man? *What* was he?

And was it my imagination, or was he getting hairier?

When I spotted the bushy tail extending from Laurent's ass, I realised I knew the answers to my questions. On the plus side, I now knew where one of the elusive werewolves had been hiding out. On the minus side...fuck.

When I went hunting for werewolves in the Carpathian Mountains with Joseph, I figured that if the beast wasn't friendly, we could just leeper on out of there. But now that wasn't an option, not if it meant leaving Lola behind. The only positive was that she was currently inhabiting Delphine's body, and Laurent wouldn't harm his own sister. Would he?

She was safe as long as he didn't suspect I'd switched out their souls. All she had to do was—

Lola caught me by surprise when she bit my hand, and her scream made my ears bleed. I tightened my grip, but it was too late.

For a second, the burning fury in Laurent's eyes turned to puzzlement. Lola was screaming at him, not at me. And Delphine had known, hadn't she? She'd known that her brother was a monster in more ways than one.

And now it was down to me to do what I'd failed to do before.

Protect Lola.

Save her soul.

"Run," I told her. "When I let you go, run. Do you understand?"

"Mmmfh."

Dammit. I loosened my hand slightly.

"Y-y-yes."

Laurent was fully transformed now. He seemed to favour four legs rather than two, but he still stood almost as tall as me. When he raked a paw through thick, lustrous hair, it stood up in a quiff that reminded me of Elvis, but obviously he lacked the man's charisma. Until this moment, I hadn't understood just how expressive an animal's face could be. Laurent was gloating. Gloating at my shock and no doubt planning to dance on my corpse once he'd torn me to shreds. Well, I had a few surprises of my own.

I shoved Lola to the side. "Go!"

She ran.

And I realised I should have been more specific. Because instead of fleeing back to the Porsche and locking the doors as I'd intended, she sprinted barefoot toward the house, shrieking as she went.

For Dad's sake...

Laurent lashed out with claws longer than Taylee M's, and that was another suit ruined. I jumped back before he managed to draw blood and hurled a fireball at him. Smug superiority gave way to a hint of shock.

"Oh, did it never occur to you that there might be other preternatural creatures in this plane?"

"This what?"

Hmm, werewolves could speak? Fascinating. Aurelia would no doubt be thrilled to learn of the discovery. She spent a ridiculous amount of time reading through the celestial archives, and she'd grown especially curious about shape-shifters after Myrtle's first unfortunate transformation. And right now, I was wishing I'd paid more attention when she'd rambled on about her research over dinner because how in Mount Malum's name was I meant to kill one of these things? Laurent had dodged my fireball with alarming ease, and as we circled, sizing each other up, I caught sight of Lola running through the mansion's open front door.

Because I clearly didn't have enough problems already.

"Plane Five? Earth?"

"What the fuck are you talking about?"

"You're a werewolf, but you know nothing about your origins?"

He swiped at me again, eyes glowing yellow, and I leapt sideways. I could reach the mansion in no time, but from what I'd seen of Laurent, he also had the gift of celestial speed, so he'd be right behind me. And I didn't want him anywhere near Lola or Wren.

"My origins?" He barked out a laugh. "A friend decided

to hold his *enterrement de vie de garçon* in Transylvania, and this was how I returned."

Curiosity got the better of me. "You encountered a werewolf in Romania?"

"How the fuck should I know? I was so damn drunk, I don't remember what happened. My friend buried his life as a boy that night, and I lost my life as a human." His fangs showed as he grinned. "It took a while for me to figure out the benefits."

"Celestial abilities are meant to be used for the benefit of mankind, not for personal gain."

"What are you, the supernatural police?"

"Far from it. I was Lord of the Underworld."

This was a strange conversation to be having, but my goal was to keep Laurent away from the house, and better to be talking than fighting. I was equipped to deal with unruly souls, not fiendish beasts who'd quite possibly been blessed with immortality. Aurelia would know what to do. The temptation to leeper away and ask her was almost overwhelming, but in the moments I was gone, Laurent could do untold damage to the women I loved. Two connected souls, two very different bonds. I couldn't lose either of them, not again.

"Did they kick you out for being too soft?" Laurent asked.

"I'm here to learn more about sin, and it seems I came to the right place."

"You're here to fuck with my business."

"When your business involves harming innocent women, I have a duty to intervene."

"Innocent? Stupid, more like. Caria never did what she was told."

Anger bubbled up inside me. "And Wren?"

"That was Caria's fault. She couldn't keep her mouth

shut." Laurent shrugged his hairy shoulders. "A bitch plays with fire, and she's gonna get—"

I hurled another fireball at him, bigger than the last, and this time, he didn't dodge fast enough. The fur on his side caught alight.

"—burned," I finished as he roared in anger and pain and dropped to the ground, rolling to extinguish the flames.

"Motherfucker!" he growled, his wolf voice much deeper than his human one.

My turn to duck as Laurent leapt at me, his fur still smoking, the vile aroma of singed hair permeating the air. In hindsight, I wished I'd just kept talking because fighting really wasn't my thing. I'd barely scraped through my combat skills module at the Celestial Academy. Where was Joseph when I needed him? He'd aced every class, albeit in demon form.

I got in a punch as Laurent flew past, but his skull had the strength and substance of a rock. My knuckles throbbed as we both lined up for another strike, but a blood-curdling scream from the house made us both whip our heads around.

Laurent sprang toward the mansion.

I blocked him with a wall of flame, forcing him to a halt as my heart stuttered. Who had screamed? Why?

And more importantly, what the hell could I do about it?

CHAPTER 34

Wren

"Wake up. Wake up!"

I shook Caria again, but she just groaned and tried to roll away. Even in the gloom, I couldn't miss the bruises shadowing her pale skin. Blood had crusted under her nose and worse, on her thighs, but she was alive.

She was alive, and so was I.

Before Laurent went to meet Blane, he'd nodded toward me and ordered Rick to, "Put her with the other one."

Rick had retorted that, "I'm not your servant," but when Laurent stormed out, Rick shrugged and followed his instructions anyway. I couldn't quite work out their relationship. Rick didn't seem to like Laurent or even respect him, and yet he was staying in the man's house. Maybe they were bound together by some kind of supernatural bond, the way Blane claimed he and I were?

Whatever the reason for their relationship, I'd found myself in a small room at the back of the house, a space the size of my bathroom at home, lit by a single yellowing bulb.

When Rick had shoved me inside, I'd stumbled, tripped, and landed right on top of my best friend.

She'd barely stirred.

"Mmmmf."

Was Caria drunk? Drugged? Or worse, did she have a head injury? How were we supposed to get out of this house of horrors if she couldn't even stand? I rattled the door—locked—and looked around desperately for something I could use to break through the wood. But the room was almost empty, cleared out to be used as a makeshift prison. An unopened package of potato chips sat on a tray in the corner beside a full bottle of water, and a coat lay crumpled on the floor. There were more coats hanging on a rail, coats that probably never got worn in Vegas.

I wrenched off the bottle cap and splashed water on Caria's face, holding her steady when she squeaked and struggled.

"Sit up. You have to sit up, okay?"

She glared with unfocused eyes, and I hauled her upright. Somehow, we needed to escape from this nightmare. Would Rick come back? Or maybe...maybe Blane would save us? After what happened at Club Dead, I was scared of him, but Blane was definitely the lesser of the evils lurking in this luxury hellhole.

I heard footsteps approaching and held my breath. Friend or foe? Should I try yelling? There were guards in the mansion—I'd seen a pair of them striding toward the front of the house as Rick hustled me through the hallways, his hand clamped around the back of my neck.

"Help us!" I cried, but the footsteps kept going. A shadow passed across the sliver of light at the bottom of the door and disappeared. I backed up and then ran at the door, but rather than it flying open, I bounced off the wood with my shoulder throbbing. A sob threatened to burst free as I begged Caria again.

"Please, you need to get up. Because the next time this door opens, I'm really gonna need some help."

I put my eye to the keyhole and squinted, but the key was still in the lock, so I couldn't see anything useful at all.

Wait...

The key was still in the lock.

If I could wiggle it out and then work it back under the door...

Quickly, I grabbed one of the wire hangers from the rail and straightened out the hook. A moment later, the key hit the tile, and I prayed it hadn't bounced out of reach. I slid the hanger under the door and worked it around, hoping... There! I felt it move. I tried again to snag the key, focusing every ounce of concentration on listening for that faint metallic sound, then jumped out of my skin when I heard distant gunfire.

Perhaps that was why I missed the footsteps?

But I didn't miss the rattle of the key in the lock.

I scrambled back, shielding Caria, hoping for Blane but terrified that Laurent would be back to finish what he started. In that moment, I envied Caria her oblivion. My heart was threatening to give out.

The door creaked open, and I blinked in the light.

It wasn't Laurent.

It wasn't Blane either.

It was... "Vee?"

"Hurry, we need to get out of here. Is that Caria?"

"Yes, but she can't even stand. I don't know what they've done to her."

In a heartbeat, Vee slung a groaning Caria over her shoulder as if she weighed nothing, and suddenly, having a vampire on my side didn't seem quite so bad after all. She'd come to help me, and so had...

"Blane," I choked out. "Where's Blane? He came to see Laurent, but Laurent...he isn't normal."

"We realised that."

"No, I mean I shot him in the chest, and he didn't fall. It's like he's one of...one of you people."

"He's definitely not one of us," she said, and she sounded annoyed by the mere suggestion.

"I didn't mean a friend or anything. Just that he won't freaking die. And there's this other guy—"

"Shhh! Do you want to attract the attention of every guard in the place?"

No, of course I didn't. I wanted all of us to get out of this place without dying, and if Laurent was on the rampage... An unearthly howl sounded from outside, and I hurried to keep up with Vee.

Only to bump into her as she stopped short.

Oh, hell.

Rick was right in front of us, and even though he wasn't exactly friendly with Laurent, I wasn't sure he'd let us walk out of there either. But Vee was a badass. And also a vampire. Couldn't she suck out his blood or something? Yesterday, heck, even a few hours ago, the mere idea of that would have filled me with horror, but that was then and this was now. At this moment, I was cheering for the fangs.

But Vee didn't leap into action as I expected. No, she backed up and stepped on my foot. A little squeak escaped my lips.

"Well, hello, *ma petite épine*."

Wait, they knew each other?

"*Mon Dieu*," Vee whispered.

Caria fell to the floor as Rick grabbed Vee by the arm and hauled her toward him. Her scream froze my blood.

And...and I didn't understand. Vee was so strong, so confident, and yet this arrogant Frenchman was pulling her around like a rag doll.

"Hey! Let her go!"

Rick finally seemed to notice I was there.

"This doesn't concern you."

Anger overrode my last scraps of common sense, and I put my hands on my hips. "Are you freaking kidding me? You kidnapped my friend, you locked me in a closet, and now you're trying to dislocate my other friend's shoulder?"

"It's okay," Vee tried to reassure me, but I could see from the terror in her eyes that it was anything but.

"Women aren't possessions. You can't just order us around."

"This one belongs to me," Rick said, jerking Vee's arm. "Although she seems to have lost her wedding ring."

Wait, what? Was he saying what I thought he was saying? Vee was his *wife*? Married or not, she clearly didn't want to be anywhere near him, and wasn't she dating a cop? I grabbed her other arm and pulled, and the last thing I remembered was flying through the air.

Then everything went black.

CHAPTER 35

Wren

"Wren? Wren?" Someone was calling my name, but from a distance, or at least it sounded that way. "Wren, wake up."

The muffled words were followed by a searing pain, and my eyes flew open in time to see Myrtle raking her claws down my arm.

"Hey! Get lost."

Was I late giving her breakfast or something? Making me bleed sure wasn't the right way to ask for extra maple syrup. But Myrtle scratched me again, on my leg this time. What was her problem? I sat up to shoo her away, and when I saw Caria lying at my side and Delphine-slash-Lola kneeling over me, the memories came rushing back. Laurent, Rick, Vee... Where was Vee? I looked all around, but she was gone.

"Where's Vee?" I asked, although I didn't expect an answer, not when the only person capable of replying was a four-year-old stuck in somebody else's body.

"I didn't see her."

Which meant Rick had dragged her away. I'd found Caria but lost another friend instead. And now I knew the truth—Vee *was* a friend. Yes, she was a vampire, but she'd come here to save me, only to land in grave danger herself.

And Blane... He might have been the literal devil, but Laurent was the real monster.

Yelling came from outside. Had a neighbour called 911 yet? Was anyone close enough to hear the commotion? We needed help, but what could cops do against a man who shrugged off bullets and thought nothing of breaking the law? Vee was gone, I had no idea where Blane and Joseph were, and I was left with a cat, a preschooler, and a barely conscious Caria.

I had to keep them safe.

"What should I do?" I whispered, more to myself than anyone else.

"Mom says that if I'm scared, I should call her," Lola said.

I thought of Marianna, lying motionless on the floor under Aurelia's watch. "That won't work."

"But I have a phone. I found it in my pocket."

Should we run or hide? The only thing I knew for certain was that we couldn't stand around in the hallway. Where were all the guards?

"I know the number by heart," Lola said.

Pulse racing, I cracked open the nearest door. The room was in semidarkness, lit only by the full moon and a few decorative lights around the pool beyond, and as my eyes adjusted, I could make out couches grouped around a coffee table, squashy couches, not like the style-over-comfort furniture in the great room. I herded Lola inside, relieved when Myrtle followed, and then went back for Caria.

"Wren?" she mumbled.

Thank goodness. "Yes, it's me. Can you stand?"

In answer, she slumped against the wall. Dammit!

She'd always been much slimmer than me, and now she

was positively skeletal, but it still took an effort to haul her into the small living room where we were taking refuge. I dragged her behind the nearest couch, although if a guard appeared with a gun, the cushions wouldn't do much to stop a bullet. Where were the guards? I'd seen several earlier, but now the house was eerily quiet. All the noise was coming from outside.

"Mom?" Had Lola managed to make a call? "I want Mom."

"Shhh," I told her, mindful of Vee's words earlier. "Don't make a noise."

She held out the phone. "The lady wants you."

Tell me she isn't talking to an emergency dispatcher. What would I even say? *Oh hey, ma'am. I'm trapped in a house with two immortal psychos, one of them just grabbed my vampire saviour, and the devil is outside trying to help.* Did we need a SWAT team or an exorcist?

I pressed the phone to my ear. "Who is this?"

"Aurelia." Oh, thank goodness. "Where's Blane?"

"I don't freaking know!"

"Who's with you? Just Lola?"

"Caria, but she's delirious, and Myrtle too."

"Put Myrtle on the phone."

"How? Myrtle's a damn cat."

"She changed back? Oops, awkward."

"Changed back?" The horrifying truth suddenly dawned. Cat-Myrtle. Girl-Myrtle. The fact that I'd never seen the two of them in the same place at the same time. "You have to be kidding me."

"She doesn't have much control over the whole shape-shifting thing." Aurelia giggled. "Just find a spot to hunker down and wait for Blane and Joseph and Vee to do their thing."

"Vee's gone. Some guy grabbed her and I must have

blacked out, but I don't know how long for." A memory flitted past, and I closed my eyes and caught hold of it. "A wedding ring. He said something about a wedding ring, but I thought she was dating a cop?"

Silence.

"Aurelia?"

"I'm thinking. It might be Voltaire."

"Who's Voltaire?"

"Another vampire."

Another vampire? I tried not to hyperventilate. "He said his name was Rick, and he was strong enough to overpower her." Plus he'd grabbed my gun in a blink. "And fast. He was fast too."

"Okay, that sounds like Voltaire. Try to keep out of his way."

No kidding. "What do you think I'm doing? And there might be two of them. I shot Laurent and he didn't die, so I don't think he's human either." Another horrifying thought popped into my head. "What about the guards? Can they create more vampires?"

"Uh, probably?"

Great. Just great. My voice dropped to a whisper. "And Delphine? What if Lola's in a vampire body?"

"No, no, that's impossible. She died, and now her body has Lola's soul."

Thank goodness for small mercies. "We have to find Vee."

"To do that, you need to find Blane and Joseph first. They're the only ones strong enough to take on Voltaire."

I glanced out the window. The yard looked so peaceful, but danger lurked around every corner. Vampires, guards with guns, and— Holy crap! An enormous dog ran around the corner, and the dog was on fire. The beast launched itself into the swimming pool with a high-pitched howl, and water exploded upward like a geyser. Lola shrieked as it splattered against the window in front of us.

"What happened?" Aurelia demanded.

"A giant flaming dog just jumped into the swimming pool."

"Like, a guard dog?"

"How should I know?" It scrambled halfway out of the water, huge paws resting on the pool deck, and shook water off its head. Our gazes met through the glass, and I found myself staring into angry yellow-orange eyes.

"I don't like that doggy," Lola said, taking a step backward. I tried to join her, but my knees threatened to give way.

"Oh, shit."

"What?" Aurelia asked through the phone.

"The dog saw me."

"It's still outside, right?"

I eyed up the thin pane of glass between us as the beast climbed fully out of the pool and tilted its head to one side, probably trying to decide whether I'd be one bite or two.

"Yes, but I'm not sure that matters. And I'm not sure it's a guard dog either."

"So what is it?"

With its fur burned away, the creature reminded me of Zuul out of *Ghostbusters*, but that was just fiction. Wasn't it? I mean, I'd always assumed *Interview with the Vampire* was a figment of the author's imagination, but I'd clearly been wrong about that, hadn't I?

"Do you have a Gatekeeper in your world?" I asked Aurelia. "A Keymaster?"

"Uh, no? We don't have gates in the conventional sense."

Phew. "Okay, so maybe this thing is a...wolf?" I swallowed hard. "Its eyes are glowing yellow."

"Yellow? You're sure?"

"It's staring right at me."

And I knew, I just knew, that it was sizing me up, readying itself to smash through the glass. The moment I tried to run, it would spring. It was toying with me the way a cat—not Myrtle, obviously—would play with a mouse.

"Then it must be a werewolf," Aurelia said, slightly breathless. "How exciting. You need to find wolfsbane or a silver bullet."

Exciting? *Exciting?*

"I don't even know what wolfsbane is, and where the hell am I meant to find a silver bullet?"

"Wolfsbane is a plant with purple flowers, more of a weed really."

"It grows in Vegas?"

A pause. "Perhaps the silver bullet would be easier to get ahold of. Or a silver knife might work? As long as it goes right into the werewolf's brain, that's the important thing."

Oh sure, all I had to do was stick a silver object into its brain. Simple.

"Tell Blane I want to be buried rather than cremated."

"Don't be so negative. Blane and Joseph can help."

"Blane and Joseph are missing in action." And so was Laurent.

The werewolf took a step forward, its mouth curved in what seemed to be a grin, but when Lola clutched at my arm, those yellow eyes blazed as if it couldn't decide whether to be amused or annoyed by these pathetic humans who dreamed of survival when there was no way to escape.

Ticktock, ticktock.

Time was running out.

"Did you ever play hide-and-seek with your mom?" I asked Lola, and she nodded. "When I tell you to run, you need to hide, okay?"

I'd always known that coming here would be a suicide mission, and now I had one final job to do: draw the werewolf away from Lola, away from Caria, away from Myrtle. I wasn't scared of death, not anymore. Because thanks to Blane and Aurelia, I knew it wasn't the end. I'd be back, and next time around, I'd make smarter decisions. In my twenty-seven years of life, I'd only seen the surface of this world, but now I knew there was so much more to it than I'd ever imagined, some good, some bad. The devil had taught me about love, and the charming, hot guy with the sexy accent had taught me that looks could be deceiving. Maybe Blane would put flowers on my grave?

The werewolf sprang.

"Run!" I yelled, but before I could spin around, a blur came out of nowhere and barrelled into the beast. Another almighty splash, and this time, the wall of water carried with it a lawn chair that cracked the window. My turn to scream, and not just from the shock.

Because I recognised the man grappling with the werewolf in the pool. His clothing was in tatters, and his skin was shredded too, but it was unmistakably Blane.

And now there was only one thing that mattered.

Finding something sharp and silver.

Flowers on a grave.

I knew where to look.

CHAPTER 36

Wren

I sprinted blindly along the hallway, only to find myself sprawled on the floor, skidding along on my front as if I were on a slip 'n' slide, if the slip 'n' slide were made from Italian marble and the hose were spraying blood. Trying not to puke, I ploughed into a lump at the end and found myself face to face with a pile of entrails and... "Joseph?"

"My apologies. Things got slightly messy."

The metallic stench of blood hung thick in the air, and ruby drops fell from the huge, curved knife in his hand. His eyes glowed red. Instinct sent me scrambling backward, but I didn't get very far before I starfished onto my ass.

Joseph nudged the guard's body with a shiny leather shoe. "Relax. I've disposed of most of them, but there are a couple left somewhere at the rear."

Don't puke, don't puke, don't puke. Since I was already way, way beyond horrified, I accepted Joseph's offer of a hand because what was a little more blood between friends?

"What about Laurent?"

"Blane is taking care of Laurent."

"Blane is wrestling with a werewolf."

"Yes, exactly."

After the day I'd experienced, I don't know why I hadn't guessed.

"Laurent is the werewolf?" I asked, just to check.

Joseph chuckled. "We thought they were all in Eastern Europe, but what do you know? There's one right here in Vegas."

"Don't just stand there. Help Blane!"

"Blane can hurl fire at him for a few more minutes while I finish off the guards."

"Not in the swimming pool, he can't."

"They're in the swimming pool?"

"That's what I said, isn't it?"

"Oh. Oh dear. Blane only passed his hand-to-hand combat course because he slept with the professor."

"I did *not* need to know that," I snapped, and Beauregard had the grace to look chagrined. "According to Aurelia, we need something silver and stabby. Or a silver bullet, but who the heck has one of those?"

"Decima. It's her good-luck charm." He glanced around. "Aurelia's here?"

"No, we spoke on the phone while you were busy with your own personal remake of *Scream*."

"Being disembowelled slows people down. If they try to run, they trip over their... Never mind. So...silver, huh? Maybe we could stick a fork in his eye?"

"That would blind him, but I doubt it would reach his brain."

And I couldn't believe we were even having this conversation.

"Depends on how hard one drives it in there. Do you have a better idea?"

"Maybe."

I took off at a run again, feeling marginally better now that I had backup. And if Joseph had taken out most of the guards, then Caria, Lola, and Myrtle had a good chance of living. Blane and Vee were in the most danger, but Aurelia said I needed Blane to help Vee.

In the great room, I ran to the coffee table and snatched one of the long-stemmed silver roses out of the skull vase, squinting for a hallmark. *Please, please, please.* Judging by the decor in this place, Delphine had expensive taste, and I hoped she hadn't skimped when it came to the artwork.

Joseph quickly realised what I was doing, and he grabbed a flower as well.

"925 silver. Let's go."

Huh. Guess he had superhuman eyesight too.

And a better sense of direction than I did, because he set off without hesitation.

"Uh, now that we have the silver, how are we supposed to ram it into Laurent's brain? Don't you think we should address that before we go outside?"

"I'll take care of it."

He'll take care of it. As I hustled after him, it struck me that this was my opportunity to flee. Most of the guards were gone, and Laurent was preoccupied. I could grab Caria and run. I still had Blane's car key. But when I thought of him in the water, bruised and battered—for me—I realised I could no sooner leave him than leave my own soul.

Whether I liked it or not, whether I wanted to believe in his world or run screaming into the night, we were connected.

If I left him to his fate, I wouldn't be able to live with myself.

When we burst out the back door, Laurent was standing at the edge of the pool, his back to us, but Blane was nowhere in sight. But Joseph saw right away what I missed, and he didn't hesitate. He sprinted across the terrace with a rose in his outstretched hand, poised to leap at Laurent.

The gunshots came out of nowhere.

Bullets ripped into Joseph's chest, and he stumbled, looking more surprised than anything else.

The rose slipped from his fingers as he fell to his knees.

My own knees went weak as two guards stepped out of the pool house, their guns raised, firing again, focused only on the man dying before them. And Joseph *was* dying. Demon or not, his mortal body couldn't hold up against the bullets thudding into him. With the last of his strength, Joseph raised his knife, and I thought that maybe he'd try to take at least one of the men out.

I gasped as he turned the blade on himself, slashing a thick wound across his stomach.

Then I screamed as the darkness escaped.

For a moment, it was all around us, a swirling, rushing malevolent cloud that knocked over lawn chairs and tore plants out of the ground. A shower of dirt hit me, and I blinked grit out of my eyes in time to see the cloud adopt a humanoid shape and start advancing toward the guards.

The men dropped their weapons and ran.

Hell, I wanted to run too, but then an arm broke the water in front of me, and I realised where Blane was.

He was drowning.

And I was the only one with a rose.

I didn't stop to think things through. If I'd done that, my next stop would have been Texas. Instead, I ran across the terrace and leapt onto Laurent's back, gripping slippery tufts of fur as I clawed my way forward. He stank of charred steak, and the roar as he tried to shake me off was unreal. But I clung on, digging my fingernails into burned and blistered skin, hoping I hurt him as much as he'd hurt the women of Vegas. One giant paw rose, but he couldn't swipe me, not on his back.

"That's for Caria," I screamed as I plunged the stem of the rose into his left eye, right up to the petals.

His roar turned into a high-pitched yowl, and I plummeted into the pool as I finally lost my grip. It all happened so fast that I had no time to take a breath, and my lungs felt as if they were about to explode as I desperately tried to work out which way was up. But I had no time. Laurent toppled into the pool, the light in his eyes dimming, and I found myself forced down, down, down, and it didn't matter that I could see the moon. I'd never reach it. Laurent was too big…too heavy… I couldn't stand the burning in my chest any longer…

The last thing I saw was Blane's beautiful face.

Then I closed my eyes and…sprawled across the pool deck?

"Breathe, dammit." Blane thumped me on the back, and I vomited water over his feet. "Have you lost your mind?"

"Didn't…didn't want…you to die," I choked out. Literally choked. How much water had I swallowed?

"I can't die, my darling. I was just keeping him busy so he didn't turn his attention to you."

"But…but you're bleeding."

"I'm fine. The question is, are you okay?"

I burst into tears. Blane held me as I sobbed against his shoulder, my tears trickling down his now-flawless skin because honestly, there wasn't much left of his clothing.

"That's a really dumb question," I blubbered.

"That's fair." He kissed my hair, and even in the midst of the devastation, I felt an inexplicable sense of peace. "If you killed a werewolf to save me, does that mean I'm forgiven?"

I'd killed a freaking werewolf. *Me.* And I didn't even feel guilty about it.

"You still have a lot more grovelling to do."

He *had* come here to help me, but that didn't make up for all the half-truths.

"Anything." Another kiss. "Anything, I promise." Then he leaned back to look at me, and I saw the deep-seated pain in his amber eyes. "Is Lola...? Is she...?"

"I told her to hide. Most of the guards seemed to be dead by then"—dead, freaking *dead*—"and Joseph dealt with the rest, so I think she's okay. But Vee..." A sob welled up in my throat. "Laurent had a friend, and he took Vee. I think I blacked out, so I don't really know what happened, but when I woke up, she was gone."

"A man couldn't just take Vee."

"He wasn't a man." Another wave of emotions washed over me. "I th-th-think he was a vampire. Maybe her husband?"

"Fuck. Voltaire? Voltaire took her?"

"He told me his name was Rick."

"Cédric Voltaire. Joseph!" Blane called. "We have another problem."

Was this ever going to end?

CHAPTER 37
Blane

A man ran out of the house, a stranger dressed in ill-fitting khaki clothing, and I focused on his soul. It stayed firmly stuck. Planes above and below, how many celestial beings were in this place? I tucked Wren behind me and prepared to get my hands dirty again, but then I saw the twitching.

Joseph.

"What happened to your other body?"

"It broke, and this was the only one available. What do you think of it? Feet too big?"

The whole thing was hideous.

"Forget the feet. Voltaire has Vee."

"Voltaire? How...?"

"He was here. We need to search every building." I kissed Wren chastely on the lips. "Start with the pool house —if it's clear, Wren can wait in there."

"Are you serious right now?" Wren went back to glaring. "You survived a fight with a werewolf—the safest place in the world is in your shadow."

She was correct, but if Joseph and I had to take on

Voltaire, that wasn't something Wren needed to witness. One of the reasons Joseph was in admin rather than enforcement was his tendency to make a mess.

"You've seen enough blood for today, my darling."

"No kidding—I already slipped in entrails. But I'm still not staying here on my own. Plus Caria's drugged, Myrtle turned into a cat, and we need to find Lola." Wren blew out a breath. "*Myrtle turned into a cat.* That's a sentence I never thought I'd utter, and I can't believe you kept that from me as well."

"Would you have believed me if I'd told you?"

Wren deflated slightly. "Probably not. Unless I saw her transform, I guess."

"That might happen. She has no control over it."

No, she just itched like crazy for a minute or so—her signal to get out of sight—and *pop.* She changed form. Interestingly, Laurent had appeared to shift at will, so perhaps there was hope for Myrtle? Although Laurent had also been able to speak in his animal form, so maybe they didn't have much in common after all.

"Can we just hurry up and rescue Vee?" Wren asked.

Back at the apartment, she'd been timid and reserved, flight rather than fight. But here at the monster's mansion, I was seeing a different side of her. Throw Wren into the middle of a crisis, and she found the confidence normally lacking.

Forget the aetherbond, that courage alone made me want her more. How many of my kin found a woman willing to go head-to-head with a werewolf in a foolhardy quest to save an immortal? Grovelling aside, the love I felt for her wasn't one-sided. She felt it too.

Laurent floated motionless, his remaining eye staring sightlessly at the stars. The first werewolf I'd ever seen outside of ancient journals, and hopefully the last. Were they all like him? Intolerable assholes? Or were they like vampires and humans—a mix of good, bad, and indifferent?

"Stay behind me," I instructed Wren. She'd picked up a gun one of the guards had dropped, and I wasn't about to suggest she leave it behind, not when she had her mouth set in a thin line and her eyes narrowed.

She gripped my hand as we headed inside, and Joseph brought up the rear. It was easy to see the path he'd taken through the house. Blood trails, random lumps of flesh, brain matter splattered on the walls... Freed of his mortal bounds, he turned into a twilight tornado. Once again, I'd need to explain the concept of moderation, but this wasn't the time or the place.

"It's possible they've left already," I said as we skirted a mangled corpse. Wren studiously looked away from the mess. "Even on foot, they could be far away by now. Vee moves supernaturally fast, and I suspect Voltaire has the same gift."

"Voltaire also has a car. A black Mercedes. He parked it out front."

"You saw him arrive?"

"Uh, yes?" Her cheeks flushed. "He might have given me a ride for the last part."

I stared at her.

"He seemed polite," she defended.

"I didn't say a word."

"But you're thinking it." She heaved a sigh. "I always thought I was a good judge of character, but these past two weeks have been a real eye-opener."

Was that a dig at me? I thought it might be, but we didn't need to get into a fight, not at this moment.

"Joseph, check for the car."

He stumbled as he hurried off, still unaccustomed to the new body. The twitching was worse than usual this time.

Explaining why my assistant had morphed from a slender, reasonably handsome lawyer into a muscle-bound fool who dressed in tasteless cargo pants would also be a challenge, but one I'd tackle later. I nudged open the nearest door and found a minimalist half bath. Empty.

"I'm worried about Caria," Wren whispered. "Lola too. What if Voltaire finds them?"

"If he has Vee, he won't be interested in anything else."

Joseph returned quickly. "There are no vehicles parked in front of the house."

"Dammit all to Plane Three. We need to find them."

"We're not leaving without Caria and Lola," Wren said. "And what about Myrtle?"

"Myrtle understands priorities, and she'll get herself out."

But of course we needed to find Lola. She had neither the knowledge nor the ability to make her own way home, and if Caria was drugged, she'd need help too. But every second we wasted in this house was another nail in Vee's coffin, metaphorically speaking. Vampires didn't really sleep in coffins. Well, it was possible Voltaire did, but Vee had a California king with far too many pillows. Callahan complained about them constantly.

Joseph tilted his head to one side. "I think I hear crying. Kind of muffled, though. These ears are full of wax."

That was a visual I didn't need. "Which direction?"

He considered for a moment, then pointed toward the front of the house. "Through there."

When we reached the hallway, Joseph stopped, and I heard the soft sniffles myself. But there was nobody around. Unless... I yanked open the door of the credenza by the Medusa stairs, and Lola tumbled out.

"Ow!" she yelped.

How on earth had she managed to fit in there? In her previous life, Delphine must have been a contortionist.

Wren dropped to her knees. "Are you okay?"

"My legs are all tingly."

"I'm not surprised," I said, and that earned me another glare from Wren.

"I want to go home."

"Soon, sweetie," Wren promised. "I can drive you after we find Caria."

"I want Lucian to drive me."

"Lucian has to help Vee. A bad man has her."

"The man who hit her?"

"Yes." Wren gave a wet-sounding sniffle and nodded. "I'm so sorry you saw that."

"The man didn't take Vee."

What?

I crouched and gripped Lola's arms. "What do you mean, he didn't take her?"

"It...it went dark and scary."

Lola's turn to sniff, and Wren reached over to loosen my fingers. Lola's skin had turned white, and the old feelings of guilt resurfaced in a crashing wave. Fuck. I let go and gripped her hand instead.

"It's okay. It's okay. Just take your time."

"The dark went everywhere." *Joseph.* When anger filled him, he literally couldn't contain himself. "And the man who hurt Vee ran down the stairs, and he was saying all the bad words. And then he ran out the door."

Why? Why would he leave alone? Vee was scared enough of Voltaire that when she realised he was in Vegas, she'd almost skipped the country. Only Callahan's job and the fact that I'd promised to protect her had kept her in Vegas.

It was another promise I'd broken.

The devil had a reputation for lying, but I'd never done

so intentionally, not to my friends. Turned out that my father had been right after all—I was a screwup.

And if Lola was correct, then Vee was upstairs.

Wren must have had the same thought because she stared toward the mass of writhing silver snakes and bit her lip.

"What did he do to her?" she asked softly.

I didn't want to find out.

But I had to.

I ran for the stairs with Joseph, and we thundered up to the second floor. How many rooms did this place have? Doors, so many doors. I kicked open the first and found a bedroom, one that hadn't seen a housekeeper in weeks. Clothes strewn across the floor, dirty mugs on a chest of drawers, tangled bedding. No Vee.

The next room was set up for fun and games. A spanking bench, a Saint Andrew's cross, a rack full of whips, chains, and assorted leather implements. This was the logical place for Voltaire to have brought Vee for punishment, but there was no sign of her.

I turned for door number three and nearly tripped over Myrtle.

"Look where you're going," I snapped.

She must have been taking glaring lessons from Vee because she fixed me with a death stare. If cat-Myrtle had been able to talk, every word would be bleep-worthy.

"Wait in the car," I told her, and of course she ignored the instruction. Instead, she lashed out with a claw and left deep gouges in my shin, then ran deeper into the house.

I was about to curse her again when I glanced down at the damage.

An arrow.

She'd carved a fucking arrow into my leg.

And then I understood.

And I ran.

She led me through a bedroom to a closed door, one that might have been to a bathroom or a walk-in closet or a... personal tanning room.

The barely audible whimpers coming from within tore my heart apart for the second time this decade, but as I ripped the power cable out of the socket, that heartache turned to fury. I had no idea how to kill a vampire, but I'd spend the rest of my life working it out.

Voltaire was a dead man.

He'd imprisoned Vee in the tanning bed, a heavy chain and padlock—presumably borrowed from the room of kink—fastening it shut. She might not have been able to die, but the air was thick with the smell of burned flesh, and she was terrifyingly still. There were some fates worse than death.

"Lock picks?" I asked Joseph.

"I left them with my other body."

"Get them. Hurry!"

"They probably got shot to pieces. We need a plan B. Can't we just tear the tanning bed apart? Or shake her out the end?"

The chain wrapped around the ends, and wasn't she in enough pain already? Punching glass shards into her raw wounds would only make matters worse.

"Vee, we're trying to help you," I said. "We're here."

"What's that smell?" The voice came from the doorway, and I spun to see Wren. She hung on to Lola to stop her coming any closer, and with her other hand, she held the pistol in a death grip. "It's like well-done—" Her expression turned to horror. "Oh no."

Oh yes.

"Give me the gun."

"Why?"

But she held it out anyway, and I studied the padlock. "I saw this in a movie once. Take Lola into the hallway."

"Uh, is shooting at a padlock safe?"

"Does it matter? It's not as if I can die. Joseph, go with them. You don't want to ruin another body, and there isn't a spare."

Wren was absolutely right about the safety aspect. It took three shots to shatter the padlock, and a shard of metal lodged itself in my thigh, dangerously close to my left testicle. The wound healed fast, but it still stung like a bitch.

Although that pain was nothing compared with Vee's. I flung back the lid of the tanning bed, and for the first time in my life, I felt nauseated. It wasn't just the melted flesh, or the blistering, or the stink; it was the fact that Vee was a friend.

Wren did throw up. Lola was crying, even as I tried to shield her from the sight of Vee's animated corpse.

"What do we do?" Wren whispered. "If we get her to a hospital...?"

"A hospital can't help. Usually, she heals almost instantly, but the UV light has caused damage beyond her ability to repair."

"There must be something... We could call Aurelia? She might know?"

"There's only one thing." And it was the request I could never make, not of Wren. Not when she'd already been thrust into a world she'd never wanted to be a part of. "Blood. Vee needs blood."

CHAPTER 38

Wren

Blood.

The word rang in my ears as I stared down at Vee. Except she wasn't Vee anymore. She was a pile of reddened flesh and sinew, with grey-white bones visible through her peeling skin.

And she was my friend.

She'd come here to save me.

"How much blood?" The words stuck in my throat, but I choked them out.

"Honestly, I don't know."

People donated blood in hospitals every day, didn't they? I could live without keeping all of mine. The prospect of being vampire food terrified me, I wasn't going to lie, but the thought of leaving Vee in this state was a hundred times worse. I didn't want to lose a friend. Yes, realising she wasn't entirely human had been a shock, but today, I'd also learned there was true evil in the world. And I'd rather hang out with the good team of supernatural beings than risk dying at the hands of the bad.

My arm trembled as I held it out.

"I don't know what to do."

"Hold your wrist to her mouth."

It took a moment to even work out where her mouth was, but suddenly one of her eyes opened, and I saw a spark of hope among the bloodshot veins. Sharp teeth pierced my skin, but it didn't hurt. I'd expected it to hurt.

Vee drank greedily, and one slimy hand came up to hold my arm. Her grip tightened when Blane pried her away from me. I staggered backward, and Joseph caught me by my armpits.

"That's enough. No more," Blane said.

"I can't...I can't..." Vee's voice was the whisper of a breeze through the trees, so quiet I had to lean close to listen. My blood had helped, but it wasn't enough. And now...now my wrist had healed. I'd expected the wound to keep bleeding, but the holes closed up as I watched and there was nothing but unblemished skin.

"She needs more."

Blane shook his head. "It's not safe. We're not risking your health."

"Then...Lola."

"I can't."

I understood what he meant: that he wouldn't ask her. That he *couldn't* ask her. Guilt had finally caught up with him, guilt for violating both my and Nevaeh's trust, and remorse had hit at the worst possible moment.

Which meant it was down to me.

I stroked Lola's hair. She was taller than me, even barefoot, but she was no woman. Inside, she was still a little girl, and using her would leave me racked with guilt too. But better to offend my conscience than to let Vee suffer.

"Lola, you need to give Vee your wrist."

"I don't wanna."

"It won't hurt, I promise. Vee really, really needs you."

"It's yucky."

"Close your eyes."

Maybe I'd go to hell for coercing her into this, but if Blane's sister ran the place, then that might not be too bad. I kept telling myself that this wasn't really Lola's body, that we'd set out down this dark path so she could be a normal four-year-old girl again.

Vee bit into her wrist, and Lola giggled.

"It tickles."

"Only for a minute."

Vee was getting stronger—I could see it in the way she fought Blane when he decided she'd had enough from Lola —but she wasn't healing. Why wasn't she healing? The concern on Blane's face was all too obvious.

"I'll bring Caria," Joseph murmured.

"She's at the back of the house," I told him. "We were in a room overlooking the pool."

After he left, Blane and I looked at each other, and he answered my unasked question with a shrug. *What if it's not enough?*

"Could you or Joseph...?"

"I don't know," he admitted. "Not Joseph. He doesn't even bleed if you cut him."

Vee was pitiful. That was the best word to describe her. She'd always been so friendly and full of life, and now she was knocking on death's door, but he wouldn't let her in. Watching her struggle, I understood the true meaning of the phrase "ignorance is bliss." If I'd never found out about Dom's affair, if I'd stayed in Wyoming, I might not have been happy, but I would have been oblivious to this dark new world I found myself thrust into.

Joseph dumped Caria at Vee's side, and if there was one thing to be grateful for, it was that the drugs hadn't worn off yet. She had no idea what was going on.

Vee drank, and I gripped Blane's hand as Vee's shallow, ragged breaths became deeper.

"Is that good?" I asked.

"I think so."

But Blane had to stop her. After everything we'd gone through to save Caria, sacrificing her wasn't an option, which left only one possibility. Himself. And we didn't have time to agonise over the pros and cons—sound travelled, and even though we were out in the desert, there was a chance that the cops were already on their way.

Joseph checked his watch. "Hurry up and make a decision. You know if Great-Uncle Tiberius were here, he'd do it."

"You're not exactly selling this. Remember when Great-Uncle Tiberius created the cencorn? I heard that was something to do with angel blood."

Cencorn? "Dare I ask what that is?"

"Half man, half unicorn, constantly grumpy, great hair."

Vee groaned from the tanning bed, and I couldn't even offer her a hug.

"Just do it," I said. "We can't leave her here, and we can't stay either."

Blane gave the heaviest sigh, muttered words under his breath that might have been a prayer or a curse, and offered Vee his wrist. He winced when she bit. Gritted his teeth as she drank. And like magic, her skin began to reform, pale, so pale it was almost translucent. Her hair came back, although now it was blonde rather than turquoise. Vee became Vee again. She didn't grow horns or hooves or claws. No, she sat up, blinked a few times, and spat out a mouthful of blood.

"Yeuch. You taste disgusting."

"You're welcome."

She closed her eyes for a long moment and worked her neck from side to side. Bones popped.

"*Mon Dieu*," she whispered.

"It's okay." Blane smoothed her hair. "You're okay."

"Voltaire was here, and I couldn't... He grabbed me, and he's stronger than ever." A sob burst from her. "I have to get out of Vegas."

"We can discuss that later."

"What if he's still here? What if he's hiding downstairs? Or outside?"

"He left. His car is gone."

"No. No, he wouldn't just..." Vee gasped. "We need to go. Right now. Run."

"Is running a good idea?" Blane asked. "Three humans have each lost over a pint of blood, and until two minutes ago, you were more or less dead."

"You don't understand. The only reason Voltaire would have left was so he could hurt me more. He called the cops, I know it."

"To his friend's home?"

"Voltaire doesn't have friends. He has people he uses and then throws away."

"He didn't seem to like Laurent much," I put in.

Blane didn't hesitate any longer. "Find Vee something clean to wear while Joseph and I fetch the vehicles. Wait by the gates."

Then he disappeared. He took Joseph by the arm, stepped forward, and vanished into thin air. Vee's jaw dropped.

"You never saw him do that before?" I asked.

She shook her head. "No. You?"

"Nuh-uh."

"Can we go home yet?" Lola tugged at my hand. "I don't like it here."

"Sure, we can go home."

CHAPTER 39

Wren

Vee's Porsche was a definite step up from Blane's car. If I ever won the lottery, it might even be at the top of my list. Lola was sitting in the passenger seat with cat-Myrtle on her lap, pointing out things that began with G. We'd already done A through F. Caria was lolling sideways in the back seat, carefully belted in, and with the sun peeping over the horizon, Vee was curled up alongside with a blanket covering her. The last thing she needed today was more UV damage, especially since Blane wasn't with us.

He'd stayed behind with Joseph to handle the cleanup at Laurent's mansion. Rumours of werewolves were best left to conspiracy websites and kooks, and if Laurent's corpse remained in the pool, it would end up on the front page of the *National Inquisitor*. Nobody except Voltaire wanted that.

And Vee was right about the cops. As I drove steadily toward Club Dead, making sure to stick to the speed limit, I heard the sirens in the distance, heading toward the edge of the desert. My job was to get us back safely, and I wasn't going to mess it up.

But somebody else already had.

As we neared the Medical District, traffic backed up, and I saw flashing lights ahead. A car accident. A black Mercedes crumpled into the side of a dump truck, blocking the roadway. Cops were directing the traffic, sending people off down a side street, but everyone was slowing to look at the wreck.

Including me.

Because I thought that maybe I recognised the car.

I'd ridden in one remarkably similar earlier this evening.

"What's happening?" Vee asked. "Why are we going so slowly?"

"There's a car crash ahead. I think it might be Voltaire."

"What?" She sat up, the blanket still on her head, like a dark ghost in a funhouse. "No, no, no, it's a trap."

"It might not be him. It's just that the car looks similar."

"Turn around." Her voice rose an octave. "Turn around right now!"

"Turn around, turn around, turn around," Lola sang. Why wasn't she tired yet?

"He didn't even know we'd be coming this way," I told Vee. "And it's daylight now. Doesn't he have to stay inside in daylight?"

"Yes, but he could have another accomplice. He always thinks ten steps ahead. Please, I can't be here."

"Okay, okay." I spotted a gap in the traffic and made a U-turn. "We'll go the long way."

I should have looked behind me.

Dom had always told me to use my mirrors more, and maybe, just maybe, he'd been right about that one tiny thing.

The siren made me jump, and I prayed it was for someone else, but then the flashing lights lit up the inside of the car, and my guts clenched in fear. Laurent had cop friends. What if Voltaire was cosy with them too? Was Vee right? Was this all a setup?

"Don't stop," Vee said.

For a long second, I considered trying to outrun the police. In Blane's car, it would have been impossible, but this was a Porsche, and I had a quarter tank of gas left. Would that be enough? What if a helicopter joined the chase?

Then I saw more traffic ahead and realised I had no choice.

"I have to. Just stay quiet and let me handle it."

There were witnesses, drivers crawling along in their cars and folks out walking their dogs before it got too warm. And I wasn't alone. A corrupt cop might have been able to abduct Caria, but he wouldn't be able to snatch four people, especially when one of them had the belligerence of a toddler.

I slowed.

Rolled down the window.

Waited.

"Ma'am, do you know why I pulled you over?"

"Uh, no?"

"You made an illegal U-turn." Then he peered past me. "And it isn't safe to have a cat riding loose in your vehicle. It should be in a carrier."

"C is for cat," Lola announced proudly.

"I'm aware of that, miss." The officer turned back to me. "I'm going to need to see your driver's licence."

Shit. "I... Uh, I do have a licence, but I left in a hurry this morning, and my purse is at home."

I mean, probably? It might have burned up in the fire.

"Driving without a licence in your possession is a misdemeanour, ma'am."

"I know that, and I swear, this is the first time I've forgotten it."

"If I had a buck for every time I've heard that line... Gimme your full name and date of birth."

"Wren Margaret Gillebrand, and I was born on August ninth—" The groan from the back seat made the cop's head snap up and my heart sink. Dammit, Caria! "That's my friend. She's not feeling so good."

Now the cop had his face pressed to the rear window, squinting through the tinted glass. Uh-oh.

"What the...?" His radio crackled, but he ignored it as he backed up and drew his gun. "Ma'am, step out of the car."

Once more, I considered trying to run, but a crowd was gathering now. More police were heading our way. My pulse ratcheted up as I unlocked the door and climbed out, and the cop looked me up and down, eyes wide. Yes, okay, I was an absolute mess. Thank goodness I'd fallen into the pool, or the blood would have been all too obvious.

"Hands where I can see them."

"I don't have any weapons."

The gun was back at Laurent's home, thank goodness. The only weapon in the car was Vee, and I had no idea what she would do if she was cornered. Run? Fight? Dissolve into a pile of smoking flesh again?

"What's under the blanket?" the cop asked, ignoring the blip of his radio for the second time.

"My friend. She's tired."

"Your friend is sitting up."

"There are two people in there."

"One, two, three, four, five, six, seven," Lola chipped in.

"What's up with her?" the cop asked, his brows pinching together.

"She has some difficulties."

The main one being that her four-year-old soul had been

dumped into a thirty-something body, but I'd be committed if I told the cop that.

"Ah," he said and pulled open the rear door. My heart leapt into my throat as he aimed his gun at Vee. "You under the blanket. Sit up."

Caria was blocking the sun, but Vee couldn't see that.

"It's all right," I told her. "You're in shadow."

The cop gave me a funny look, and I glared at him. What? It wasn't illegal to tell somebody where the sun was.

Vee slid the blanket off her head and sat up, squashed against Caria. "I wasn't driving."

"No, but you were riding in a moving vehicle without wearing a seat belt. The fine for that is twenty-five bucks, and I'll have to issue a citation."

"Thatsh mean," Caria slurred, and *this* was the moment she chose to wake up? I was beyond happy to hear her voice, don't get me wrong, but a few more minutes of silence would have been good.

"Ma'am, are you okay?" the cop asked.

"She's drunk." The last thing I needed was for him to take a closer look.

"Drunk? Ma'am, have you taken any illegal substances?"

"Like, probably?"

His grip on the gun tightened. "Everyone, get out of the vehicle."

Oh, hell. "I was the one who made the illegal U-turn. Can't you just give me a ticket and let us go?"

A female cop was approaching, plus another squad car had pulled up. Running wasn't an option anymore. From the corner of my eye, I saw Myrtle jump off Lola's lap, and what was she planning to do? Scarper? Claw the cop? She'd get herself picked up by animal control, and couldn't just one thing go right today? The urge to sit and rock was almost unbearable, and a tear slipped down my cheek.

"I'm sorry, okay? I'm sorry I ever came to this freaking city."

"Wren said a bad word." Lola managed to get her seat belt undone and scrambled out of the car. "You're not supposed to say bad words."

"'Freaking' isn't a bad word."

"It isn't?"

"You can say 'freaking,'" the female cop on the other side of the Porsche agreed. She came across as more chill than the guy with the gun, and an amused smile played across her face. "It's the other F-word that's the problem."

"Fox?" Lola asked, puzzled.

"Something like that."

The sound of retching came from the back seat. *Oh no.* Good Cop had fast reflexes as well as a sense of humour, and she yanked the door open. Caria staggered out, and the female cop jumped sideways just in time to avoid Caria puking on her shiny black shoes.

But my attention was on Vee. She fell backward, and sunlight splashed across her face. I waited for the sizzle or the smoke or whatever happened when she faced her nemesis, but...nothing. Her skin stayed smooth and milky.

And she seemed as surprised as I was, if her frown was anything to go by.

"Out of the car," Bad Cop said again, and gingerly, Vee stepped into the daylight, looking ready to run at any moment. The sequins on her borrowed cocktail dress sparkled—it was the first item of clothing we'd happened upon that fit. "Ma'am, I need your name."

"Genevieve—"

"Stubbs, you got a problem with your radio?" The next newcomer wasn't wearing a uniform, but I could tell he was a cop. His bearing and attitude gave the game away, as did the gun at his hip.

Bad Cop snapped his head around. "I'm in the middle of a stop here."

"There's a serious incident out past Iron Mountain. The captain wants you over there."

"He does?"

"Right away."

"I can handle the stop," Good Cop offered. "You know Captain Lindsay hates ditherers."

Getting into the captain's good graces was clearly more important than a traffic violation, because Stubbs climbed back into his car and took off toward Iron Mountain. I only hoped Blane had successfully disposed of Laurent's corpse, or I could be charged with considerably more than a moving violation. What was the penalty for killing a werewolf in Nevada?

"You okay?" the newcomer asked Vee, and there was a familiarity in his voice that hadn't been there before.

"I'm okay. It's been a long night, is all. Wren, this is Shep. He's a friend of Jack's." She nodded toward Good Cop. "And this is Jack's partner, Daphne."

Daphne grinned as she passed Caria a tissue. "Stubbs is such an asshole. But don't make any more U-turns, okay?"

"I swear I won't. What happened up there?"

"Some douche in a Mercedes was speeding, and *bam*. He came out of nowhere and hit the dump truck."

"Was the driver injured?" Vee asked.

"Who knows? He ran off, so I guess he wasn't hurt too bad. What happened at Iron Mountain?"

"A fire," Shep said. "From the way the place went up, the CSIs suspect there might've been a meth lab at the property. Folks are travelling out there to watch and getting in the way."

Blane had incinerated the mansion? Laurent's house of

horrors had also been his funeral pyre? That was...brilliant. Nothing less than he deserved.

"I should head to the station and meet Callahan," Daphne said. "I'm not even supposed to be here."

"And you should head indoors," Shep said to Vee. "Don't you get a rash if you stay outside too long?"

"The photosensitivity is a little better at the moment."

The words seemed to stick in her throat, and I knew why. Not only why they stuck, but why she wasn't burning up. Blane's blood had changed Vee on some fundamental level. Whatever she'd been before, that wasn't what she was now.

Shep studied her for a long moment before offering a smile. "Good, that's good. Daphne, the car is registered to a Raphael Laurent. Probably stolen. The address is out near Iron Mountain."

"It's all happening over there today. You want Callahan and me to pay him a visit?"

"You mind? My shift finished an hour ago."

"We'll go."

Huh. Might be tricky.

"Well, we should get out of your way," I tried. "It looks as if you have a lot to deal with this morning."

Shep looked from me to Vee, and then his gaze fell on Lola, and Caria, and Myrtle, who'd ambled back to the Porsche and jumped onto the hood.

"That your cat?"

"It's Blane's cat." Vee smiled brightly. "She escaped again. So, uh, good luck with the accident investigation."

CHAPTER 40

Wren

I t felt like a lifetime ago that I'd left Club Dead.

And maybe it was? Like Vee had experienced, something in me had fundamentally changed since yesterday. Not physically, but I was a different person now. Against the odds, I'd survived the trip to Laurent's lair, and now I was stuffed with fears for the future, a thousand bad memories, and secrets I could never tell.

Caria was tucked up in a guest room in Vee's penthouse apartment. Thanks to the drugs, she'd remained more or less oblivious to the otherworldly goings-on last night, and that was the way it needed to stay. Vee had offered a place for her to sleep it off while we dealt with the aftermath—the mess in Blane's apartment, Lola's fate, and for me, a very uncomfortable talk with my former beau.

I was dreading that part.

But the thought of walking away and never seeing him again? I hated that too.

"Are you okay?" I asked Vee as I turned the Porsche into the parking lot at Club Dead. Lola was asleep in the back seat, Myrtle too, although I figured Myrtle was only pretending. She was sneaky. And Vee seemed kind of...nervous.

"This is the first time in over two hundred years that I've purposely sat in sunlight, and I keep waiting for my skin to start smoking."

"After everything that happened last night, you should enjoy the fairy-tale ending."

"Fairy-tale ending? As in, the clock strikes midnight and everything goes back to the way it was?"

I let out a sigh. "If only."

Vee glanced across at me. "You're worried about what happens next?"

"How can I not be?"

"I know how you feel."

"Do you? No offence, but you're a freaking vampire, and Blane can kill people with his mind."

"Honestly, I was terrified after Voltaire got his teeth into me. The day after he forced me to marry him, I jumped off the Pont Neuf, and that was when I realised I couldn't die. And worse, neither could he. It took years for me to get away, and I thought I'd be alone forever, but then I met Jack, and... Now it's all falling apart again."

"I can't believe you're married to that psycho. I mean, he seemed okay when I first met him. Kinda charming. And then...yikes."

"He's a monster. But Blane is no Voltaire."

"I'm not sure I can trust anyone anymore."

"That's understandable."

Curiosity got the better of me. "How did you and Jack end up...you know? I guess you didn't list your origins on Tinder?"

Vee choked out a strangled laugh. "Tinder?" She shuddered. "I don't date. I mean, I didn't date. The last thing I was looking for was a boyfriend. But my friend died, and he was investigating her murder, and he just kept showing up."

"I'm sorry about your friend."

"Her name was Serenity. I miss her so much."

"Did Jack find the person who did it?"

Vee nodded. "Yes, he did. And then the guy shot him," she added softly. "Blane's sisters saved his life, and then my secrets came out. I was going to leave because I didn't think Jack could possibly want me anymore, but he looked past the vampire thing and saw me. Really saw me. So I stayed."

"And he's okay with giving you blood?"

"I only need a little."

Wow. That must be some relationship. "Does Blane have any...unusual needs?"

"Not that I'm aware of. He comes across as a bit awkward and standoffish, but once you get past his outer shell, he's a good man. Kind. Protective too, but I think you've already seen that side of him."

"You think I should stay with him?"

"I think you loved him before you found out about the planes, and beneath the unusual abilities, he's still the same person you fell for."

"But he tried to keep all that stuff from me. I'm not sure he even told Nevaeh."

"Because he was scared of rejection. And quite rightly so."

I blew out a long breath. "I don't want to get hurt again."

"Think positive—if Blane finds it hard to meet women, he's less likely to cheat."

"Oh, please. What about the three-hour girls?"

"Did you know he called Barry McKee two days ago and told him to clean out his personal suite at Tilt?"

"He did?"

"Going forward, it's to be used as a regular guest room."

"Really?"

"He doesn't want the three-hour girls. He only wants you."

Wasn't that what I'd always craved? For somebody to want me? My parents hadn't wanted me. Dom hadn't wanted me. The only constant in my life had been Kayden, but he had a career, a girlfriend, his own hopes and dreams. Blane cared. Even if he sometimes showed it in strange ways, I couldn't deny that he cared.

And Vee was right—I had loved him.

Maybe I still did.

The man who'd fought a freaking werewolf for me.

"I need to talk with him."

"Just promise to listen."

"Ohmigosh! I can't believe you found a real werewolf." Aurelia ran across Blane's apartment and flung her arms around me. "How big was it? Did it walk on two legs or four? This is *fascinating*."

"Fascinating? I was terrified."

"Why? Blane was with you, wasn't he?" She glanced behind me. "Where is he now?"

"Cleaning up."

Vee walked past, carrying a still-sleeping Lola in her arms.

"Don't go into the big bathroom," Aurelia called. "I put the bodies in there."

Yeuch, I'd almost forgotten about the first lot of bodies. If we managed to get Lola's soul back to its rightful home, how much of last night would she remember? I hoped not much at all. I looked past Aurelia to Marianna, still cradling her frozen daughter. She hadn't moved an inch. Pablo was sleeping on the couch, and judging by the laptop sitting open on the coffee table, it looked as if Aurelia had discovered YouTube.

"Is he...?" I pointed at Pablo.

"Is he what?"

"You know...frozen?"

She broke into a smile. "Oh, no. Pausing people for a long time drains me, so it was better to leave him awake. He's just tired." She pointed to a wonky house made from plastic bricks in the corner. "He's been busy building most of the day. So, what happened to the werewolf? Do you have pictures?"

The answer came from behind me. "I dropped it off at the Academy. Someone can use it as a science project."

I whirled to see Blane standing at the top of the stairs, wearing...sweats? They were too short, and he'd paired them with sneakers that reminded me of clown shoes. I couldn't help it. I burst into giggles.

"What?"

"Where did you get those clothes?"

"From a closet."

"Laurent's closet?"

His faint grimace said it all. "I suspect it might have been. Give me a moment to change, and I'll burn them. Where's Lola?"

Vee reappeared from the hallway that led to the bedrooms. "Sleeping. Her energy levels finally crashed."

"Wait, the windows." Blane leapt to pull down the blinds, but I put a hand on his arm.

"There's no need."

"There is, I can assure you. It's not just tanning beds that Vee can't tolerate."

"I've changed." She walked past him and stood in front

of the window, letting the sun bathe her in its light. "Everything's changed."

"You changed her," I told him.

Aurelia looked from me to Blane to Vee. "Wait, what's going on?"

I told her. Between tears, apologies, and the occasional sniffle, I told her everything that had happened since we left Club Dead last night. Vee helped out, and when Joseph arrived with breakfast, he added a few words too. Far from being horrified, Aurelia was equal parts annoyed and intrigued.

"I can't believe I missed all that! Why did I end up with the second-rate gift? Blane throws flames and souls here, there, and everywhere, and Decima mends people. When I work, literally nothing happens."

"That's still pretty special."

"It's so boring."

"Even with YouTube?"

"I don't understand YouTube. Girls dancing with llamas? Boys wilfully trying to kill themselves by jumping off cliffs? Are they trying to attract Decima?"

"They'd quickly regret that," Joseph muttered. "Who wants coffee? I brought pastries from Gerard's."

"Can we sit on the terrace?" Vee asked.

Aurelia and Joseph followed her outside, and I noticed Aurelia angled her seat so she could still see Marianna and her family through the glass.

"Does the 'direct visual contact' thing apply to her too?"

"Yes and no. She needs direct eye contact to stop time completely, but she can slow time by visualising a particular place. Long-distance work exhausts her, though. It's more likely to happen by accident when she's emotional."

"Like, she gets upset, and somewhere on the planet a plane falls out of the sky?"

"The plane doesn't fall. It just doesn't go anywhere, and the airline blames the delay on a strong headwind. Or sometimes it arrives at its destination too fast."

"And then it's a tailwind?"

"Exactly." Blane's eyes narrowed as Myrtle jumped up onto a stool. "You, outside. This is a private conversation."

Wow, until today, I never realised a cat could give the finger.

As Myrtle stalked off, Blane leaned against what was left of the kitchen island, and I realised that there were advantages to the grey sweatpants. I forced myself to look him in the eye. That magic dick was the reason I'd jumped feet first into a relationship with him, and I couldn't afford to get distracted now.

"I did some thinking on the drive from Laurent's place."

"So did I. Wren, I know I screwed up. I find it difficult to put things into words, and there were secrets I kept because I feared that spilling them would be worse than holding them close. I didn't keep things from you because I wanted to hurt you."

"I know that."

"And I'll understand if you don't want to be with me, but I still need to keep you safe. You're not going back to your apartment. I'll find you a place in a building with excellent security, and you'll need a vehicle too."

"You'd rent me an apartment?"

"No, I'd buy you an apartment. Real estate is a good investment."

"It's a nice offer, but I'll have to say no."

"Your safety is non-negotiable. You'd rather have a house?"

"I'm saying no because I figured I'd stay here for a while longer."

"Here? With me?"

"Unless you're planning to move out? But you were right about the kitchen needing a refresh."

A slow smile spread over his face, and I stepped forward into his arms. Jack Callahan had given Vee a chance, and now I needed to do the same with Blane. As Vee said, he was no Voltaire, and he was no Dominic Winchester either.

And now he was mine.

That now-familiar feeling of absolute rightness spread through me, and I knew without a doubt that Blane would do everything in his power to protect me. Being loved by the devil was the best feeling in the world.

This new life wouldn't be easy, but I had friends now. Blane, Vee, Joseph, Myrtle, Aurelia. Plus Caria and Kayden, of course. I wouldn't have to worry about my job, or taking the bus home late at night, or whether I had enough money for groceries as well as rent.

Security.

I finally had security.

The rooftop hot tub was just an added bonus.

CHAPTER 41

Blane

"What the hell happened in here?"

At the *ding*, I'd glanced up from the couch. Callahan began complaining before he left the elevator.

"Why does the place smell like smoke and Lysol?" he continued.

"Would you believe I burned dinner last night?"

"No, because you never cook anything. And this is the second fire I've had to deal with today." His gaze fell on Vee. "What happened this morning? I tried calling, but you didn't answer, and then Daphne said you were outside in daylight..."

"I lost my phone."

Callahan rubbed his temples with his fingers. "Tell me you didn't lose it on the other side of Iron Mountain?"

"Uh..."

"I only ask because last night you asked me where Raphael Laurent lived, and this morning, his house went up in flames."

"A terrible coincidence," I told him. "Coffee?"

We'd spent the day cleaning up the apartment as best we could. Marianna was resting in a guest bedroom along with Aurelia and Lola's original body, the dead assholes had been loaded into suitcases ready for disposal, and Joseph's new coffee machine was sitting on the sideboard in the dining area. We'd need to replace the kitchen units, of course, but the granite countertops had survived, and once we'd wiped the blood and soot off the tiles, the place didn't look as bad as I'd expected.

Callahan ignored my offer. "Laurent is missing, and his vehicle was found wrecked in the Medical District. Vee, I have to ask—were you chasing him?"

Her shoulders dropped an inch. "No, definitely not. We were just driving home when we got stuck in traffic, and some jobsworth pulled us over when Wren tried to turn the car around."

Callahan wrapped Vee up in a hug, and for once, I didn't feel that hot bud of envy. The envy that another man had found what I'd lost. Because against all the odds, I had Wren. A slightly nervous, uncertain Wren, but she hadn't sprinted off into the sunset, so I was counting it as a win.

"I was so worried about you. Laurent isn't a man you want to mess with."

"Laurent wasn't even driving the car. Voltaire was."

I groaned. Joseph groaned. Wren groaned. Even Lola groaned, but that was more because she was copying everyone else.

"Vee, my sweet, sometimes less is more."

"I can't lie to Jack."

"Maybe you could just leave some parts out?"

Wren kicked me in the shin as Callahan leaned back to look at his beloved. "Vee, what's going on?"

"Do you promise you won't yell or arrest anyone?"

His turn to groan. "Tell me."

"You have to promise first. This is all off the record."

"I'm a cop, not a journalist."

"Okay, fine." Vee shrugged. "What do you want for dinner? Should I book a table at La Nostra Casa?"

"You're putting me in an impossible position."

Joseph got up to make coffee anyway. "To be fair, the 'impossible position' part happened months ago when you got shot in the heart."

"Wait, who are you?"

"Joseph."

"You're not Joseph."

"I changed my hair. Do you like it?"

"Vee..." Callahan stared at her. She stared right back, and of course, it was he who gave in. No mortal could beat a vampire in a battle of wills. "Fine, I promise." Then quieter, "I'm going to hell anyway."

"Technically, that might not be possible," Joseph put in. "Either a vampire or one of the Electi would have to kill you first."

Vee shushed him. "Don't you think there's been enough talk of death today?"

"No?"

Another groan from Callahan.

"Laurent kidnapped Wren's friend," Vee said quickly. "We were just trying to get her back."

"And Wren is?"

She raised a hand at the same time as I said, "My girlfriend."

Wren leaned into me, tension rolling off her in waves. But I wasn't too worried. Callahan couldn't talk. Firstly, he'd lose Vee if he did, secondly, nobody would believe him anyway, and thirdly, he'd find himself with a first-class ticket to another plane if he spilled our secrets. Probably Plane Four, but I wasn't fussy.

Callahan turned to Lola-slash-Delphine. Caria was still holed up in the apartment Vee shared with him, recovering from her ordeal, so that would be a fun introduction this evening. Wren and I had visited earlier to make sure she was comfortable, and Wren had asked her to sit tight for a day or two while we got things straightened out. Caria had readily agreed.

"And you're Wren's friend?"

"Yup," Lola said. "I'm everybody's friend. Mommy said it's nice to be important, but importanter to be nice. Are you important?"

That detective brain picked up on the disparity between Lola's appearance and her mannerisms right away, and he sighed.

"You're gonna have to start from the beginning."

So we did. Vee took the lead, and we explained how a cop had handed Caria to Laurent, how Zion had double-crossed us in our quest to get her back, and how we'd been forced to take matters into our own hands. When Vee got to the part about Voltaire, Callahan looked visibly furious, which I had to take as a good sign.

"He locked you into a fuckin' sunbed? He's a dead man."

"Good luck with that," Joseph muttered, and then he began twitching again.

"He said I needed to learn my lesson. That nobody defies him and gets away with it."

"Pretty harsh lesson—he left you there to die."

"That wasn't his plan. I think he just wanted me compliant so I didn't fight him, but then the whole house went dark as if someone cut the power. Then there was this... I can't really put it into words, but this feeling of overwhelming malevolence, and he took off. But then the electricity came back on, and I couldn't get out, and...and..."

Callahan kissed her hair. "It's okay. I swear he won't get near you again."

"You can't stop him."

"*We* can stop him," I said firmly. "You're not alone in this."

"And you're stronger now," Wren reminded her. "Blane's blood has given you an advantage."

"You drank from *Blane*?" Uh-oh. Callahan sounded pissed.

"He tasted gross," Vee said, presumably to make Callahan feel better.

"No need for jealousy," I added. "She'd already been through Wren, Lola, and Caria, and it was a last resort."

"Lola? As in Marianna's daughter? You took a *child* on this insane rescue mission?"

"Not exactly?" Vee said. "Laurent's sister came here to kidnap Wren, but she ended up shooting Lola instead, so Blane stuffed Lola's soul into Delphine's body, and now she's stuck there until Decima gets back from the fifty-fourth realm."

Callahan sank onto the arm of the couch. "I need a drink."

"Joseph, fetch a bottle of champagne."

"A stronger drink."

"Scotch?"

"That works."

I nodded to Joseph, and he disappeared into the elevator. Callahan might not have liked the situation, but there wasn't a damn thing he could do about it, and at least nobody had mentioned the three body-filled suitcases stacked in the master bath.

"Is there much in the way of evidence at Laurent's place?" Vee asked, crouching next to him.

"The arson investigator said it burned hotter than a

cremation furnace, and there was no sign of an accelerant. Lot of head-scratching going on today."

I'd done a good job, if I said so myself. Creating that amount of heat had left me a little tired, but then again, I was used to keeping the fires of Plane Three stoked, so it hadn't been too much of a chore.

"We couldn't leave Wren and Caria to die."

"Yeah, I know that. At the moment, the working theory is that an insider burned the place down, either by accident or for an insurance job, and took off in the Mercedes. We figured it was Laurent, but you're telling me he's dead?"

Vee nodded.

"And he was a fuckin' werewolf?"

"It came as a surprise to us too," I said.

"Who did it?"

"Professor Plum by the swimming pool with a silver rose."

I wasn't about to let Wren take the blame for Laurent's death. If anyone was going to fall on a sword, it would be me.

Callahan cursed under his breath. "My solve rate is gonna look like shit this year."

"Maybe we could help with one of your other cases?" I suggested.

"Hell no. Do me a favour and stay far away from the criminal underworld."

"Does that include Voltaire?"

"I might make an exception for Voltaire." Callahan rubbed Vee's back. "We'll keep you safe."

"He knows I'm here now. In Vegas. He'll never stop looking for me."

"Wren's right—you have an advantage now. If you move around in daylight rather than at night, he won't see you."

"What if it wears off?"

Callahan looked to me.

"I'm not sure the Celestial Council would approve of me being used as a soda fountain," I said, and Wren poked me in the ribs. "Okay, fine. If Vee needs a top-up, I'll provide it."

Whether it broke the rules or not, I'd look after my friends. Aurelia wouldn't spill the beans, not intentionally, although she struggled to keep her mouth shut at times. The mysteries of celestial gifts fascinated her, and the moment she found out about Vee's new ability, she'd begun chattering about blood samples and microscopes.

And perhaps research wouldn't be a bad thing? Knowledge was power, and we'd need everything in our arsenal to defeat Voltaire. Leaving him free wasn't an option. I had three women to protect now—a good friend, a bonded child, and my future wife—and I'd kill to do it.

But that was tomorrow's problem. Today was a time to celebrate.

Laurent was gone, Caria was safe, and Wren was mine.

When Joseph returned with the drinks, I poured Callahan a generous measure of Scotch and popped the cork on the champagne.

"Here's to friendship."

CHAPTER 42

Blane

"Can't I get five minutes' peace?" Decima grumbled. "What have you done this time?"

Three days had passed since Delphine had invaded my apartment, and my older sister had finally returned from the fifty-fourth realm. Late, and with a smile on her face, which meant she'd probably hooked up with some poor schmuck who wasn't yet aware of her dragonish reputation. Or possibly several schmucks, if the rumours on the celestial grapevine were to be believed.

"I didn't do anything. A madwoman broke into my apartment and shot Lola."

"Lola? That child you're weirdly obsessed with?" Decima looked Joseph up and down from her seat in my former office. In my opinion, she spent too much time behind a desk and not enough time getting to know Plane Three's varied guests. "And what happened to you? Did you lose your other body in a poker game?"

"I'm not weirdly obsessed with her. Our souls are bonded."

"Bonded, schmonded. You know the celestial-human

aetherbond is a myth, don't you? Someone on the Celestial Council made it up when they couldn't get enough volunteers to fill the monitoring roles in Plane Five."

"I thought that too until I felt it." Aurelia had taken great delight in saying "I told you so," and it was then that I began to take more of an interest when she talked about the weird and wonderful texts she found in the library. Decima, on the other hand, was yet to have an "aha" moment and remained a firm sceptic. "Rather than getting into an argument you can't win, will you just come and fix Lola?"

"You can't win either."

"I'm aware of that, which is why I'm not going to bother explaining how meeting your soulmate is better than a hot-tub party with three lacrosse players and an assistant professor from the ninety-third realm."

Decima's cheeks turned scarlet. "Who told you about the hot-tub party?"

"So it's true?"

"I'm not going to dignify that with a response."

"I'll never bring it up again if you come and fix Lola."

My darling sister glared at me.

"Ooh, Thaddeus, turn the jets on higher. Yes, yes, that feels so good."

"Shut up! And Thaddeus isn't an assistant; he's a full professor now."

"I'm not sure that's much better, but you do you." Although she'd passed the corrections course he was teaching with a glowing report, so Thaddeus had clearly been satisfied with the experience. I glanced at my watch. "Lola's waiting."

"Fine, I'll come, but you have to do me a favour first."

"What kind of favour?"

"Three Category M prisoners escaped their bonds and fled to Mount Malum."

"Guests. We call them guests, or residents in a pinch. 'Prisoners' doesn't foster a community spirit."

"Whatever. You need to get them back."

"Give me five minutes."

The three assholes from maximum security were chilling on a boulder halfway up the volcano, and I ignored their protests as I herded them back to their shackles. Apparently, Decima had cancelled the weekly movie night, so they'd left because they were bored. Banning movies was such a petty move, but that was Decima all over. She never saw the bigger picture.

Anyhow, we were soon back in Vegas, and Wren gaped as Decima healed the hole in Lola's chest. To give Decima credit, she always did an excellent job with healing, partly due to her natural ability but also because she liked to show off. She never left a scar.

I was about to return Lola's soul when Joseph interrupted.

"Wait."

"What now?"

"If Lola's going back, then she won't need the hot body anymore, will she?"

I should have known this was coming.

"I suppose not."

"So, can I have it? This one doesn't suit me. It has heartburn and indigestion, and I think it's allergic to whatever they put in your shampoo."

"Why are you using my shampoo?"

"I ran out."

For goodness' sake, the grocery store was five minutes away. But I had to admit, a body swap wasn't the worst idea Joseph had ever come up with. No, the worst idea was hand-grenade-dodgeball because those fragments got everywhere.

A DEVIL IN THE DARK

"Let him swap," Wren whispered, crinkling her nose. "Please."

I understood where she was coming from. Joseph 12.0 passed wind constantly, and I suspected the new body also had a faulty sense of smell because he didn't seem to notice the problem. No amount of scented candles could cover up the stink.

"What should we call you? Josephine?"

The switch only took a moment, and Joseph began twitching afresh before running to the mirror on the closet door.

"Hey, look at my ass. I need a whole new wardrobe."

"Can I come to the mall?" Aurelia asked.

"Sure, bestie. And after we've shopped till we drop, we can get mani-pedis and catch a show."

Heaven help me, he was going to drive me insane.

But if he was going on a shopping spree with Aurelia, at least I'd have some time alone with Wren for the first time since the shooting. Decima wouldn't hang around. And my relationship with Wren was still on shaky ground as we learned to navigate the new normal.

Lola sat up and stretched, yawning.

"Wake up, sleepyhead," Aurelia said. "You got a little something on your shirt. How about we go find you a clean one?"

"I'm hungry."

"What do you want to eat?"

"Cookies."

"Sure, we have cookies. You want chocolate chip or oatmeal and raisin?"

"Oatmeal is yucky."

As Aurelia left the room with Lola, she released her hold on Marianna, who blinked slowly as she took in her surroundings. Wren and Vee had been caring for Pablo while

305

his mother was resting, and that was another problem for the future. I could see how good Wren was with the little boy. What if she wanted children? I had no idea whether it was physically possible for me to grant that wish, or what might happen if I tried. Aurelia had found references to a handful of human-celestial hybrids throughout history, but the logistical details were hazy. Nev hadn't been maternal. I hadn't needed to consider that conundrum before.

"Why am I here?" Marianna asked. Her gaze landed on Decima. "Who are you?"

I sat on the edge of the bed. "You weren't feeling too good. Probably a bug of some kind. We thought it best for you to stay here for a few days while you fought it off."

"A few...days?"

"You slept for most of it. Don't worry; we've had a full complement of babysitters. This is Decima, my older sister."

Marianna pushed herself up to sitting. "You have two sisters?"

"Unfortunately. How are you feeling now?"

"Tired. So tired. Where's Lola?"

"She's with—"

"I'm here, Mommy!"

Lola ran into the bedroom in a clean T-shirt, dropping cookie crumbs as she went, and I swallowed hard to force down the lump in my throat. I'd been sent to Plane Five to learn about sin, and I'd done that, but I'd also learned about love. I knew now that it came in many different forms. Love between friends, love between family, and all-consuming romantic love.

In truth, being fired was the best thing that had ever happened to me, not that I'd ever confess that to Decima.

Wren handed Pablo back to Marianna and then took her place at my side. Right where she belonged. Death, destruction, and difficulties with Voltaire aside, life in Vegas was better than it had ever been.

"How do you feel about going out for dinner tonight?" I whispered to Wren as we moved back to give the Vasquez family some space.

"Like a date?"

"The first of many."

"I don't have anything fancy to wear."

"You don't need fancy clothes to look beautiful, but I'll buy you as many dresses as you want."

"You don't need to do that."

"No, but I want to. Wren, you've done more for me than you could ever know. You accepted me for who I am. I love you, and I'm going to spend an eternity proving that."

"You...you love me?"

"How could I not?"

"I...I..."

"You'll say it when you're ready. We have all the time in the world now."

"I think I'm getting there."

"Good." I kissed her hair. "Italian? Chinese?"

"Chinese."

"I'm done here," Decima announced. "This place smells weird, by the way. You should get different candles."

"Say hi to Cathy and Ivan for me."

Decima huffed and strode out of the room, out of Plane Five, and out of my life, albeit temporarily. With Voltaire around, I had a horrible feeling I'd have to grovel for her services again, sooner rather than later.

But not tonight. Tonight, I was going to enjoy this new beginning with Wren.

CHAPTER 43

Wren

"I think I ate too much."

"Nonsense."

"I definitely drank too much." I giggled as Blane lifted me out of the back seat and carried me across the parking lot. Joseph had decided that he—she—was taking the evening off, so Blane had called a limo service. A freaking limo service. I tried to tell him a regular cab would be fine, but he insisted.

Was this going to be the new normal?

Dom had been pushy, and so was Blane, but in a totally different way. Dom used to insist I iron his handkerchiefs and vacuum three times a week, even if the floor wasn't dirty. Blane insisted I spend eight hundred dollars of his money on a blue dress because the colour matched my eyes.

A sigh escaped as I ran a hand down his beautiful face. I knew which I preferred.

Blane, the handsome devil who treated me like a princess.

Music was pumping out of Club Dead, but Blane assured me that the management team could handle things for a few days. Maybe he'd check on things later? He'd confessed that he needed much less sleep than I did, only two or three hours a night, so he'd do some of his work while I rested. As for my job, whether I went back to Tilt was up to me. Blane said I should work if I wanted to, but money wasn't an issue anymore. My bills were covered, and yesterday when I checked my bank balance, I'd found it had grown significantly. Stubborn Blane told me to give the money to charity if I didn't want it, but he refused to take it back.

Over egg rolls and rice and chow mein, we'd talked about a vacation. He owned a vineyard in Italy and a villa in the Caribbean, but the destination was up to me. Blane was from another world, and now I found myself in one too, but I loved it.

I loved him.

I wasn't ready to say it out loud yet, but my heart knew.

Upstairs in our apartment, Blane set me on the floor and steadied me as I walked across the foyer. In the kitchen, I paused. The units would be ripped out soon, and memories would leave along with them.

"The designer is coming next Monday," he said. "It's the soonest she can squeeze us in."

"That's not what I'm thinking about."

"Do you want a midnight snack?"

"Maybe?"

"What kind of snack? I can get it delivered if we don't have it."

"You."

"Me?"

Since the Laurent incident, we'd been sharing a bed, but that was all. Blane had kept his dick to himself, no pushiness in that department. A perfect gentleman. He was waiting for me to make the first move, but now that I'd made it, he looked more confused than anything. Another one of those missteps.

"Yes, you. Naked."

"Here?"

For Pete's sake. "You've done a great job with the chivalry, but five days of abstinence is long enough. Strip me, bend me over what's left of the counter, and fuck me until I forget my own name."

My words surprised even me. Around Dom, I'd learned to mind my language, but Blane never criticised the way I spoke.

"Caerus above," he muttered. "You're a siren."

"Whoever Caerus is, he's not invited."

Blane just laughed, and I jumped as all the scented candles flickered into life. Like, thirty of them.

"Do you have any other party tricks?"

"I can give you a literal out-of-body experience if you want."

"Uh, I'll pass on that one. The night I burned the stir fry, did you extinguish the flames?"

"Of course."

"Amazing. That means there's another reason to keep you around besides your Grade A cock."

"There are more than two reasons. I always put down the toilet seat, I toss my dirty clothes in the laundry hamper, I— Wait, was that sarcasm?"

"You're getting it."

"And so are you, my darling. Possibly in more than one orifice."

Blane grinned as he reached for me, but I shrieked and leapt backward.

"Careful with the dress!"

"All evening, I've been dreaming of ripping it off you."

"How about we settle for unzipping it gently?"

He nuzzled my neck. "For you, anything."

There was something wildly hot about being slammed onto a cold counter and feeling a man nudge your legs apart. Blane draped my beautiful dress neatly over a stool and then slapped my ass. Now that we'd bared our souls to each other, he didn't try to hide the raw power that rolled off him in waves, or his strength as he positioned me just the way he wanted. In his hands, I felt like a delicate little doll.

And in return for being his plaything, I gained his protection.

Best trade ever.

Dom had liked to boss me around in the house, but in the bedroom, he'd expected me to do all the work. Blane was the complete opposite. He took charge of my pleasure, feathering kisses down my spine as he leaned over me.

"Did you tell the kitchen designer that the island has to stay?" I asked.

"Absolutely. Planes above and below, you're beautiful like this. Not that you're not beautiful in every other way, but—"

"Blane, stop talking."

He turned me over and pushed my legs apart, hooking my knees over his arms as he raised my ass higher, higher. I gripped the edge of the granite for support, and how was I ever meant to eat breakfast here again? His tongue slid through my folds and dipped inside me, and I bit my lip to stop from crying out.

Wait, why did that matter? The music downstairs was loud enough to cover gunshots; I knew that from experience.

"Oh, Lord."

"A bit formal, but acceptable."

The tip of his tongue flicked against my clit, and he didn't let up until I screamed his name, my back slip-sliding across polished stone slick with sweat. Now I understood all those romance novels where the good girl falls for the villain.

And when Blane flipped me with effortless ease and unzipped his pants, his hard cock springing free, I embraced the darkness and licked my lips. My new favourite colour was morally grey with a hint of hellfire.

~

"What did my brother do to you last night?"

I regarded Aurelia through bleary eyes. She looked so damn perky. As for me, there wasn't a part of my body that didn't ache. The devil had stamina, and he had the skill to match. When I was ten years old, one of my foster parents used to wag her finger at every indiscretion and tell me, "If you keep that up, you'll be going to hell, young lady." I so, so wished I could go back in time and tell her I was looking forward to it.

Wait, hold on a second...

"Please, don't ask me for the details. Can you rewind time? Like, by seventeen years?"

"No, I can only slow it down." Ah, well. "Why?"

"Doesn't matter. Are those Danishes from Gerard's?"

"Joseph picked them up. Josephine. I have to remember to call her Josephine."

"Has he...she ever changed gender before?"

"As in a body swap? Once or twice. In Plane Three, she's more gender neutral."

"Wow. It's going to take me a while to get used to."

"Don't worry; she won't get offended if you get it wrong, and her given name is actually Grimwald. Joseph is her middle name."

"Grimwald?"

"Yup, and her sister is Grimalda. Grimalda was born ten

minutes earlier, so if you want to get on Josephine's nerves, just call her Little G."

"Does she hate it?"

"Detests it."

"Awesome."

Aurelia laughed along with me as I made myself a mug of coffee, but when I turned back to sit at the island, I found her expression had grown serious.

"Is Blane awake?" she asked.

"He's getting dressed. Is everything okay?"

"Yes, yes. I just found out something interesting."

"About Laurent?"

"No, about you."

"Me?"

"Your internet is a wonderful thing. Well, mostly. Some people are mean, and others lie a lot, but you can find so much information if you look in the right place. Like you can find out about whole families."

Had she dug up dirt on my mom? I didn't appreciate the idea of Aurelia snooping through my background, and why hadn't she just asked me? I'd thought we were becoming friends.

"My mother is in prison. I've never tried to hide that."

"I'm so sorry to hear it, but this isn't about her."

"My father? I don't know who he is."

"This is about your sister."

"I...I don't have a sister. Only a brother."

"But you did once. In another life."

"What's going on?" Blane appeared behind me, and I needed his steadying hand on my shoulder. "Don't upset Wren before she's even had breakfast."

"I don't mean to. Did you know Nevaeh had a second sister?"

Blane took a seat beside me, and he looked as shocked as I felt. "A second sister? She only ever mentioned Esther."

"If her parents were the control freaks you said they were, she might not even have remembered. Aerin Michaels died when she was three years old. They were twins."

He gripped my hand. "And you think..."

"I don't know. But I'm saying it might be possible. Likely, even."

I'd once been a twin?

A memory sparked. "When I first met Lola, before anyone told her my name, she called me Rin. I thought she was trying to say Wren, but what if...what if she'd meant *Aerin*?"

"We already know her soul wasn't properly wiped because she remembers Blane. I think she remembers you too."

Of all the things that had happened in the past two weeks, of all the things I'd learned and horrors I'd seen, that was the revelation that turned me into a weeping mess. I cried for Aerin and I cried for Nevaeh, two girls who'd never been able to reach their full potential. And there was guilt too. Guilt that Lola and I were here with Blane, and they weren't.

And Blane? He just held me and let me cry it all out.

"Don't be sad." Aurelia put an arm around me. "Great-Uncle Tiberius wrote in his journal that once souls are bonded, they always find their way back to each other. You have this life with Blane and Lola, and someday, you'll have another with them too."

"How do souls become linked?"

"Even Great-Uncle Tiberius didn't know the answer to that. He thought that maybe one of his predecessors designated a matchmaker to take the regular human aetherbond and amplify it between the planes, although that's purely speculation. The Creatori were terrible at keeping records. There are journals and notes and scraps of parchment going back for millennia, and until I took over at the library, none were in any discernible order."

"Aurelia's spent years filing," Blane said. "She's being groomed to take over in Plane Two when Mother and Father finally retire, but that's centuries away. So for now, they're happy for her to while away her time on a project that keeps her out of trouble."

"Don't you ever get bored?" I asked her.

Blane let go of me to give his sister's shoulders a squeeze. "She loves it."

"I do," Aurelia agreed, but before she replied, I saw something else flash in her eyes. Resignation? It was only there for a second, and I might even have imagined it. "And speaking of the library, I have a new assistant starting today. Well, yesterday, and I just know I'm going to get a lecture from Mother because I wasn't there to greet him."

"Is that the exchange student?"

"From the nine hundred and sixty-third realm?" Aurelia's sigh suggested she wasn't thrilled about the arrangement. "Yes. His name is Lysander. Meggie said she'd show him around."

"He can't be worse than the girl from the thirty-second."

"That's what I keep telling myself."

"Do you still have the earplugs?"

"In my desk drawer. My last exchange student didn't stop talking for a month straight," Aurelia explained. "I kept thinking she'd go hoarse, but no. In the end, we had to reinstate the rule of silence, and of course she took it personally."

"If you need to get away for a couple of days, you could

always come to visit again," I suggested. "We could go see a show."

"I'd love that." Aurelia drained her coffee and gave me a hug. "No rest for the wicked."

And then she was gone.

Blane took the seat she'd just vacated and studied me, those amber eyes assessing.

"Are you okay? Aurelia has a habit of speaking without thinking sometimes."

"You mean about the Aerin and Nevaeh thing? I'm not gonna lie—it freaks me out a little. But there's nothing I can do about it, and even Aurelia can't turn back time. Are *you* okay?"

"I'll always regret that I didn't get to spend more time with Nev, but the aetherbond brings me comfort. I'm always going to outlive any human I fall in love with, so knowing you'll be back, that I only have to wait a while until I see you again... It helps to dull the grief." He tucked loose hair behind my ear. "Negligible senescence brings its own challenges."

"Negligible what?"

"Immortality, more or less. You'll age while I won't. People will look at us differently. And when I remain youthful while the world around me changes, I'll have to move away and reinvent myself so others don't ask questions. We'll both live many lives, but in different ways."

I'd been so busy surviving that I'd barely thought about the future, not long-term. But now I realised he was right. Both immortality and the aetherbond would be a blessing and a curse. We'd never lose each other. But the connection wouldn't always be one that society approved of.

Life wouldn't always be easy.

But how I handled the situation was up to me.

I could laugh about it or cry.

"What are you meant to do? Date Lola when I age out?"

The look of absolute horror on Blane's face made me snort. "No! I couldn't, not after I've watched her grow up." He kissed my hair. "I'll just have to go home and annoy Decima for a few decades while I wait for you."

"You can never die?" I asked. "Won't the immortal world get overcrowded at some point?"

"The universe is forever expanding. New realms are created, and staff are always needed. My uncle and his family were shipped off to Realm 73,927 centuries ago, so we don't see them much these days. Then there are the other dimensions... And yes, we can die."

"How?"

"Are you planning to get rid of me already?"

My turn to be horrified. "Never! I'm just curious. It's not every day I hook up with an immortal."

"I should hope not." Blane took a sip of my coffee and helped himself to a Danish. "There's a substance called tirrium. If we spend too much time near it, we weaken like Vee in the sunlight, and eventually we die."

"I've never heard of it."

"It's mostly found on our penal planet. The Celestial Council sends immortals there if they're found guilty of gross misconduct, but thankfully, that doesn't happen often. Usually, it's just a threat our parents use when we're young—be good, or you'll be sent to Tirria."

"Gross misconduct? Like drinking someone else's coffee, you mean?"

He glanced down at the mug he was holding. "Sorry. I'll make you another cup, and then I need to head over to Tilt."

Blane moved to the coffee machine, and I replayed his words in my head. "What did you mean by 'mostly'?"

"Huh?"

"You said tirrium was *mostly* found on your penal planet. There's none here on Earth, right?"

"There are small quantities elsewhere. We know of a piece in Brazil. It lives in a crumbling temple in the Mala Valley."

I shuddered. "Have you ever been to Brazil?"

"I tend to avoid the area, but not even regular tourists visit. The temple is guarded by the Karaza tribe with terrifying ferocity, and they worship it as a god. The valley is the only place on Earth where coco du ciel trees grow, but that's a story for another day." Blane checked his watch. "I really do need to leave. Sheikh Mahbrouk is in town, and his wife's dog got loose last night and ate a poker chip."

"Batman?"

"I'm sorry? I can't fly, if that's what you're asking."

"No, the dog. The cute little fluffy one. She named it Batman because its ears stick out."

"Ah. I wasn't aware of that."

"You want me to come help? The sheikha is a sweetheart, but she always seems nervous around people she doesn't know."

Blane beamed at me, the full hundred-watt smile. "Your presence is always appreciated."

"This decor has to be fifty years old." Caria ran a fingertip across the scratched surface of the former VIP bar. The Devil's Den wasn't just tired; it was practically catatonic. "See these chairs? There's an upcycler I know over near Spring Valley—she'd pay twenty bucks each for them."

"They have character."

Vee poked at a hole in the velvet seat. "It's like everything—give it a generation, and it comes back into fashion."

"What's old is new again?"

"That's right."

And she should know—she'd been around to see it happen enough times.

Josephine unscrewed the cap on a bottle of top-shelf liquor. The previous owners of the resort hadn't packed up before they left, and apart from a layer of dust, the bar looked the same as it had the night it closed.

"You think this is still drinkable?"

"Try it and see," I suggested.

Six weeks had passed since Laurent's death, and we'd begun to settle into the new normal. The kitchen was refurbished, and somehow, we'd ended up with two islands. For variety, Blane said. Josephine had helped me to collect my things from my old apartment, and thanks to her stolen body, she'd also managed to inherit the burned-out remains of Laurent's mansion, several properties in other states, a yacht, a collection of cars, and half a strip club. Yes, she was now the proud co-owner of the Pink Squirrel. As yet, we hadn't worked out who owned the other half or what the heck we were supposed to do with it.

Blane didn't have time to run the place—he was too busy with the Devil's Den. The paperwork was signed, and now the mammoth task of turning it into a luxury casino had begun. And I was helping.

He'd told me that as his partner in soul and in love, I could do whatever I wanted with my time, and after two weeks of shopping with Josephine, going on lunch dates with Vee, practising yoga with Caria, and watching too much TV while I waited for Blane to finish work, I'd quickly decided that a life of leisure would bore me to death.

Meanwhile, Caria had sworn off men. Even though she conceded that Blane seemed charming, and maybe not *every* man was a psychopath, she was determined to stay single for the rest of her life. Thankfully, she barely remembered a thing about the rescue, and the snippets she did recall, she assumed were hallucinations. The guards had begun drugging her after she bit one of them and kicked another in the balls, and Laurent didn't seem to care whether she was sentient when he raped her.

When she tearfully told me what he'd done, I was so damn happy I'd killed him.

Anyhow, Blane had offered her a role as a consultant, and she was going to assist with the refurbishment of the

Devil's Den. It would be her first paid interior design job. There was still some friction between her and Josephine, mainly because Caria had met her a handful of times as Delphine, and we'd had to come up with a story where Delphine had secretly hated her brother and worked with us to facilitate Caria's rescue. Now Delphine wanted a fresh start, which included ditching her former lifestyle and changing her name to Josephine.

Didn't everyone deserve a fresh start?

The gift of happiness?

Marianna didn't remember a thing about her time slip either, and Lola was none the worse for wear after her ordeal. Vee's reprieve from photosensitivity had come to an end almost two weeks ago, when she'd had to dash home from a morning jog with severe sunburn. Blane had driven over to give her a top-up, which should keep her going until next week, and now that we knew what was needed, she and Blane had added a monthly dinner date to their schedules.

Voltaire had disappeared.

We were all twitchy, constantly looking over our shoulders, and Callahan had put out feelers to see if he showed up in Europe, but there was no sign. He had money, we knew that much. If he'd bought a new identity, we might never find him unless he chose to reveal himself.

Callahan was also keeping an eye on Laurent's mole in the LVMPD. Caria had been able to identify him, but there was no way to bring the traitor into the light without a lot of questions being asked about the showdown in the desert. So Callahan was monitoring him. Watching and waiting for him to make another mistake. Blane had offered to remove the man's soul, but Callahan thought he might be useful. If he was in bed with one criminal, there could be others.

We just needed a little time. Aurelia thought it might be possible to kill Voltaire someday, but we weren't prepared yet. The key to his demise still lay stubbornly out of reach, but last week, she'd found a cryptic reference jotted in the margin of an ancient text, a strange little verse that gave us hope.

The king of the vampires was vanquished, his heart a thousand pieces.
'Twas pierced by a gift from the queen of trees, the elder of her species.

Was that where the stake-through-the-heart myth came from? Vee said she knew from personal experience that a regular stake wouldn't work, but when I'd asked whose heart the theory had been tested on, she'd changed the subject.

Anyhow, Voltaire was tomorrow's problem. Blane had outbid him for the Devil's Den, and our job was to help make sure that money hadn't been wasted. He had the business side of things in hand, he assured us, with a project manager on board and financing in place, but he wanted our thoughts on the facilities. Our job was to visit each hotel in Vegas and check out the competition, which wasn't exactly a hardship. We relaxed in the spas, tried out the rooms, ate in the restaurants, and spent time on the casino floors. Blane had given us a generous budget to start off with, then Caria won the jackpot on a slot machine at Caesars, and now we were in profit by twenty-seven thousand bucks.

"There's an Eames chair in the Presidential Suite, and I swear it's an original," Caria said as Josephine swigged from the bottle. "Do you know how much those go for? We need to check the other rooms just in case there are more of them."

When Caria's landlord kicked her out for late payment

of the rent—she'd already been two months behind, and being abducted wasn't an acceptable excuse, apparently—Blane had invited her to use a guest room. So had Vee, and even Marianna had offered a couch. But Caria was still racked with guilt over the rescue and insisted she'd find an apartment, whereupon Blane had pointed out that he had two hundred and fifty-four empty rooms, thirty-seven of which were suites, and she might as well use one of those for the time being.

So Caria was living in the Presidential Suite, along with a vast collection of mid-century modern furniture and Nigel, the cactus she'd carted through her last eight house moves. We'd rescued him from a dumpster outside her old apartment. The Devil's Den was small compared to many of the casinos on the neighbouring Strip, but the rooms were a good size, and Blane thought it would be perfect as a luxury boutique hotel that catered to high-rollers and folks stuck on the waitlist for Tilt.

"We have the keys for all the rooms," I told Caria. "Which floor do you want to take?"

"The penthouses will have the best stuff. This place is so cool, even though it gets creepy at night."

"Blane put security in the lobby."

Two guys, and they patrolled at regular intervals.

"I know, but if there's a ghost on the twelfth floor, I'm not sure they'll be able to help."

"There's no such thing as ghosts," I scoffed, then saw Vee shaking her head in the background. Wait, ghosts were a thing? I needed to ask Blane about that. "Anyhow, back to the chairs..." My phone rang. Saved by the bell. "Kayden?"

Silence.

"Kayden?" My pulse sped up. With Voltaire on the loose, I was jumpy, and my mind went straight to the worst-case scenario. "Are you okay?"

"Sarah cheated on me."

"That's all?"

"Damn, Wren."

Shit! "Sorry, I'm sorry. What happened? I mean, how did you find out?"

In Hawaii, he'd asked her to marry him, and she'd said yes. How could things have fallen apart so quickly?

"I went to tell my boss about the bachelor party that trashed the fifth tee, and she was sitting on his desk."

"Maybe he just ran out of chairs?"

"She wasn't wearing a shirt."

"Oh."

"And her panties were stuffed in his mouth. I think I broke a knuckle."

"Tell me you punched the wall and not his face."

More silence.

"So you don't have a job now?"

"Or anyplace to live. The lease was in Sarah's name."

"Do you still have a car?"

"Most of my stuff is crammed into the back of it."

Okay. Okay, we could deal with this. Two months ago, I'd have offered my couch and silently prayed that my tips would stretch to extra groceries, but now, I had options. Two hundred and fifty-three of them, to be precise.

"Come to Vegas. I have a place for you to stay."

Caria perked up when I told her she'd be getting a roommate. So, unfortunately, did Josephine. In fact, she looked a little *too* happy.

"Good luck with the furniture," she said. "I need to visit the salon."

"Hey, you said you'd help us."

"You have everything under control. I have the utmost faith in you."

What had I done?

~

That evening, over a dinner of pan-fried risotto and a green salad—no, I hadn't made it—Blane chuckled as I recounted the conversation. Josephine had shown up at the Devil's Den, primped and preened, a half hour after Kayden arrived. Her offer to "show him around" had been gratefully received, and now I was having regrets. Big regrets.

"Why didn't you tell me that Josephine was into Kayden?"

"When she was Joseph, I didn't think it was important. Kayden had a girlfriend."

"This is a nightmare."

"Look on the bright side—Josephine would never hook up with Kayden's boss." Blane couldn't quite keep a straight face. "I'd throw her into Mount Malum if she even thought about cheating."

"This isn't funny. Kayden needs time and space to mend his broken heart, not a rebound fling with a literal demon."

"You don't think hot sex might cheer him up? Take his mind off things?"

I buried my head in my hands. "Kayden is my *brother*. I don't even want to think about that." But I couldn't help it. "Can Josephine even...? She just dove into that body, and what if parts got rearranged?"

Now it was Blane's turn to grimace. "I hadn't considered it in that level of detail. At least I don't have these worries with Aurelia and Decima."

"I just don't want anyone to get hurt. Kayden's been through—"

"Did I hear my name?"

Aurelia strolled in from the terrace, but she wasn't alone. A petite brunette trailed behind her, eyes wide as she glanced around in utter bewilderment. First time in Vegas?

She had the palest skin I'd ever seen, and when the light from the new chandelier hit her, she looked almost ethereal. Who was she?

Blane rose to hug his sister and then kissed the brunette on the cheek. "Megara, you look lovely as always. To what do we owe the pleasure?"

Aurelia dropped into the chair beside me and motioned to Megara to sit next to Blane. She perched on the very edge of the seat, looking ready to flee at a second's notice.

"Lysander."

Blane frowned. "Lysander sent you here?"

"No, we came here to get away from him."

The frown turned darker. "Did he do something to hurt you?"

"No, no! He hasn't laid a finger on me. I mean, maybe if he had…" Aurelia gave her head a shake. "He's so…so nice."

"And that's a problem? I thought women liked that?"

"Well, we do. But sometimes, we also like a man who'll tear our clothes off and throw us on the bed, you know?"

"Please, Aurelia. You're my sister."

But Blane caught my eye and smirked, and I tried desperately not to laugh. It didn't work. Megara's gasp was a testament to that.

"Lysander isn't that type of man?" I ventured.

"Lysander would hang my clothes neatly in the closet, iron the sheets, and have me fill out a questionnaire with my likes and dislikes before he even touched me. There's no spark whatsoever. None."

"Does that matter? Can't you put him to work cataloguing books until it's time for him to go home?"

"He asked me to have dinner with him. And I thought it was just a platonic meeting to discuss the new filing system, but over dessert, he asked me how I like to be kissed."

Blane paused with a forkful of risotto halfway to his mouth. "Awkward."

"It gets worse," Megara whispered.

"What was I meant to say? In all the romance novels I've read, people just work it out as they go along. And then yesterday, Meggie overheard Mom and Dad talking, and it turns out that Lysander isn't only an exchange student. He's also a suitor."

Blane dropped the fork. "What?"

"He's a prince from Realm 11,593, and I'm supposed to marry him. Then we head to the other side of the universe to run the second plane there and live happily ever after." Aurelia slumped over the table and rested her head on her arms. "I can't do it. I just can't. I don't want to live in another realm, and I especially don't want to live in another realm with the most boring man I've ever met."

"That's understandable, but—"

She looked up at Blane with pleading eyes. "Can we stay here for a while?"

Blane adored his little sister. He wouldn't want to see her leave for another realm any more than she wanted to go. There was only one answer he could give. I reached across the table and squeezed his hand to let him know I agreed.

"Of course you can."

What's Next?

The Planes series will continue with Aurelia's story, release date to be announced.

~

My next book will be the fourth novel in the Blackstone House series, *Hard Luck*...

Jerry Knight's ex taught her one important lesson: never lose your heart to a man. They mess with your career and they screw with your sanity. These days, Jerry's too busy saving the world to get ensnared in a relationship anyway, but there's nothing wrong with a one-night stand. Unless of course you bump into a hit squad while doing the walk of shame...

Cole Gallagher's ex taught him one important lesson: never lose your heart to a woman. They tear you up from the inside out. These days, Cole's too busy trying to rescue Uncle Mike's failing casino to consider another entanglement, at least until he crosses paths with a certain enigmatic brunette. Would a little one-night stand really be so dangerous?

Jerry doesn't do rest and she doesn't do relaxation, but when a stroke of bad luck leaves her in San Gallicano with nothing to do but Cole, she's forced outside her comfort zone. Weeks of downtime. It's her worst nightmare.

Fortunately, some new acquaintances decide to liven up the trip, and Jerry soon finds herself in a game of cat and mouse with the criminals of the Caribbean. Cole isn't quite so happy about the situation, but who cares? He's nothing more than a pretty face and a little light entertainment. Isn't he?

For more details:
www.elise-noble.com/hard-luck

If you enjoyed *A Devil in the Dark*, please consider leaving a review.

For an author, every review is incredibly important. Not only do they make us feel warm and fuzzy inside, readers consider them when making their decision whether or not to buy a book. Even a line saying you enjoyed the book or what your favourite part was helps a lot.

Want to Stalk Me?

For updates on my new releases, giveaways, and other random stuff, you can sign up for my newsletter on my website:
www.elise-noble.com

If you're on Facebook, you might also like to join Team Blackwood for exclusive giveaways, sneak previews, and book-related chat. Be the first to find out about new stories, and you might even see your name or one of your suggestions make it into print!

And if you'd like to read my books for FREE, you can also find details of how to join my advance review team.

Would you like to join Team Blackwood?

www.elise-noble.com/team-blackwood

facebook.com/EliseNobleAuthor

instagram.com/elise_noble

goodreads.com/elisenoble

bookbub.com/authors/elise-noble

tiktok.com/@EliseNobleWrites

threads.net/@elise_noble

Also by Elise Noble

Blackwood Security

For the Love of Animals (Nate & Carmen - Prequel)

Black is My Heart (Diamond & Snow - Prequel)

Pitch Black

Into the Black

Forever Black

Gold Rush

Gray is My Heart

Neon (novella)

Out of the Blue

Ultraviolet

Glitter (novella)

Red Alert

White Hot

Sphere (novella)

The Scarlet Affair

Spirit (novella)

Quicksilver

The Girl with the Emerald Ring

Red After Dark

When the Shadows Fall

Phantom (novella)

Pretties in Pink

Chimera

The Devil and the Deep Blue Sea

Blue Moon

Blackwood Elements

Oxygen

Lithium

Carbon

Rhodium

Platinum

Lead

Copper

Bronze

Nickel

Hydrogen

Out of Their Elements (novella)

Blackwood UK

Joker in the Pack

Cherry on Top

Roses are Dead

Shallow Graves

Indigo Rain

Pass the Parcel (2025)

Blackwood Casefiles

Stolen Hearts

Burning Love (TBA)

Baldwin's Shore

Dirty Little Secrets

Secrets, Lies, and Family Ties

Buried Secrets

A Secret to Die For

Blackwood Security vs. Baldwin's Shore

Secret Weapon

Secrets from the Past

Blackstone House

Hard Lines

Blurred Lines (novella)

Hard Tide

Hard Limits

Hard Luck (2024)

Blind Luck (2025)

Hard Code (2025)

Hard Evidence (TBA)

The Electi

Cursed

Spooked

Possessed

Demented

Judged

The Planes

A Vampire in Vegas

A Devil in the Dark

An Angel from the Ashes (TBA)

The Trouble Series

Trouble in Paradise

Nothing but Trouble

24 Hours of Trouble

The Happy Ever After Series

A Very Happy Christmas

A Very Happy Valentine

A Very Happy Halloween

A Very Happy Easter (2025)

A Very Happy Thanksgiving (TBA)

Standalone

Life

Coco du Ciel

Twisted (short stories)

Books with clean versions available (no swearing and no on-the-page sex)

Pitch Black

Into the Black

Forever Black

Gold Rush

Gray is My Heart

Audiobooks

Black is My Heart (Diamond & Snow - Prequel)

Pitch Black

Into the Black

Forever Black

Gold Rush

Gray is My Heart

Neon (novella)

A Very Happy Christmas

A Very Happy Valentine

A Very Happy Halloween (2024)

Dirty Little Secrets

Secrets, Lies, and Family Ties

Buried Secrets (2025)

A Secret to Die For (2025)

www.ingramcontent.com/pod-product-compliance
Lightning Source LLC
Chambersburg PA
CBHW030557170726
48283CB00002B/362